THE

Rx

FACTOR

J. THOMAS SHAW

LANGDON STREET PRESS

MINNEAPOLIS

Langdon Street Press
212 3rd Avenue North, Suite 290
Minneapolis, MN 55401
612.455.2293
www.langdonstreetpress.com

ISBN-13: 978-1-936782-89-5
LCCN: 2012932034

Distributed by Itasca Books

Printed in the United States of America

END OF DRUG TRIAL
IS A BIG LOSS FOR PFIZER

The news came to Pfizer's chief scientist, Dr. John L. LaMattina, as he was showering at 7 a.m. Saturday: the company's most promising experimental drug, intended to treat heart disease, actually caused an increase in deaths and heart problems. Eighty-two people had died so far in a clinical trial, versus 51 people in the same trial who had not taken it.

Within hours, Pfizer, the world's largest drug maker, told more than 100 trial investigators to stop giving patients the drug, called torcetrapib. Shortly after 9 p.m. Saturday, Pfizer announced that it had pulled the plug on the medicine entirely, turning the company's nearly $1 billion investment in it into a total loss. . . .

—Alex Berenson, *New York Times*, December 4, 2006[1]

PROLOGUE

Dr. Rosenberg delivered the diagnosis: ovarian cancer, stage IV, the most advanced and lethal stage of cancer. Jessica Barringer was given three to six months to live without treatment and two additional years with an aggressive plan of surgery, radiation, and chemotherapy. A third choice, and an extreme long shot, was participation in a new clinical trial of an experimental drug being tested against Jessica's particular type of cancer. The trial was scheduled to commence within thirty days and Dr. Rosenberg informed Jessica that she would have an excellent chance to qualify for participation in the trial if she was interested in registering. Of course, Dr. Rosenberg explained, even if the drug were effective, there was only a fifty-fifty chance that Jessica would receive the experimental drug, since half of the participants would be placed in a control group and only receive a placebo. A fifty-fifty chance to get an untested, unproven drug were not the odds she'd been hoping for.

Prior to learning their cruel twist of fate, Ted and Jessica Barringer were living the ultimate American dream. Ted had been the youngest associate ever to make partner at one of the most prestigious law firms in San Francisco. From there, he quickly worked his way up to senior partner by generating scores of new clients over the course of several years.

Despite Ted's success, it was his wife, Jessica, who earned the windfall that afforded them the five-million-dollar home with the panoramic view of San Francisco Bay, the forty-two-foot yacht they sailed on summer weekends, the skybox season tickets to their favorite sporting events, and their million-dollar chalet in Lake Tahoe.

Passing on the six-figure salaries being offered by the big boys, Jessica had joined a start-up technology firm after graduating with an MBA from Stanford. While the small company could not compete for her services via salary, they made up for it with generous stock option grants. Less than four years later, her gamble paid off and her firm went public. Before the paint could dry on their dream home, Jessica had cashed in her options for a net of nearly $20 million.

* * *

The man did not bother with greetings or small talk. When he approached Jerry Cottle sitting alone on the park bench, he held out his hand and Jerry filled it with an envelope that he had stuffed with hundred-dollar bills prior to leaving his office. In exchange, the man passed along a manila file folder, which Cottle knew contained information that could be worth millions. The man turned and walked away, but Jerry did not notice as his eyes were already scanning the contents of the folder.

The details revealed inside filled in the blanks from the phone call he had received a few hours earlier; Jerry knew he would need to act fast. Jessica Barringer was scheduled for surgery in three days and if he was going to extract her money, he had no time to spare.

He pulled out his cell phone and dialed the unlisted number that had been revealed to him in the file folder. When Jessica Barringer answered on the third ring, Jerry explained that he was with New Hope Cancer Alternatives, or NHCA, and that Jessica's name had been passed on to him as a possible candidate for the services that NHCA had to offer. Jerry explained that very few get this opportunity and asked to meet with Jessica and her husband to discuss her options. Though wary, Jessica's spirits were lifted by the caller's thorough knowledge of her particular situation and his assurances that NHCA had cured many patients with her same diagnosis. She agreed to meet with him the next day at his office.

The Barringers arrived early for their meeting, but Jerry was already waiting for them in the lobby. He didn't have to remind them of the seriousness of a stage IV diagnosis, or the scant odds of survival, but he did anyway. He emphasized that the NHCA had a drug that, while not FDA approved, was available at the organization's clinic outside of Puerto Vallarta, Mexico; Jessica's dire circumstances made her a perfect candidate to receive treatment at the NHCA clinic.

Ted inquired about the drug's success rate. Why should he entrust his wife's life to such a questionable venture? Jerry was both soothing and encouraging as he advised the couple of the high success rate of this drug, its minimal side effects, and the quick response that could be expected.

Ted was quick to jump on these claims. Why hadn't the wonder drug received FDA approval? Jerry chose his words carefully as he explained the long and costly process of obtaining approval. He assured Ted that someday the drug would be approved by the FDA, but unfortunately not in time to save Jessica's life.

Jerry began to sense hope and excitement in the desperate couple and moved in for the close. "Here are the facts. We have a drug that has cured stage four ovarian cancer on numerous occasions and all those who have received the treatment remain in full remission. When you meet with the clinic director, view our five-star facilities, and hear the testimonials from other patients, I am sure you will be convinced that this is the best—actually, the only—real option you have. I am sure that Dr. Rosenberg has already communicated to you that with the current diagnosis, there is almost no chance of long-term survival given the low quality of care that is available in the United States. And if you get started with our treatment plan and are not satisfied with the progress, you can always return to the care of Dr. Rosenberg."

When the couple hesitated, Cottle increased the pressure.

"If you like, I can arrange our departure flight for tomorrow morning. We can tour the facility, have our team of American physicians answer all of your questions, and then you can make your decision from there."

Ted pondered the offer, then, eyes narrowing, said, "Okay, so what's the bottom line? Something this valuable must have a fancy price tag."

"Yes, you're right, Ted. Access to this medicine is not cheap. The total is five million. One-third up front, one-third at the end of treatment, and the final one-third will be held in escrow to be released once we document that the cancer is in complete remission."

Ted was speechless as he contemplated the payment plan. He Looked at Jessica. She quivered as she smiled at her husband "This sounds promising, but it is a lot to digest. Ted and I will discuss it, and we'll call you with our decision."

Taking his cue, Jerry rose from his chair and walked the Barringers to the door. He handed Ted his business card, shook hands with Jessica, and fixed them with a piercing gaze that managed to convey sympathy, seriousness, and dependability all at once. "I am sure you will make the decision that is right for you."

Four hours later, Ted phoned Cottle and told him to book the trip. Jerry had been anticipating the call. "Consider it done. I will have our service pick you up tomorrow morning. Seven thirty sharp."

PANEL FAULTS PFIZER IN '96 CLINICAL TRIAL IN NIGERIA

A panel of Nigerian medical experts has concluded that Pfizer Inc. violated international law during a 1996 epidemic by testing an unapproved drug on children with brain infections at a field hospital.

That finding is detailed in a lengthy Nigerian government report that has remained unreleased for five years, despite inquiries from the children's attorneys and from the media. The *Washington Post* recently obtained a copy of the confidential report, which is attracting congressional interest. It was provided by a source who asked to remain anonymous because of personal safety concerns.

The report concludes that Pfizer never obtained authorization from the Nigerian government to give the unproven drug to nearly 100 children and infants. Pfizer selected the patients at a field hospital in the city of Kano, where the children had been taken to be treated for an often deadly strain of meningitis. At the time, Doctors Without Borders was dispensing approved antibiotics at the hospital.

Pfizer's experiment was "an illegal trial of an unregistered drug," the Nigerian panel concluded, and a "clear case of exploitation of the ignorant." . . . Pfizer contended that its researchers traveled to Kano with a purely philanthropic motive, to help fight the epidemic, which ultimately killed more than 15,000 Africans. The committee rejected that explanation, pointing out that Pfizer physicians completed their trial and left while "the epidemic was still raging."

The panel said an oral form of Trovan, the Pfizer drug used in the test, had apparently never been given to children with meningitis. There are no records documenting that Pfizer told the children or their parents that they were part of an experiment. . . .

An approval letter from a Nigerian ethics committee, which Pfizer used to justify its actions, had been concocted and backdated by the company's lead researcher in Kano. . . .

The panel concluded that the experiment violated Nigerian law, the international Declaration of Helsinki that governs ethical medical research and the U.N. Convention on the Rights of the Child.

Five children died after being treated with the experimental antibiotic. . . .

Aspects of the affair remain mysterious, such as why the report remains confidential. The head of the investigative panel, Abdulsalami Nasidi, said in a brief telephone conversation from Nigeria, "I don't really know myself" why the report was never released.

"I did my job as a civil servant," said Nasidi, who is quoted in the report as saying he has been the target of unspecified death threats.

—Joe Stephens, *Washington Post*, May 7, 2006[1]

CHAPTER 1

Mayday, Mayday, Mayday! Piper Foxtrot X-ray. Nassau, Nassau. Sixty miles northwest of George Town, altitude 7,500 feet and falling, heading 270. Tail exploded, ditching aircraft, six souls on board. Piper Foxtrot X-ray. Nassau, Nassau!

As the aircraft burst into flames a few hundred feet over the Atlantic, Ryan Matthews bolted upright. His heart pounded and a cold, clammy sheen of perspiration covered his trembling body.

Swinging his legs over the side of the bed, Ryan glanced at the clock and dropped his sweaty face into his hands.

Hell, you didn't even make it to 6 p.m. this time.

He was drenched as he sat in the dim room, head spinning, while his heart returned from the racing panic of his nightmare. He wiped his face with the sleeve of his T-shirt. *My god! Has it been five years?* Time hadn't eased his longing for Cindy and the kids. Even the most fleeting thoughts of them caused a searing pain that gripped him in his waking hours of sobriety almost as often as in his repeated nightmares. He switched on his bedside radio to one of the island's few stations, his sole company most days, and picked up the half-empty bottle of Jameson. He poured a glass, took a swig, and lit up a cigarette from a pack of Marlboros on the nightstand.

Well, I guess you're starting this evening earlier than usual, Matthews.

Alcohol was the best jump-start he knew and the thing he did these days when he was not busy attempting to escape reality fifty feet below the sea or training for the marathon that he would never run. It was in pushing his limits that he felt he might escape the stranglehold of grief.

As he sat on the edge of his bed, his bleary eyes panned the room, from the tropical bamboo furniture to the kitschy flamingo photo on the far wall and finally to the deep-sea fishing calendar. He stood up and ripped off the sheet that read *January*, crumpled it up, and flung it toward an overflowing trash can in the corner. Lying back down, his eyes hypnotically followed the rotating ceiling fan, and he could feel himself cool down.

His usual drinking post was Rosey's, a place run by his friend Roosevelt Aranha. Rosey's was one of those quaint drinking places in George Town right on Exuma's Elizabeth Harbor that the tourists sought out for the breathtaking views. The joint had the unique ability to capture all the flavor of the island in a single setting. In some ways, it was the epitome of the Bahamas, catering to both tourists and locals alike—unpretentious, welcoming, and friendly to all.

The fronds of a coconut palm outside his window were beginning to whisper in the tropical evening breeze. The reddish-purple leaves of a nearby bougainvillea added a papery rustle to the air. The sun had ceased shimmering on the vast ocean and was starting its descent to the other side of the world, leaving the sky a brilliant orange-pink.

By the time he had taken a quick shower, run a razor over his face, and left for Rosey's, darkness had fallen. Ryan turned the key and the jeep lurched to life. It was time to hit his stride.

* * *

Rosey's Place was just beginning to stir. As Ryan scanned his familiar evening haunt, he noted a smattering of locals spread out among the small tables and a few brightly festooned tourists talking too loudly as they leaned against the polished bar. Behind the bar, a mirror reflected an impressive array of liquor bottles set up in rows along the shelves, capturing a spectacular panorama of the ocean. Even at night the mirror made the place look bigger than it was, scattering the fleeting hints of the moon's trail on the waves through the bottles and glasses. Rosey's had no need for artificial air-conditioning, as it was open on all sides to the soft, balmy trade winds.

Ryan sauntered over to his accustomed spot at the bar and ordered his usual, Jameson on the rocks. He was well into his second drink when his buddy Franklin Rolle slid in next to him.

"Hey, champ," Franklin said, patting Ryan's shoulder.

"Good to see you, Frankie. What would a night at Rosey's be like without you?"

In a subtle gesture reminiscent of a baseball manager giving the steal sign, Franklin ordered a Kalik, the local beer of the Bahamas, with just a nod and an index finger to the side of his cap.

Ryan had met Franklin—who hated being called "Frankie"— several years back at Rosey's. A volunteer with the Bahamas Air Sea Rescue Association (BASRA), Franklin was a regular, and stopped by for a beer or two after work most days to socialize with friends and tourists.

Rosey delivered the Kalik to Franklin and topped off Ryan's glass without his asking. Franklin clinked his bottle to Ryan's glass and took a long swig of his icy brew before sharing the news of the day. "Did ya hear about them tourists who ran their boat aground today, mon?"

"Not yet Frankie, but I'm sure that I'm about to. Let me guess. They're from the States."

"Ya mon, these two were a real piece of work. Said they got a fishing lure stuck on some coral and tried to maneuver the boat in position to get it unsnagged." Franklin laughed and took a gulp from his bottle.

"Sounds reasonable to me. What's so funny?"

"Patience mon, I'm gettin' to that. Once da boat was almost

on top of da lure, dis real fat guy leaned over to try to free da line, but fell overboard when a wave side-swiped the boat. Then de other guy panicked, threw the throttle in full speed reverse and plowed the back of da boat right up onto a reef. Ended up burning up the motor and put a crack in the hull."

Franklin cackled even louder this time and took another swallow of his beer before continuing. "When the fat guy tried to swim to shore, he somehow lost his shorts and got his legs all scratched up on the coral reef. He was sunburnt, half naked and looked like a beached whale by the time we got to him and his friend."

Ryan snickered at the image that popped into his mind before taking a jab at Franklin. "I suppose a by-the-book hard-ass like you levied a fine against these tourists for damaging the coral reef."

"That is not in my jurisdiction, but I probably would have reported him had dey not already been out many thousands of dollars for da boat repairs."

Franklin drained the remainder of his beer, then jumped up from his barstool and took a few steps towards the door before turning back to Ryan with a jab of his own. "Besides, I have compassion for anyone who is dat damn stupid. Dese morons said dey were from North Carolina. Isn't that the same state where you came from?"

Before Ryan had a chance to tell Franklin to go fuck himself, the door to Rosey's slammed shut and Franklin was gone.

Just as Ryan drained his glass, the door to Rosey's began to open, but quickly closed with no one entering. Figuring Franklin was returning for a few more rounds, Ryan leapt from his barstool to greet his friend with the first stinger in what was certain to be a new round of gibes. Standing in the doorway and waiting to gain the upper hand, Ryan was momentarily tongue-tied when a gorgeous woman with long black hair, full pouty lips, and curves in all the right places entered the bar with an armful of shopping bags.

Stunned by the sight of Rosey's new patron, Ryan hypnotically held the door open with his foot while simultaneously relieving her of the shopping bags.

"What a gentleman. Thank you so much," she exclaimed.

"Table for one, madam?" Ryan teased.

The woman looked at Ryan with a cautious grin and hesitated before responding. "No thanks, a seat at the bar will do just fine."

"Very well then, right this way please."

Ryan escorted the woman to the barstool where Franklin had been sitting a few minutes earlier and set her bags on the floor between the bar and toe kick. He then held her barstool and waited for her to position herself up onto her seat.

"Thank you." She hesitated and then smiled. "I don't recall Rosey's having a maître d', and you don't look Bahamian, but it's a very nice touch."

Ryan hopped back onto his barstool and gave the lady a devilish smile. "Just having a little fun. The name's Ryan."

The woman looked surprised before composing herself and extending her hand. "Hello Ryan, my name is Jordan. Jordan Carver."

As Ryan released her hand, Rosey came up to the couple. Seeing Rosey beside her, Jordan jumped up off her barstool and gave him a big hug.

"You two know each other?" Ryan asked.

"She has been visitin' Exuma for years mon. Her aunt and uncle too. Comes here every year. She's my favorite tourist."

"Hey, what about me? You know, I can go spend my money somewhere else, Rosey."

"Ah, come on mon, you been livin' here way too long. You ain't no tourist, yuse what dey call an expat mon." Rosey flashed a brilliant white smile. How 'bout a couple of drinks on da house."

"Sounds good and why don't you get Jordan here a drink as well," Ryan quipped.

Rosey smiled and shook his head at Ryan. "You got it mon, double Jameson on the rocks and, let's see, Captain Morgan, Diet Coke, and lime for Dr. Carver, correct?"

"You got it. Great memory Rosey."

"Doctor?" Ryan questioned.

Before Jordan could respond, Rosey jumped back in. "Oh ya mon. Miss Jordan is a doctor. In medical research, mon, just like you used to do."

"You don't say."

"Tis a remarkable ting, doncha agree, mon?" Rosey said, a bright white smile on his dark face. "Dat she is brilliant and beautiful, too?"

Ryan raised his eyes a fraction, enough to see Jordan's eyes lower to her drink. "Oh, Rosey, you're overdoing it," she said.

Rosey flashed another brilliant smile. "Two drinks coming up."

As Rosey maneuvered through the growing crowd to his station behind the bar, Jordan followed up on Ryan's background. "You were in medical research? What area did you specialize in?"

Suddenly sullen, Ryan hesitated before responding. "Seems like a lifetime ago. But back in the day, I ran a small biotech company that was searching for a cure for cancer."

"Wow! Very impressive. What happened? And how did you end up in Exuma?"

"That's a very long story. Let's just say that I wasn't as good at it as I thought. I sold my company for the right price at the right time and decided I had had enough of the bureaucracy and bullshit of the industry for a while. And what better place to escape that rat race then right here in the Bahamas?"

Ryan was losing the desire to discuss his background any further and felt a great rush of relief when Rosey delivered the drinks. He immediately grabbed his glass, gave Jordan a half-hearted "Cheers!" and slammed half his drink in one gulp. Gathering himself, Ryan took control of the conversation. "What area of research are you in?"

"It's a unique area."

"Unique? How so?"

"Well, I used to oversee a clinic in Chicago that ran FDA trials. And, like you, I've had enough of the 'bureaucracy and bullshit,' as you put it, for a lifetime. Now I'm getting out of the mainstream and am preparing to open a clinic in Sayulita, Mexico. My new medical clinic will offer real hope for terminal patients by providing them with drugs that can actually cure their disease as opposed to just keeping them alive until their bodies burn out or the insurance dries up."

Her response was filled with such venomous sarcasm that Ryan was taken aback. He felt that he had unintentionally entered an emotional minefield. In an earlier time and place, he had lived for riddles. He loved the taunt of a challenge and wouldn't be able to rest until he had mastered its puzzle, assailing it from every angle and pounding it into submission.

"I am well aware of the bureaucracy involved in the U.S. drug industry, but—"

"Bureaucracy is one thing," Jordan interrupted, louder than before, "but I've been dealing with complete and utter incompetence. Hell, the FDA wouldn't recognize a real breakthrough drug if it drove up and parked in its fat ass."

Deferring to her obvious passion for the subject, Ryan let her continue without comment.

"The big pharmaceuticals are only interested in coming up with their me-too coping drugs, and because of all the lobbying dollars and backroom deals, those are all the FDA is interested in approving. Sad to say, but if you really want to get good medicine, you have to leave the country. America, 'land of opportunity'? What a crock!"

Now she was striking too close to his own experience. "I agree that on top of the bureaucracy there is a sizeable dose of incompetence, but all in all, I think the FDA does a fair job of keeping bad drugs off the market." Ryan's expression turned somber, and he felt his shoulders slump. "Trust me. I know better than anyone that even the most promising drugs can turn out to be killers."

Rosey slipped in front of them on his way to deliver cocktails to a nearby table. "Jordan, I tink ya cell phone's buzzing."

Jordan thanked Rosey, grabbed the vibrating cell phone sitting on the bar behind her, and headed outside to answer her call.

Rosey smiled at Ryan. "She be a regular Madame Curie, don' she?"

"Yeah, sounds that way. I just hope she knows what she's doing. Hey! If she's been coming here all these years, why is it I never met her before?"

"We usually see her in the afternoon mon, when she is not out sailing. Aren't you usually sleeping one off around dat time?"

Ryan scrunched up his face, giving Rosey a look that he hoped conveyed the message *Screw you*, but Rosey just smiled and walked away.

Jordan returned from the outside deck just as Ryan was finishing off his drink. With a smirk, he asked, "And who was that? Did the FDA track you down already?"

"Ha ha, very funny. No, the FDA is crooked and incompetent and they couldn't track down an elephant in a coat closet." Her mouth changed expressions from a pout to a grin as she continued. "It was just my overly protective uncle wondering why I wasn't back yet."

"Does he live on the island?"

She took a sip of her drink. "My aunt and uncle own that sailing yacht out there in the harbor," she said, as though it were nothing special. "I'll be living on it for the next two weeks."

He glanced out over the bay. "You mean that white beauty all lit up like a Christmas tree?"

"That's her. The *Bulls and Bears*."

"Your aunt and uncle must be doing well. I bet they have a whole staff with them on that whale."

"They are doing very well, but they both fancy themselves as sailors with salt in their blood. They maintain the yacht themselves while at sea and hire locals at each port of call to keep her sparkling. It doesn't hurt that the yacht is equipped with the most advanced electronics and instrumentation that money can buy." Jordan smirked before adding, "My uncle is Henry Carver. He's funding our project in Mexico. Perhaps you've come across his name?" This last question came laced with an edge of condescension.

Ryan straightened up in his chair. "The Wall Street Henry Carver?"

"Yes," she said with a twinkle in her eye.

"Well, then, this must be some clinic you're starting up in Mexico."

"Yes, we are very well funded. Money is not going to be a problem."

"Then maybe I'll come down and apply for a job?"

"I can't imagine you have already run out of the money you received from selling your company, but if you did come down to Mexico, then maybe I would hire you."

Ryan laughed and ordered a couple of shots of tequila. Handing Jordan the shot glass filled with the generous pour from Rosey's hand, Ryan declared, "Then let's celebrate—Mexican style."

It was nine o'clock when the music started playing and Ryan and Jordan realized they were starving. Ryan ordered the conch chowder and a batch of conch fritters and Jordan decided on the fresh grouper with rice and beans. As the food was being prepared they moved to an open table, shopping bags in hand. They enjoyed their freshly caught meal over the jubilating sounds of the usual Thursday night three-piece calypso band that was jamming to its own special blend of Caribbean jazz.

As Ryan and Jordan finished their dinner and their plates were being cleared, the band started in with "Day-O". Jordan immediately jumped to her feet, grabbed Ryan by the hand, and dragged him to the makeshift dance floor that was starting to overflow with Rosey's well-lubricated patrons. As the band and the audience sang the refrain for the seventh time, Ryan shook his head and smiled. He was staring into Jordan's eyes but began to think back to his honeymoon when he and Cindy were here in the same place, dancing to the same song, not a care in the world.

As the last refrain echoed through the bar, Ryan returned to reality and immediately felt uncomfortable when Jordan kissed him on the cheek. It was a fleeting sense of remorse. Ryan quickly rebounded and gave Jordan a twirl as they headed back to the bar to refill their empty glasses.

Most of the patrons had gone home for the night when Jordan's cell phone began to buzz again. This time she did not answer, but jumped up and gave Ryan another kiss on the cheek and said goodnight before stumbling over to where Rosey was sitting to give him a big hug and tell him she would catch up with him again soon.

She was already at the door when Ryan called out to her. "Hey, you forgot your shopping bags." Embarrassed, Jordan returned to the table where they had moved her bags and thanked him before heading back outside.

She was still on the deck when Ryan caught up with her. "How do you plan on getting back to your uncle's yacht? Is someone coming to pick you up?"

"I have a dinghy in the harbor."

"You're in no condition to run a dinghy in the dark," Ryan lectured.

She lowered her gaze, mischievous. "And I suppose you are?"

"This is my natural condition. Besides, I can drive a boat better drunk than you can sober." She started to protest but he had already taken two of the bags from her and was stomping off toward the dinghy mooring. "Let's go! I can bring the dinghy back out to you in the morning."

Jordan directed Ryan to the spot where the dinghy was tied down. He put her shopping bags in the boat and held out his hand for hers. As Jordan stepped aboard, the dinghy lurched suddenly to starboard, but Ryan's firm grip and unwavering balance saved her from a cool night swim.

He started the outboard after a couple of drunkenly over-zealous pulls, unmoored the vessel and guided the dinghy out of the docking area. He set a course for the ostentatious yacht rocking slowly on the harbor swells. The full moon hovered over her main mast. Ryan was just thinking how elegant she was when a violent blast shattered the still night, filling the sky with eye-searing light. With mouths agape, Ryan and Jordan watched as the blinding flash of flame and smoke sent the beautiful yacht skyward in thousands of pieces.

Ryan stopped the dinghy dead in the water just before the outer ring of falling debris. Jordan stared in horror at the carnage. She began swaying from side to side, emitting sounds of disbelief, tears coursing down her cheeks. "Oh my god! Oh my god! Auntie! Uncle! This isn't happening."

At that moment, déjà vu struck Ryan hard as he relived his own words five years before. *"No, no! This isn't right, can't be. My god, Cindy, Jake, Karly! No!"* He gazed thunderstruck at the roaring, ravenous flames, hypnotized by their beautiful and horrendous power. Yet Ryan did not see the yacht's devastation before his eyes. Instead, the image of a raging, fiery plane wreck was superimposed over what was left of the boat's burning hull.

He was experiencing his nightmare again, but this time he was awake. Horribly awake and abruptly sober. An uncontrollable shuddering overcame him, filling him with a foreboding that his life's course had once again been forever altered.

CHAPTER **2**

Ryan and Jordan sat in the bobbing dinghy, mesmerized by the inferno. The bright, leaping tongues of fire lit up the night, casting an array of dancing shadows over the harbor. Jordan's lamentations had subsided into soundless sobs, her body shaking with grief. The distant crackling of flames was all that could be heard in the otherwise eerie silence.

Speechless, Ryan turned the dinghy back to shore. Jordan protested. "We can't leave them here!" Oblivious to their own safety, she lurched up and reached out her hand as if to grab Ryan, nearly capsizing the launch.

Ryan forced his voice to remain calm. "If they were on the boat, there's nothing anybody can do for them now. We've got to get away from the boat. There could be more explosions."

Jordan sank back to her seat, her grief giving way to anger. "Damn this island," she snarled. "God knows how long it will take for help to get here. Get this thing moving!"

A small crowd had gathered by the time they reached the dock. Stepping off the dinghy with the stern line in hand, Ryan shouted, "Has anybody called BASRA?!"

An onlooker told them that BASRA had been called and within a few minutes, Franklin and two of his Bahamian colleagues arrived in time to see the smoldering hull slip beneath the dark waters. All that remained was a smattering of floating debris and a pall of black smoke rising into the moon-lit sky.

With a tone that implied he knew the answer, Franklin asked the growing crowd, "Did anyone here see what happened?"

The crowd muttered and shook their heads. Ryan motioned to Franklin to come over to where he and Jordan were standing on the dock. Jordan was frozen, staring like a zombie out into the harbor, so Ryan decided to skip the introductions. He put his arm around Franklin's shoulder and led him down the pier away from Jordan.

"Jesus Christ, Franklin, I'm shaking like a leaf on a tree. It was an unbelievably horrible sight."

"What exactly happened and who is dat women you were with? She looks horrified."

"Her name is Jordan Carver. We met tonight at Rosey's. I was giving her a ride on the dinghy back to her uncle's yacht when the damn thing exploded into a million pieces."

"Dat's terrible. Was dere anyone on board at de time?"

"Right now we are assuming both her aunt and uncle were on board when it blew. Jordan is beyond distraught."

"Don't sound like dere's much of a chance dey survived."

"From the force of the explosion, I would say zero chance if they were on board."

"Thanks for the information, Ryan. My boat's pulling up now. I will get in touch as soon as we have scoured the area."

On his way to meet the boat, Franklin stopped to offer his condolences to Jordan.

"Ms. Carver, my name is Franklin Rolle. I'm with Bahamian Air Sea Rescue. Ryan explained what happened. I'm terribly sorry. Me and my men will be going out now and searching the area and I will get in touch with you as soon as I know more."

Jordan had a blank face and did not respond to Franklin's statement. But as Ryan approached and Franklin hurried off to meet up with the BASRA boat, Jordan snapped. "I can't stand here and do nothing. I'm going back out there." She headed for the dinghy.

Knowing the authorities wouldn't let them return to the blast site by themselves, Ryan took hold of her arm and called out to Franklin. "Hold on. We're going with you."

Franklin slowed his stride. Glancing at Jordan's distraught face, he gave in. "I shouldn't, but let's go."

A few minutes later, they were bobbing over the grave of the *Bulls and Bears*, surrounded by wreckage. Spars, ropes, and shards of teak decking littered the sea in an ever-expanding field of debris. They cruised back and forth through the floating remnants for over an hour. Jordan's eyes scanned the water with desperation.

Finally, Franklin announced, "There's nothing else we can do tonight. At first light I'll have divers in the water."

Jordan glared at him. "Why can't they get started now?"

Franklin shook his head. "Can't see nothing down there, Ms. Carver." He peered at Jordan before shooting a glance at Ryan. "I think it would be best if we meet here tomorrow, first light."

Jordan was unresponsive. Returning to shore, they disembarked before Ryan turned to her and said, "Look, it's too late for you to find a hotel. You can stay at my place. We'll come back out together in the morning."

Jordan's face was blank, and he wondered if she had heard him. He gave her a gentle shake. "Is that okay?"

Almost in a whisper, she said, "You're too kind," before turning one last time toward the harbor.

* * *

It wasn't until he opened his front door, switched on the lights, and led Jordan inside that Ryan realized how out of control his life had become. Clothes and other detritus covered almost every flat surface, dirty dishes were piled high in the sink, and two bags of trash lingered in the kitchen. As Jordan stood blinking in the light, Ryan swept through the room and snatched up as much as he could, carrying it off to the laundry room.

Back in the living room, he found Jordan rooted to the same spot. Pointing down the hallway, he said, "The second door on the left is the guest bedroom. You can bunk there. I'll get you a bathrobe." As he moved off, he assured her, "It's a clean one."

When Ryan returned, he handed her the robe and a folded towel, and pointed out the bathroom. "First door on the left." He noticed she had some soot on her face. "You got some, uh . . . ," he brushed at his face as if to mirror her own. "I mean, there's a shower in there if you want one."

She moved without a word, robe and towel in arm, to the bathroom. Ryan heard the shower running and decided to prepare her a nightcap—nothing heavy on booze but something soothing to help her sleep. He settled on an Irish coffee. He found a crumpled bag marked *decaf* on a shelf hidden under a stack of assorted coffee filters that didn't fit his machine. The beans were stale, but it wouldn't matter. Hot coffee with a dash of whiskey, a splash of cream, and a generous spoonful of sugar would help Jordan take the first step on the path to restoring her sanity. *A path I know all too well.*

When she emerged in the bathrobe, her hair damp, he handed her the drink. "A little something to calm your nerves."

She seemed grateful. They both sat, him in his favorite chair, she with her knees clamped together on the sofa, eyes distant.

As they sipped the coffee, Ryan said, "I'll set the alarm for five thirty to make sure we make it to the harbor by daybreak. Okay?"

She nodded. He looked into her eyes, but after a few seconds, she dropped her gaze.

She needs some time. A lot of time, he thought. *Best to leave it alone for now.* He rose from his chair, leaned down, and hugged her. "You need anything, just yell."

She managed a weak smile that never quite made it to her eyes.

* * *

In the gray of predawn, Ryan awoke to the rattle of tambourines reverberating from his clock radio. He jumped out of bed and slammed down the off button, slipping into swim trunks and a T-shirt before staggering into the bathroom to splash water on his face.

In the living room, he found Jordan up and dressed. As she handed him a fresh cup of coffee, Ryan noticed she had changed into tan shorts and a black tank top, items evidently purchased on her shopping trip the day before. He noted her glazed expression. "Did you get any sleep?"

"Not much. I think I finally dozed off around three a.m."

He sipped the coffee while she paced. When she stopped, she raised a quizzical eyebrow. "It looks like you're going swimming," she said, gesturing toward his bright blue swim trunks.

"I'm a licensed diver," he explained. "I sometimes help Franklin out when extra divers are needed. I'm sure he'll have no objections." He threw back the last gulp. "I'll get my gear."

Ten minutes later, they were in his jeep and heading for the harbor. The sky was flushing out in a pink dawn. The blazing tropical sun wouldn't be far behind.

It was light when they got to the dock. Franklin and two divers were drinking orange juice from paper cups and chewing on buttery croissants.

"Morning, folks," Franklin said. "We made another surface sweep of da area about an hour ago." His tone told them they had found nothing. "And I got some witness statements from a group of tourists on a neighboring yacht." He pursed his lips. "The explosion dey described sounds odd."

"Why's that?" Jordan asked.

"Well, boat explosions, while rare, can occur as a result of de build-up of fuel fumes combined with something to ignite it. Starting the engine could be enough to do it."

"And?" she questioned, waiting for more.

"From da eyewitness reports, it appears dat de explosion rippled through de boat from bow to stern."

"What does that mean?"

"I don't know yet. But an accidental fuel explosion wouldn't go off like dat. It would most likely be a single massive blow without de rippling action. And if there were secondary explosions, dey would happen seconds, even minutes later, not like de chain reaction dat was described by da folks on da nearby yacht."

"I didn't notice a rippling explosion. From my vantage point, it was just one massive explosion."

"Yeah, I agree with Ryan. It was just one massive explosion."

"I'm sure dat is what it seemed like from da distance, but dese other folks were a lot closer and they all reported hearing a rippling of small explosions a second or two before da massive blast. We will of course check out all possible causes. Nothing is being ruled out at dis point." Franklin glanced around and saw two more of his divers walking toward one of the BASRA boats. "Looks like everybody's ready to go."

Ryan swung his tank and gear onto the boat's deck and helped Jordan aboard. The boat skimmed straight to the scene. The four Bahamian divers completed their preparations and entered the water as Ryan made adjustments to his tank, checking his gauges and hose lines while Jordan watched. Ready, Ryan sat on the gunwale, his back to the water. He slipped on his mask, popped it a few times to get suction, and took one last look at Jordan before turning his face up to the pale blue morning sky and dropping backward over the side.

As usual, the water was crystal clear as he kicked his way down. On the harbor floor he spotted two of the BASRA divers swimming around the small portion of the bow that still clung to the yacht's keel. Ryan swam away from them toward a mass of wreckage nearby. He could make out the main engine, generator, and the charred remains of the stern. He turned to look at the other divers nearly 120 feet away. The boat had been split violently in two from the force of the explosion.

A ravenous school of scavenger fish passed about fifteen feet from Ryan, gliding along like geese on migration. All at once, without signal, they switched direction as one mass toward another part of the wreckage just behind Ryan. Following their lead, he saw beneath the jagged edge of the splintered main spar the remains of a body pinned to the sea floor. It was a gruesome sight and Ryan momentarily turned away in disgust before regaining focus. From Ryan's vantage point through a cloud of fish, the body appeared charred beyond recognition. Using a piece of railing, he chased the fish off. Since he was not a Bahamian official, he knew he shouldn't touch the corpse. He headed for the nearest BASRA diver and directed him back to the dead body.

A few minutes later, Ryan ascended to the surface to prepare Jordan for the news. He worried how she would handle the gruesome sight of her loved one's remains. Between the mutilating burns and fish feeding frenzy, he was sure it would take more than a visual to identify the body.

He climbed onto the boat and was removing his scuba gear when two Bahamian divers hefted the body from the water up to Franklin and another BASRA volunteer. Ryan, standing to block Jordan's view, put a wet hand on her arm. "I don't think you should see this. The body is in bad shape."

Jordan gulped and shifted her eyes in nervous anticipation. Returning her attention to Ryan, she fixed him with a steady gaze and said, "It's all right. I'm a doctor, after all. I've seen my share."

Ryan reached out his hand and pulled her up from her seat to guide her over to the still form on the deck. As he felt her sway, he moved his arm around her shoulders, tucking her in beside him. "You sure you want to do this?"

"How can I not?" Her voice brooked no further dispute, and they walked the short yet interminable distance as she clung to him, eyes downcast. Once there, she squeezed her eyes shut and seemed to garner strength from some reservoir deep within that allowed her to take in the pitiful human remains before her. She gasped when she opened her eyes and turned her face against Ryan's chest. "Uncle Henry."

She began trembling, and Ryan tightened his hold on her.

"How can you be sure?" Franklin asked.

"His ring. My aunt gave it to him on their twenty-fifth anniversary." She pointed to the diamond-studded gold ring with a large ruby insert on his left hand.

"We're so sorry for your loss, Ms. Carver." Franklin bowed his head for a moment and then turned away and noted the identifying information in his logbook.

Jordan regained her composure and turned her gaze to her uncle one last time. Then tears filled her eyes and she grasped for Ryan. Ryan held her tightly as she began to sniffle. "He was the nicest, most compassionate and giving person I have ever known."

Jordan attempted to say more, but her words were inaudible. Ryan caressed the back of her head and tried to come up with the words that would provide her some comfort, but nothing came to mind. This was not surprising; no words had ever comforted him during his own personal tragedies.

As Jordan began to calm down, a shout came from the water and everyone turned starboard to see two more divers ascending with a second body. Franklin and his partner retrieved the body from the divers and placed their cargo next to the other corpse. It was in the same sad condition.

Franklin approached Jordan. "Ms. Carver, can you identify this one?"

She took a deep breath and nodded. "It's Aunt Jenny."

"You're sure?"

"Yeah, I'm sure."

Avoiding direct eye contact, Jordan moved toward the stern with her back to the others. Ryan saw her shoulders heave as a soft sob escaped her.

Franklin gave her some time, then asked, "Do you know how many people were aboard?"

"Just my aunt and uncle."

"Are you sure?"

"Positive," she insisted. "They ran the yacht themselves and had no staff. They did use locals in each port of call, but that was only during the day and only for general maintenance and cleaning. I spoke to my uncle about an hour before the boat exploded. They were getting ready to turn in for the night and if anyone else was on board, he surely would have mentioned it to me."

"When was da last time you were on board da yacht, Ms. Carver?"

"Yesterday afternoon. Aunt Jenny and Uncle Henry picked me up at the airport and we came straight to the yacht. I unpacked and relaxed for a few hours, then took the dinghy back to shore to pick up some supplies and see some old friends."

"When you were on board, did you happen to notice any strange smells? Any hint of even de slightest odor of fuel?"

"No. I didn't smell anything out of the ordinary. The yacht was state of the art with all the conveniences of a luxury home. If there was anything out of the ordinary, I would have noticed it, and Uncle Henry and Aunt Jenny would have, too. They were both sharp as a tack."

"Okay den, thank you Ms. Carver."

"I think Jordan has had enough for now Franklin. Can you call over one of the other boats to give us a lift back to shore?"

Franklin grabbed his radio and requested a pickup from the voice on the other end. Within a few minutes, another BASRA boat had arrived to return Ryan and Jordan to shore.

Soon after they left, one of the divers resurfaced with news that made Franklin's throat tighten. He radioed Superintendent Everett Pritchard of the Royal Bahamian Police.

"Everett? Franklin here. Ryan and Ms. Carver are on dere way in. I think you'd better detain her for more questioning. This wasn't an accident."

CHAPTER 3

One hundred and twenty-five nautical miles northwest of George Town, William Craven stepped outside into the muggy Nassau air, leaving behind the air-conditioned comfort of his hotel lobby.

No sweat, he thought. He was cool, meticulously cool, from the top of his balding head to the soles of his black leather oxfords. He wore a black Armani blazer over a white dress shirt, sans tie, and had artfully slung a small carry-on bag over his right shoulder. The sleek black bag housed his golfing apparel, but he had a different game to play this morning.

He pointed at a lime green cab as it approached, and jumped in before it had come to a full stop. "Take me here," he said as he handed the driver a matchbook with an address scrawled on the back.

The driver, sporting dreadlocks and chewing on an unlit, hand-rolled cigarette, lowered his shades as he studied the address. "You sure you wanna go here, mistah?" he asked.

"Go," Craven said, and he settled back into his seat.

"Yes, sir, mistah, sir." The cabbie jumped on the gas.

Nassau, the capital city of the Commonwealth of the Bahamas, was home to nearly a quarter million people, roughly 70 percent of the island chain's inhabitants. Despite the languid heat and the tropical vibe, it bustled with a dirty, frenetic energy, the kind of manic, fast-paced oomph that Craven craved. The overflowing sidewalks bulged with tourists, hawkers, and businessmen and women, the professionals in suits chewing up the pavement as they hurried off to their next important place.

Craven, for his part, never hurried. He moved quickly when needed, but hurrying meant losing control, and Craven, whatever he did, never lost control. He planned methodically and executed ruthlessly. His trigger finger never paused long enough for him to ask *what if*, because he had already studied all of the options, mapped out an entrance and exit strategy, and walked himself through every contingency a dozen times. He was a professional, in every sense of the word.

As the cab left the hotel district behind, the palms lining the streets grew sparser and the road rougher. The cabbie, no doubt an experienced hand who knew every corner of the city, looked uneasy. Given his profession, he probably lived out here, on the outskirts of Nassau's disintegrating concrete jungle, but how many times had he taken a Westerner into this urban inferno?

Craven lit a cigarette and inhaled deeply.

The cabbie glanced into his rearview mirror. "You like me to turn on the air-conditioning, mistah?"

Craven spotted a bead of sweat forming on one of the cabbie's sideburns. "No need."

The streets narrowed to mere alleys and the street-side buildings towered menacingly close when they finally arrived at a nondescript bar. The place could have been one of many anonymous flats in the shabby neighborhood, save for the neon beer signs hanging in the two front windows, each of which sat securely behind bars.

"Wait for me," Craven said as he got out. He eyed his bag in the backseat. "And lock your doors."

He approached the front door, which was propped open with a garbage can and camouflaged in a cloud of hazy smoke, and paused just long enough for his eyes to adjust to the dimly lit room. In the back of the mostly empty bar, seated at a table beneath a yellowing map of the islands, was his contact, a Haitian man with short cropped hair and a gap-toothed grin. The man stood up to greet him, but Craven's frown put him back in his seat.

"Hello, Mr.—"

Craven raised his hand to cut the man off. "Don't talk," he said. "Just listen." He pulled out a chair, turned it around, and sat with his arms resting on the back, ready to interrogate the man before him. The Haitian averted his narrow eyes, still smiling, as he waited for Craven to begin. As the clock ticked on without a word being spoken, the Haitian began to fidget in his chair. When he opened his mouth, Craven once again cut him off before the man could complete an audible word.

"I don't need an update, Junior." The man's name wasn't actually Junior, but it was a favorite pet name Craven reserved for his underlings. "I know all about your punk's fuck-up."

"But—"

Again, Craven cut him off. "I arranged for this meeting simply to watch you squirm and to give you one more chance to get it right. You've got forty-eight hours to tie up the loose ends." He let the sentence end abruptly.

"No loose ends," the man said, nodding, his eyes now widened with a grimace replacing the smile. "We'll fix every-thing. You'll see."

"Yes, I will see. And if the mission is not accomplished by then, you will become the loose end, and I will handle it personally."

Sweat began to drip down the Haitian's forehead and his right hand started tapping on his leg, but Craven was not ready to release the man from his attention yet.

"And no more explosions. Christ, the whole commonwealth is ready to come undone, which doesn't make your job any easier. How are you planning on communicating with your men, now that security has tightened on Exuma?"

The Haitian scratched his clean-shaven face. "I will travel to George Town tomorrow morning and speak with them person-ally."

"How will you travel?"

"There is a passenger service. . . ."

Craven shook his head.

"I suppose I could charter a fishing boat."

Craven nodded in the affirmative, though still unimpressed. He stood up, reached into his blazer, and tossed a hotel business card onto the table. "Call me when you have the charter arranged and I will meet you at the docks. I'm coming with you."

The Haitian squirmed in his chair before reaching for a paper napkin sitting on the table next to him and wiping his sweating forehead. He composed himself to a degree before responding. "I understand your concern, but that is not necessary. I already assured you that I will make sure all loose ends are tied up in short order."

Craven lifted his eyebrows and offered a snarl of a grin. "You assured me the last time and that did not work out so well, now did it?" Craven did not wait for a response before continuing. "I think you need supervision, Junior. And lucky for you, I just happen to be here. Call me with our travel details tonight."

Back outside, he dialed his secretary on his cell phone as he ducked into the cab.

"Fisher Singer Worldwide, this is Angela Marks," a woman answered. "May I help you?"

"Hey, Angie," Craven said.

"Oh, hello, Mr. Craven," she said cheerfully. "How's everything going at the convention?"

"Swimmingly so far," Craven said. "Listen, I need you to postpone my flight to Puerto Vallarta."

"But aren't you scheduled to meet with the clinic director tomorrow?"

"Yes, but things have changed. And the director can wait."

CHAPTER **4**

Everett Pritchard was a third generation law enforcement offi-
cial: his grandfather served in the Royal Bahamian Police Force
for over thirty-five years, and his father was warden at the Carmi-
chael Penitentiary in Nassau where, seventeen years ago, he was
stabbed and killed by several Haitian inmates during a full-scale
prison riot.

At the time of the riot, Everett was a rising star in the Nassau
police force, having been promoted to the rank of inspector after
being the lead investigator in a task force that had broken up a
sizeable international drug-smuggling operation. Following the
death of his father, he requested, and was eventually granted, a
transfer back to his home island of Exuma. Despite his love of
the law and the excitement that came with working big cases, his
devotion to family and the need to care for his widowed mother
were greater than the rush of stalking the shady characters that
made Nassau their base of operations. Since returning to Exuma,
he had been promoted to assistant superintendent and, with the
retirement of Superintendent Burrows a few years back, he was
handed the top cop position.

In his fifteen years as a law enforcement official in Exuma,
there had been only a handful of serious crimes and one murder,
which turned out to be an open-and-shut case. Except for the
occasional petty crime or domestic squabble, Everett's day-to-

day routine was more as a goodwill ambassador to the visiting tourists. His body had produced less adrenaline in the fifteen years since returning to Exuma than it had in a good month in Nassau. . . . until now.

The woman who had introduced herself as Dr. Jordan Carver sat on the hard wooden chair in front of Pritchard's desk. Pritchard watched her take in the array of family snapshots, the two potted palms flanking his desk, and the vase of fresh azaleas lingering on a small adjoining table. She nodded toward the official portraits on the wall. The woman didn't miss much.

"I thought the Queen was passé in the islands nowadays," she said.

Pritchard poured them both a cup of coffee, then glanced up at the framed portrait hanging beside the flag of the Bahamas. "I am a sentimental man. I'm proud of our independence, but I am still a stickler for tradition." He leaned back in his chair and eyed her carefully before continuing. "Franklin notified me of the discovery of your aunt and uncle's remains this morning. I am sorry for your tragic loss, and grateful for your cooperation, Dr. Carver."

"Why wouldn't I cooperate?" Notes of surprise, indignation, and even a little wariness intermingled in her voice.

Pritchard paused, not rushing, watching her reaction with a Zen-like patience. "I realize this is a difficult time for you, but we must move forward with the investigation and I am afraid I may have a few unpleasant questions to ask."

"I understand. I'm sorry. How can I help?"

"Three strangers got friendly with one of the waitresses at Rosey's shortly after she finished serving your aunt and uncle lunch. The waitress remarked that these strangers seemed impressed with your aunt and uncle's yacht. Has anyone approached you recently with questions regarding the vessel?"

"No. I only arrived yesterday morning. My aunt and uncle picked me up at the airport and we went straight to their yacht. I came ashore yesterday evening to pick up a few items, but I haven't had contact with anyone on the island other than small talk at the stores and at Rosey's. But it doesn't surprise me that those people were asking questions about the yacht—everybody is always impressed with her." She paused, then corrected herself. "Well, they *were*, anyway."

"These fellows asked questions that went beyond simple admiration."

"Like what? Have you spoken to them?"

"Not yet, but I have my best man out looking for them. They were asking about the owners and the guests, and they seemed curious about arrival and departure information. They said they were looking to buy one for themselves and the waitress didn't think anything of it until, of course, the boat exploded. Then she searched us out."

"And if your best man cannot find these people, what's next? Are you suggesting that these people may have had something to do with the death of my aunt and uncle?"

Noting that Dr. Carver was beginning to control the direction of the questioning, Pritchard diverted the momentum to get the ball back in his court. "Let's not jump the gun just yet. I have no idea if these people had anything to do with the explosion and until we have evidence to the contrary, the explosion is being investigated as an accident. A very tragic accident. I'm not equipped to pursue the exact cause of the explosion, so I ordered some experts to come down from Nassau."

"So you're suspicious enough to check this out."

"Yes, that's true." He glanced at the notes before him. "You told Franklin earlier that your aunt and uncle were the only ones aboard at the time of the explosion, is that correct?"

"Yes."

"Then how do you explain the presence of a third body at the site?"

Jordan jerked upright but did not respond.

"Were your aunt and uncle planning on going to sail in the morning?"

"Yes. First light."

"Then it is odd that someone else would be aboard that you didn't know about."

Jordan swallowed hard. Regaining her voice with considerable effort, she choked out, "I'll say it's odd. I know nothing about that." She halted, recovering as her face flushed with anger. "Who was it?"

"At this point, we do not know, but we'll find out soon enough. I'm hoping you might help in that regard."

The calm in his voice seemed to relax her. She settled back into her chair and brushed back the dark hair that had fallen over her eyes during her outburst. "I don't have any idea who it is."

Pritchard shifted in his chair. "Tell me about your aunt and uncle."

"Do you follow American financial news, Wall Street stuff?"

"I read the regular papers from time to time. Why?"

"Then you might remember that my uncle, Henry Carver, was involved in a scandal."

"Yes, I do recall. That must be why his name sounded familiar."

"He was the CEO of a major Wall Street firm when a company pension scandal broke out. It was muddled, but in the end my uncle was handed a golden parachute and forced to retire."

"I see. And when was that?"

"About three years ago. Shortly after that, he purchased the *Bulls and Bears*. Ever since, he and my aunt have been traveling the world."

"I see," he said, jotting the details onto his notepad. "I understand that your uncle was helping to fund your new project in, uh, where was it?"

"Sayulita, Mexico. It's near Puerto Vallarta. How did you know that?"

"This is a small island, Dr. Carver. Secrets do not stay concealed long in George Town."

"Well it was certainly no secret, but—"

Before Jordan could finish her thought, Pritchard tossed out his next question.

"And would you mind telling me how much he contributed?"

"He and a few other investors contributed close to twenty million, but my uncle was responsible for the bulk of it."

"What about your parents?"

"They are both deceased."

"I'm sorry to hear that."

"Thank you. That was a long time ago. Uncle Henry and Aunt Jenny practically raised me. I began living with them when I was still in middle school."

"And where was that?"

"New York."

"I see. Did your aunt and uncle have any children of their own?"

"No, it was just me."

"Any idea on the value of their estate?"

"I'm not sure. A lot. Had to be at least one hundred million, could be a lot more."

"And you're the only heir to their estate?"

"I have no idea. I am their only living relative, but I was not privy to the specific details of their will. As far as I know, they may have left everything to charity." Jordan paused, squinted her eyes, tightened her lips, and then tilted her head a fraction before continuing. "And I do not appreciate the insinuation that comes with that question."

"There is no insinuation in my question, Dr. Carver. I am just gathering facts right now. Please do not confuse the two."

Pritchard finished up with his notes and slid his chair back. "Thank you for coming in, Dr. Carver. Will you be available if I should need you again?"

"Yes, of course. I want the facts as much as you do. And I'm not going anywhere until I have them."

CHAPTER 5

Their table out on the deck at Rosey's offered a splendid view of the assembled boats in the harbor, a forest of masts and a spiderweb of rigging. Jordan, who seemed to have little appetite, nibbled on conch fritters and nursed a daiquiri.

"Did you learn anything new from Pritchard?" Ryan asked over his margarita.

"To say the least. The superintendent informed me that besides my aunt and uncle, there was a third body on the boat."

Ryan's jaw dropped and he straightened up in his chair. "I thought you said it was only you and your aunt and uncle who were staying on board."

"That was the plan. At this point, no one can identify this mysterious third person. I think Pritchard suspects that the explosion was no accident."

"Based on what evidence?"

"I'm not sure of all the reasoning, but so far we know that the explosion was not typical for a fuel leak, an unknown person was discovered in the wreckage, and three people were suspiciously inquiring about *Bulls and Bears* a few days ago. Based on all of that, I'm about ready to sign on to his conspiracy theory."

"Don't jump the gun, Jordan. This is a small, friendly, but poor, family island. It would not surprise anyone, including Pritchard, to find out your aunt and uncle had a late-night visitor trying to sell them an extra fish or offering service in some way and then ending up in the wrong place at the wrong time."

"I guess that makes sense."

"And as far as these three people asking questions about the yacht, come on. A vessel of that magnitude was worthy of carrying an A-list celebrity or even royalty. I am sure these weren't the only three people who inquired about the *Bulls and Bears*, just the ones identified thus far to Pritchard."

"Sounds reasonable, but then why was Pritchard giving me the third degree?"

"Just doing his job. A person like Pritchard is trained not to make conclusions when uncertainty still exists."

As they finished their lunch, Ryan shifted awkwardly in his chair and asked, "Have you thought about where you're going to stay?"

She stared at him without responding.

He gave a short, nervous cough. "My place is comfortable, at least it will be once I tidy things up a bit, and it will take you out of the line of sight of curiosity seekers." He rushed on. "That is, if you want to. I mean, don't feel pressured."

She hesitated a moment, then said, "Sure. First, I'll need to do some shopping. Everything I had was on the yacht besides what I picked up yesterday."

Ryan offered to drive her wherever she needed to go. Within a few hours, they had hit most of the vendors at the open market and Jordan returned to Ryan's place with several bags filled with the latest island fashions along with personal items that she was able to purchase at the local drugstore.

After returning to his house, they went out back onto the veranda that faced the crystal-clear expanse of Hoopers Bay. As Jordan settled into the wicker couch, she crossed her legs, revealing a tantalizing expanse of thigh in the slit of her tan cotton dress. The offshore breeze flared through her hair as her eyes scanned the tropical horizon.

She rivals the views here, hands down, he thought.

Ryan served up some lemonade, not wanting her to think of him as the consummate drunk. She accepted with a "Thanks," brushing his hand with hers as she took the glass. She kept her eyes on him over the rim as she sipped. She pursed her lips from the tartness and recrossed her legs. His eyes followed.

"So, tell me," she said at last, "last night when I asked you about what area of medical research you specialized in, you said it was a long story. We've got the time now and I'm all ears if you care to elaborate."

He was torn between answering seriously and flippantly, but decided to give it to her straight. "My company was founded on the fact that with the mapping of the human genome, it was now possible to identify the markers in genes that lead to cancer. We theorized that once these markers were identified, a cure could be developed."

She smiled, her eyes locked on his. "That's a good theory, but hardly revolutionary."

"Agreed, but I had already positively identified several markers, which put us one step closer to a cure than anyone else at the time."

"Very impressive. Were you looking at all cancers or one in particular?"

"The long-term goal was to find a cure for all cancers, but our initial focus was on ovarian cancer."

"Any breakthroughs?"

"At one time I thought so. We were all but certain that we had finally identified all the markers and then developed a serum to target only the cancer cells impacting the ovaries. Through much trial and error and tweaking of the serum, we finally experienced a major breakthrough when all of the infected lab rats were cured after a series of injections of the serum."

"That is truly remarkable. So your serum cured ovarian cancer in rats?"

"A one hundred percent cure rate with no signs of remission. They lived a normal life span after a series of injections of the serum."

"Unreal. Why is the entire medical community not following up on your research?"

Ryan twisted in his seat and squeezed the bridge of his nose as he contemplated the best way to respond. "Excuse me," he said abruptly. He shoved back his chair as he rose and took his lemonade into the kitchen. Muttering to himself, he dumped a generous portion of Tanqueray into the glass before returning to the veranda. After a healthy swig, he said, "The entire medical community is thankfully not aware of this and no one is following up on my research because the FDA halted the human trials when my drug started killing people."

Jordan's eyes dropped to her drink and a somber silence hung in the air for several seconds. "I'm so sorry, Ryan. I had no idea." She set down her drink and twisted her hands nervously. In a gentle voice, she said, "We can talk about something else." She couldn't seem to raise her gaze to his.

Ryan shook his head. "I don't mind talking about it. Don't worry about me. How are you holding up?"

"As good as can be expected, I guess. Talking with you about all this is helping me take my mind off my own sorrows. I know they each had a long and wonderful life." Jordan bowed her head before continuing. "I know they would have wanted me to celebrate their life and not mourn their death, but the way they died just seems so senseless."

She raised her head up, gritted her teeth, and stared into Ryan's eyes. "I just can't get to the celebration-of-life point of view until I know exactly what happened, and why."

"That's very understandable." Ryan's face became sullen as he dropped his head down a few notches. "I guess when someone passes away of normal causes, it is much easier to celebrate their life, but when they are suddenly taken in a tragedy, mourning feels more appropriate."

"Yeah, I guess that makes sense."

Ryan fell silent and stared off into the distance. His heart was racing and his palms began to sweat. He wiped them on his shorts and then rubbed them through his hair. He drained his spiked lemonade, excused himself again, and went into the house. A few minutes later he returned with a fresh drink and a pack of Marlboros. He took a swig from his glass and lit up a smoke. As he exhaled, he shot a half-hearted smile towards Jordan. "Bad habit I know. . . ."

Before he could finish his thought, Jordan interrupted. "Ryan, clearly something is bothering you. You have known me less than a day, yet have treated me with nothing but compassion. If you want to unload, I am here for you."

"I appreciate that Jordan, but you have enough on your plate and don't need to get involved in my psychosis."

With a stern yet smiling face, Jordan replied, "Nonsense. That's it. Start talking Matthews."

Ryan sighed, took another drag of his cigarette, and then crushed it out in the overfilled ashtray sitting on the table beside his chair. "I lied to you." He paused. "Well, not exactly *lied*, just didn't tell you the whole story. I told you from the get-go it was a long one."

"Yes, you did. I'm all ears."

"It wasn't just people who died in the human trials of Tricopatin."

"Tricopatin?"

"Yeah, that was the registered name of my serum. Anyway, my wife, Cindy, was a participant in that trial." He dropped his head for a moment and then stared directly at Jordan. "And I made sure that she was not in the placebo group."

"I'm so sorry, Ryan, but you cannot blame yourself. If your wife was approved to be in that trial, then . . . I don't mean to sound callous, but that had to be her last hope of long-term survival."

"Of course I know you're right, but I have just never been able to accept my failure."

"Tell me about Cindy. How did the two of you meet?"

Ryan took a swig of his drink before continuing. "I met

Cindy at Wake Forest. She was a freshman biology major and mistakenly walked into my organic chemistry lab. I was awestruck from the beginning. She was the most gorgeous specimen I had ever seen." Ryan smiled a knowing smile and sat in silence contemplating the moment for a few seconds before continuing.

"From that day on we were inseparable. We dated all through college. After undergrad, I went to Duke for my MBA and we married the summer after my graduation. Two years later, our daughter, Karly, was born."

Jordan stared at Ryan with knowing and caring eyes. Her compassion and sincerity did not go unnoticed as Ryan sensed a level of comfort that he had not felt in years and began to speak more freely.

"It was near that time that my mom died from ovarian cancer. It was at her funeral that I made a commitment to go back to school and earn my doctorate degree and devote my life's work to finding a cure. I know now that this was a naive goal, but at the time I was as certain as a person can be that I was capable of making the miracle happen."

"There is a fine line between confidence and naivety and that is nothing to beat yourself up over, Ryan."

"There may be a fine line between the two, but it's that same fine line that separates success and failure, winners and losers, and . . ." He paused. "Life and death."

Jordan did not attempt to counter Ryan. She simply agreed with him and asked that he continue.

"Three years later, everything was going as planned. We were blessed with the birth of our son, Jake. I was still pursuing my doctorate and spending every spare moment I had working on my thesis. When I was finished, my theories drew much critical acclaim and by the time I graduated, I had more offers than time to legitimately consider all of them."

"Sounds like a good problem to have."

"It was not really a problem. I was so focused on what I wanted to accomplish that when I was approached by a venture capital firm that fancied itself as an incubator for start-up biotechnology firms with an offer of virtually unlimited funding to pursue my research, I jumped at the opportunity."

"Wow!" Jordan smiled. "That must have been some thesis."

"I guess it was, but it was only a thesis, a hypothesis, supported with facts, but, unfortunately, not yet backed up with results. As I mentioned earlier, we had some miraculous breakthroughs as we attempted to prove my theories and develop a serum that would cure ovarian cancer, but that is another fine line."

Jordan shifted in her chair and cleared her throat. "I guess that was a foolish statement I made about a fine line."

"I didn't mean it like that, Jordan."

"I know, but it was a stupid comment and condescending. I am a scientist like you and know full well the difference between close and exact. Unfortunately, if you are on the wrong side of the fine line in our work, the results are not . . . are not . . . well, let's just say it is not like the difference between a triple and a home run."

"Amen. Listen, I really do not need to dump all of this on you. After all, I am supposed to be comforting you."

"Nonsense. I am feeling very much comforted by your willingness to open up to me. Please continue."

Ryan hesitated and shook the ice in his now otherwise empty glass. "A few days after Cindy's annual OB-GYN appointment, the doctor called to tell her that routine test results indicated that she had a pelvic mass. Follow-up blood tests revealed advanced-stage ovarian cancer."

Ryan stopped and took a deep breath to steady himself. Jordan reached for his hand.

"She was given less than a year without surgery and chemo. But we both knew that that would only buy her another six to twelve months. Instead of living out the rest of her life in a hospital, we decided to move to Exuma and try to enjoy her remaining days free from the pain and misery that accompany the only treatments practiced for stage four ovarian cancer."

"Why Exuma?"

"This is where we spent our honeymoon. We fell in love with the beauty, serenity, and wonderful people. I came down before everyone else to set up our living arrangements. Cindy, Jake, and Karly boarded an island hopper in Miami for the last leg of their trip. About halfway here . . . ," he paused and looked out at the waves playing upon the bay, ". . . the plane malfunctioned and crashed into the sea."

Jordan squeezed his hand but kept silent. Even the birds had ceased their constant warbling, as if in respect for the gravity of Ryan's loss. Then, without warning, Jordan sprang from her chair and said, "Do you mind if I take a swim? The water looks wonderful and I need a pick-me-up."

Ryan had started to relax thanks to the alcohol's effect but was still plagued with the feelings dredged up from his revelations. Jordan's abrupt outburst sliced like an axe through his emotions and he began to regret opening up to her. Was his sad story depressing her and now she wanted to change the subject? *How could she be this insensitive?*

"Well . . ." he fumbled, "I don't have any women's swimsuits."

"I've got one in my tote bag. Would you like to join me?"

To his surprise, he found himself rising. "I guess I need to clear some cobwebs, too."

He remained standing, immobilized in the thought of Cindy, Jake, and Karly, while Jordan changed in the bathroom. She emerged a few minutes later wearing a lime-green bikini, ready for a frolic in the sea.

"Hurry up and get your suit," she said. "I'll be in the water."

By the time he got down to the beach, all he could see was her black, shiny hair disappearing in the crystal-clear surf. He plunged in and stroked out toward her. The ocean was cool and refreshing. The salt water buoyed his body and the exercise invigorated his spirit.

By the time he caught up with her, he was panting. She was out farther than he had thought. *Must be a good swimmer to come way out here.* She stretched out on her back and floated with her face to the sun. He followed suit. It was a transformation, a cessation of all things worldly. He could have gone to sleep, and nearly had, when she said, "We're drifting out pretty far. Better get in closer."

They set out swimming until they were in safer waters near shore. Jordan was the first out of the water, striding up the beach. Ryan followed close behind and settled onto a blanket he had brought out with him. She wrung the water from her hair before dropping down next to him, tugging at the bottom of her bikini.

Stretched out side by side, with the huge fluffy cumulus clouds racing by, both of them dozed off in the afternoon sun.

* * *

The sun was beginning to sink on the second day since the tragic explosion when a four-door Chevy, outfitted with standard law enforcement communications equipment and a government license plate, pulled into Ryan's driveway. When Ryan answered the door, he found Superintendent Pritchard and a tall, thin man he had seen several times, but never met before, standing on his front porch. Pritchard introduced the man as Neville Bradshaw, his lead investigator.

Once inside, both men greeted Jordan; neither looked surprised to see her there. The superintendent said, "I thought we might find you here. We have some information about the explosion that might interest you."

Ryan had been on friendly terms with Pritchard ever since his first visit to the island. Since taking up permanent residence, they had become true friends. They got together for dinner and cocktails several times a year and, as a result of Ryan's specialized background, Pritchard had even consulted with him on several official matters, off the record, over the past few years.

Ryan invited them back to the patio. As they took their seats around the outdoor fire pit, he offered drinks. Both men declined, as did Jordan. Noticing that Pritchard was not his usual jovial self and that the man he introduced as Neville Bradshaw was as stiff as a board, Ryan felt a twinge of tension and decided to excuse himself. He returned moments later with a snifter of Jameson mixed with a couple ice cubes.

Pritchard, who was seated between Jordan and Ryan, skipped the small talk, plunging right into the topic on everyone's mind. "Nassau surprised me with a rare bout of efficiency and sent a couple of salvage divers down yesterday."

Jordan leaned forward expectantly.

"Okay, here it is," Pritchard went on. "As I told you, I sent one of my men to follow those three strangers. Except now one of them is missing and customs has no record of his departure. This made me wonder about the unidentified charred body from the yacht. It's too early for a positive ID, but the man had a brass charm on his wrist that escaped the explosion. It was a voodoo charm, which makes me think he may have been from Haiti. Haitians, of course, are well known for their strong belief in voodoo. Anyway, we now believe we know who he is. . . . or was. He'd only been on the island for a few months and went by the name of Gerard Duval. We've identified the others as René Edmond and Manno Sanon, also from Haiti and both arriving just a few weeks ago. I'm still waiting on background checks on these men from Interpol."

Ryan took a belt of his drink before prodding Pritchard along. "And?"

"And we just received the report back on the boat wreckage that was analyzed by Nassau."

Ryan and Jordan waited, full of expectation.

"It was definitely a bomb, and a sophisticated one at that. These guys were obviously well financed. The man we suspect to be Gerard Duval was the one who placed the bomb. At this point we are operating under the theory that he screwed up the timing mechanism and it went off prematurely."

Bradshaw pulled a small notebook and pen from his jacket pocket before speaking up for the first time. "Dr. Carver, we have received information dat on da very day of the explosion you spoke with dis Duval character at Talbot's Market."

Jordan hesitated before responding, choosing her words with care. "Yes, I was out shopping and I do remember talking to a black man at the market. I had no idea who he was."

"What did you talk about?" Bradshaw probed.

"I think he was admiring my dress and hitting on me, but I had a difficult time understanding him."

"Yes, da Haitian dialect can be difficult for Americans to understand, but dat shouldn't surprise you."

Jordan bristled at the accusatory tone in the man's voice. "Wait a minute. What are you saying? I want to know wh—"

Bradshaw cut her off. "I'm sorry, Dr. Carver, but in an official investigation—and dis *is* one," he emphasized, "*I* ask da questions. *You* will please answer."

Ryan tried to intervene but Pritchard put his hand up to silence him. "Please, Ryan. It will not help Dr. Carver."

Bradshaw continued. "We have a report that you spoke to your uncle on da phone about an hour before da explosion. What was dat call about?"

Ryan interrupted. "It was her uncle wondering when she was coming on board."

Jordan nodded. "That's right."

Bradshaw jotted that down in his notebook. "We'll have to check dat out, of course." His voice was laced with skepticism. It was apparent to Ryan that Bradshaw had already drawn his own conclusions.

Not five minutes had passed before Pritchard rose to his feet. "That's all for now. But I'm going to have to ask you to remain on the island while I complete this part of the investigation. Now," he said, putting out his hand, "I need to ask for your passport."

Jordan stomped into the house for her purse. Returning, she thrust the passport at him.

"Can I expect you to be here if I need you?" Pritchard asked. She glanced at Ryan.

Ryan stood up and drained his drink. "Jordan will be staying here, Everett. But you're barking up the wrong tree."

Pritchard gently grabbed Ryan by the elbow and led him out towards the ocean. When they were safely out of earshot, Pritchard spoke. "I never bark Ryan, you know that. This is protocol and right now I need you to respect what I have to do."

Ryan started to speak, but Pritchard cut him off. "For god's sake, man, get your head on straight and lay off the booze. I just informed you that one of America's most prominent citizens and his wife were murdered in a most sinister way on our little family island and the suspects are still at large. The world is watching and I will not be taking any shortcuts or leaving any stone unturned."

Pritchard released Ryan's elbow. "And if Dr. Carver is involved in any way, she may not be safe."

CHAPTER 6

"They're ready for you, Senator."

Senator Edward McNally acknowledged his aide with a tip of his head and brushed the dust off his suit jacket. It was show-time. Even here, in some godforsaken village in the middle of Nigeria, a hundred miles from the nearest city and a world away from the game back in D.C., he could still feel a little extra jolt of adrenaline course through his veins as he assumed the role he'd been born to play. At forty-four, and midway through his third term, he wasn't the youngest member of the U.S. Senate anymore. But he was still the superstar of that legislative body, one of only a select few with legitimate presidential aspirations. Since joining the Senate at age thirty, the minimum age required for office, he had been riding a wave of popularity as media darling, brilliant young statesman, and budding political rock star all wrapped up in one. And in the last decade his reputation had only grown: he easily won reelection twice, authored a handful of important bills, cultivated crucial relationships with influential members of Congress and Washington power brokers alike, and nailed down an important leadership post as chairman of the FDA's oversight committee.

How else to explain why a gaggle of journalists, whether belonging to the *New York Times*, *Washington Post*, Fox News, NPR, or some fledgling blog on the Internet, followed him wherever he went, even to Africa? Slipping away anonymously from his hotel back in Abuja had been no easy task, but the subterfuge had thrilled him to the core. Now here he was in some dusty village, nicknamed "Dung Hill" by his security detail due to the locals' habit of burning cow shit for fuel, to witness in private what one of his most influential contributors had been doing beyond the scrutiny of the nosy regulatory agencies back home.

The senator squinted into the midday sun as he emerged from the climate-controlled, window-tinted comfort of a stylish but conservative navy-blue Hummer. Trim, just over six feet tall, and boasting a full head of sandy blond hair, he had more than charisma going for him. He still sparkled with youth, the promise of better days ahead. So what if he had already peaked? If he was already bought and paid for? Politics was the art of illusion, and Senator McNally's true talent lay in his ability to wield the disparate elements—sunny optimism, cool-headed realism, magnanimous bipartisanship, unflinching ruthlessness—and turn them into political gold like some medieval alchemist.

Before him sat a prefab building, not much more than a trailer and as dingy as its earthen surroundings, serving as a medical clinic for local villagers as well as farmers from the surrounding countryside. Lean men, worn down by years of manual labor and a life of scarcity, stood alongside children and peasant women, some of them pregnant, all of them weighed down with newborns or toddlers barely old enough to walk, in a long line that snaked through the dust from the building's entrance to a sprawling acacia tree several hundred feet away. The children had distended bellies and saucer-like eyes, the hallmarks of malnourishment. No one was starving, but no one was living, either, at least not by Western standards. These people, ghosts hollowed out by the ravages of poverty, disease, and local violence, couldn't have formed a starker contrast to the soft, fleshy pharmaceutical workers who had come to "help" them.

An American man, balding and ample around the middle, emerged from the building just in time to greet the senator near the entrance. "Good to see you, Senator," he said, offering a firm handshake. "We're pleased you were able to make the trip out— without the usual entourage."

Senator McNally shook his head grimly. "It wasn't easy. My friends in the press take a keen interest in whatever I do." *Friends*, in this case, meant bloodsuckers. *Keen interest*? Unrelenting obsession.

"Yeah, well, I suppose it comes with the territory."

"It sure does. So what have you got to show me, Gus?"

Gus Witherspoon, an expert in his field, was part scientist, part public relations manager, a knowledgeable salesman who dealt discretely but forthrightly with a select clientele made up of industry bigwigs, politicians, and other well-connected insiders. He served on the front lines of a secret war, paving the way for research and experimental drug trials on foreign soil while keeping his company out of the spotlight and beyond the prying eyes of regulatory agencies, journalists, and would-be do-gooders.

"Just this," Gus said, handing the senator a crumpled spreadsheet.

Senator McNally stared at the figures, some of them stained by coffee. "What's this? I don't speak microbiology."

Gus, placing a hand on the senator's shoulder, ushered him away from the crowd at the front door, and back along the caked-mud drive to the Hummer, where no prying eyes or ears lurked. "That, dear Senator, is a one hundred percent success rate. As of this morning, we've given the full treatment to one hundred and thirty-six patients. And we're batting a thousand."

"Impressive." The senator glanced back and surveyed the long line, which was growing steadily. "Are all these people sick?"

"No. Shoot, half of them don't even know what we're doing here. But they know we're making people better, so they're coming by the droves. We had one old man walk fifty miles to get here."

"Barefoot, I suppose."

"Who needs shoes when the floors are made of dirt?"

Senator McNally gave a polite chuckle. "But aren't you

worried about how fast the word is spreading?"

"Nope," Gus said nonchalantly. "Most of the people in line will receive a few free vaccines and a vitamin B shot—good PR for the company and a perfect cover for the program. Only a select few have been screened and given full treatment."

The senator nodded his approval and then spotted an angry villager trying to work his way past the minders at the entrance, shouting something to the people in line behind him. "What about him? Another happy FSW customer?"

Gus smiled wryly. "Oh, there's always some conspiracy nut out there who's certain we've come to castrate their men, impregnate their women, and poison their crops."

The senator gazed past Gus, toward the lonely hills that lay beyond the village. It was a move he had practiced countless times over the years, one meant to display seriousness, deep thought, gravitas. In this case, it wasn't a show. "If he only knew."

CHAPTER 7

William Craven made sure the drapes were closed before answering the door to his hotel room, which, like his accommodations back in Nassau, was tailored to the needs of a businessman who traveled first class. His new room had a better view, of course, and a more tranquil setting, but that was to be expected of any place worth the real estate it was sitting on here in the heart of tiny, picturesque George Town.

He opened the door and invited inside his Haitian contact and the man's two thugs. "You must be René," he said to the taller of the two assassins. "René Edmond."

René, bald-headed and wearing a clingy wife beater that accentuated his muscular frame, nodded menacingly.

Craven turned his attention to the other assassin, who was a few inches shorter than his partner, the sky-high afro atop his head notwithstanding. Dressed in a loose black T-shirt and a pair of cutoff jeans, he was smaller and leaner, but looked just as tough.

"You're Manno Sanon."

Manno shrugged indifferently, but his cool stare spoke volumes. He didn't appreciate the scrutiny and obviously felt he didn't need to impress a soul.

I can work with him, Craven thought. Craven knew men. Their posture, the way they returned his gaze—everything told a story. He could tell a poser from the real deal in a heartbeat. He shifted his attention to the man who until now had been his go-between, the flunky who had cowered in front of him at the bar back in Nassau.

"I gave you forty-eight hours," Craven said. "But you're just now introducing me to your boys, and the job's still unfinished."

"Who you calling *boy*?" Manno asked in a hard-to-decipher patois of African, French, and pidgin Creole. He took a step toward Craven.

But before Manno could move another inch, Craven was propping up the assassin's chin with his Glock. Craven motioned to René to take a seat on the bed behind him, and the man did so grudgingly. He then caught Manno's gaze, still unflinching, not an ounce of fear on his face.

"I like you," Craven said. "Go take a load off next to your pal there."

The look on Manno's face—somewhere between fury and amusement—slowly morphed into recognition. Perhaps he, too, could read men. Perhaps he understood that Craven, far from being an empty suit, was no stranger to death. Manno slowly, cautiously, sat down beside his partner.

"Show me the goods," Craven said.

The two men on the bed exchanged glances with each other and then stared back at Craven.

"I want to see," Craven explained, "what you're going to use to finish the job."

A faint smile spread across Manno's lips, and he produced from beneath his black T-shirt an exquisitely carved bowie knife that gleamed in the hotel room's artificial light.

René followed suit, gingerly exposing the handle of what looked to be a semiautomatic pistol hidden in his baggy shorts.

"Less messy than explosives," Craven mused. "Definitely more efficient." With that settled, he picked up where he'd left off with the only man still standing. "Now Junior, where were we? Oh, yeah. Forty-eight hours. I'm still waiting for an explanation. I should have been on a plane two days ago. Instead I'm here. With you."

The Haitian unleashed his patented gap-toothed grin. "But," he stuttered, "the islands are crawling with authorities. We can hardly move about. Even this meeting places us all in grave danger."

"I gave you forty-eight hours," Craven said, "and you give me excuses." He pulled from his blazer a silencer and fit it snugly to the muzzle of his gun.

Junior's eyes widened. "But, sir . . . no . . . wait—"

Craven, raising the gun level with Junior's forehead, didn't waste any time pulling the trigger, and the man crumpled in a heap, dead before he hit the carpeted floor. Craven turned to the bruisers, neither of whom betrayed a hint of emotion.

"Men," he said, emphasizing the word for Manno's benefit, "clean up this mess. You work for me now."

CHAPTER **8**

Jacob Stedman, president and CEO of Fisher Singer Worldwide, let his phone ring three times before picking it up. Making people wait was one way, among many, to remind those working for him that his time was precious, that he was always busy, and that no one, not even his secretary, had access to him 24/7.

"They're ready for you in the boardroom," said Ms. Moser, his dowdy but efficient secretary. "You're set to go live in seven minutes."

He reviewed his notes one last time. He'd been doing interviews for years, but they never got any easier. Reporters had a habit of leading their victims down a back alley and then knifing them in the back when they least expected it. His job, as always, was to keep the interview positive—and to steer clear of any ambushes.

For this morning's interview, a camera crew from the American Financial News Network had traveled to the sprawling FSW campus to interview Stedman about his corporation's fourth quarter and annual earnings, which had been released earlier that morning. He would be entertaining questions via remote from the popular anchor team of Allen Faber and Catherine Bailey, the former a pudgy middle-aged man with Ken hair, the latter an attractive brunette with an impressive résumé to match her winsome looks.

Assuming his game face, Stedman left his office and strode purposefully down the corridor to the boardroom, where he greeted the camera crew and took his position at the head of the table. An assistant worked him over quickly, running a comb through his hair and applying a small amount of makeup before helping him with his clip-on microphone and earpiece. And just like that, he was ready to go.

The cameraman, who Stedman guessed to be in his late twenties, began counting down silently with the fingers on his right hand, and as soon as he reached his index finger, Stedman could hear the voice of Allen Faber in his earpiece.

"We're being joined live now by Jacob Stedman, CEO and chairman of the board of Fisher Singer Worldwide, whose stock is trading at another all-time high. Good morning, Mr. Stedman, and congratulations on another blowout quarter and what appears to be the best year in the company's history."

Jacob flashed a smile at the camera. It was crucial to appear at ease without looking disinterested, confident but not flip. "Good morning, Allen. And thank you. It was another great year for the company. We grew our revenue and profits by over twenty percent for the fifth year in a row and are extremely optimistic about the future."

"My first question is," Faber began, "how do you guys continue to beat the street quarter after quarter, year after year, when your competitors are experiencing sluggish growth and diminishing earnings?"

Insincere flattery, designed to soften him up before the real questions came. "Well, Allen, I'm not qualified to comment on how our competitors execute their strategies, but I can tell you that since I became CEO at FSW we have been committed to plowing a significant portion of our earnings back into research and development. For the past several years that strategy has paid big dividends, and we believe it will continue to pay big dividends."

Faber's co-anchor joined the fray. "Hello, Mr. Stedman, this is Catherine Bailey. Congratulations on another great year."

"Thank you, Catherine."

"You just mentioned that you attribute much of the company's success to your commitment to heavy R&D spending. Your financial statements show that Fisher Singer Worldwide spent more than one billion dollars last year in R&D alone. That's a thirty percent rise over the previous year, and yet your revenue only increased twenty-two percent in the same amount of time. You already spend significantly more on R&D than any other pharmaceutical company. How long can you continue to increase your R&D budget at a faster pace than your revenue is growing?"

Was this the main thrust of Bailey's probing? Or was she setting him up for a sucker punch?

Stedman nodded thoughtfully. "FSW is committed now and will continue to be committed to growing our revenue and earnings through developing great new drugs that help make peoples' lives better. R&D represents less than fifteen percent of our revenue, so we are very happy with the ratio of R&D expense growth versus revenue growth."

Faber cut in. "You spend more than one billion now on R&D, yet you have also acquired . . . I believe it's eleven companies over the past five years, while your nearest competitor has only made two or three acquisitions over the same time period. Some of these acquisitions have turned out to be complete busts, yet amazingly, your revenue and profits continue to soar. What's your secret?"

Stedman offered another smile for the camera. "It's actually twelve companies over the past five years," he said, correcting Faber. He assumed a solemn expression. "It's true that some of the companies we acquired ended up with drugs we thought could go to market but failed. However, I don't believe any of those acquisitions should be labeled a 'bust' as you call it. With each acquisition, we also brought on some remarkable talents and technologies that have led to other breakthrough discoveries—some of which have already been launched, and many more of which are in the developmental stage—that we're extremely excited about."

Bailey cut in again. "But many analysts have been quoted as saying that you overpaid for several of these acquisitions, that you paid top dollar for companies that were years away from clinical trials. Why is FSW willing to continue to pay such a high price for these small biotech companies with no proven results?"

"Catherine," he replied, relishing the fact that she'd never know the real answer to her question, "we look beyond a company's experimental drug and focus on its technologies and human talent as well. In this business, you have to take some calculated risks; not every promising drug is going to end up passing the FDA's scrutiny." Time for an all-American metaphor. "However, we don't need to hit a home run every time to be successful. If we can hit a few singles and doubles, maybe strike out once or twice, and also hit the occasional home run, then we'll continue to meet and exceed all of our goals. This is the business we're in, and I'm confident our strategy will continue to prove the best course to follow."

"Well," Faber responded, "you can't argue with success. Jacob Stedman, CEO and chairman of the board at Fisher Singer Worldwide, once again, congratulations on another fantastic year, and thanks for joining us."

"It was my pleasure," Stedman lied.

The cameraman lowered the camera, and with that, the interview was over. A crew member helped Stedman remove his earpiece and microphone and thanked him for his time.

"No, thank you," Stedman said. "You guys did a bang-up job—like always."

He offered a round of handshakes, and then he exited alone.

"Fucking reporters," he muttered to himself as soon as he was out of earshot.

CHAPTER **9**

On the third morning following his chance meeting with Jordan, Ryan awoke just after sunrise with a splitting headache and the final words of Pritchard from the night before stuck in his mind: *And if Dr. Carver is involved in any way, she may not be safe.*

Ryan reached for the bottle of Jameson on his nightstand. There wasn't much more than a few swallows left. He scratched his head, tilted the bottle to a forty-five-degree angle and held it there for a few moments before deciding to set it back on the bedside table, its contents undisturbed.

As Ryan showered, he pondered Pritchard's statement. He analyzed the facts of the incident and concluded that Pritchard was being overly cautious due to the magnitude of the case. Even so, he decided to change routine and keep on alert. After all, Jordan was the niece of Henry Carver. If the yacht explosion was an act of revenge against the former Wall Street tycoon, then the psycho pulling the strings may not be satisfied until the entire Carver clan was wiped out.

Ryan wondered what it was about Jordan that intrigued him. He had initially tried to pretend that the bond was formed as a result of her tragic circumstances, but, in a sober moment, he acknowledged to himself that he had been taken with her from the moment he laid his eyes on her. Exuma was a vacation paradise and there was never a shortage of good-looking female tour-

ists, ready and willing for some fun. But up until now, he had had
no interest. What was it about her?

After they had breakfast, Ryan suggested a tour of the island.
Jordan was concerned about Pritchard, but Ryan assured her that
she was free to move around as she pleased so long as she did not
leave Exuma. As Jordan showered, Ryan cleaned up the house and
then they set off down the road. Despite the rattling muffler, faded
red paint, and healthy layer of dust, the open-topped rig of Ryan's
fifteen-year-old jeep provided a fine 360-degree-view riding tour.

They were a few miles down on Queens Highway before he
said, "This old jeep isn't much to look at, but it handles well on these
crummy old island roads. Besides, I don't need anything fancier to
get to the few places I need to go." He took his eyes off the road
long enough to flash her a grin. "To tell you the truth, about the
only places I go are Rosey's and the harbor. Once in a great while,
I'll take my diving gear and go up the coast to really be alone."

"Haven't you had enough of the solitude?" she inquired.

He turned toward her, a note of surprise in his voice. "Yeah.
Yeah, I guess I have." Then, concentrating on the winding road,
he said, "I don't do it for the solitude. Solitude gives you time to
think and remember, and I don't need that."

"Then why hide away?"

"Good question. I guess I'm doing what comes naturally
and not necessarily what's best."

"Do you miss your work? The research?"

"Sometimes. On a rare occasion, I'll sit and think up new
ideas and rehash old projects that I left incomplete."

"Have you ever thought about getting back into clinical
research?"

"Not really."

She frowned, disappointed. "And I thought you were going
to apply for a job at my clinic."

"I still might." Ryan smiled. "But who ever said I was going
to apply for a position as research scientist? I'm sure you'll need
a maintenance engineer."

"Ha! I've seen your house and there is no way I would ever hire you to be in charge of sanitation."

Ryan shrugged. "Touché."

"Seriously," Jordan continued. "When you rehash old projects, what becomes of that?"

"Nothing, usually. I wind up drinking and forgetting my ideas."

"That's a waste of a good research mind."

"How do you know I'm any good?"

As they hugged the curve of the road entering Emerald Bay, he said, "There's a five-star resort up ahead, but I just got a better idea." Passing the grand hotel—resplendent and luxurious, yet sterile—he geared down and continued up the road. "Maybe you can tell *me* something."

Her eyes sparkled. "Try me."

"Most women as engaging, smart, and . . ." He cut the sentence short, wishing he'd begun differently. "What I want to know is—"

"Why I'm still single," she said flatly. She ran a hand through her long mane in a gesture that was neither contrived nor inhibited. "Let's just say I'm passionate about my work."

"You can't work *and* play?"

"Sure, but can you keep up?"

Ryan chuckled. The woman knew how to dance.

After a few more miles of empty road, they ended up at the Conch Shack, overlooking the ocean in the hamlet of Steventon. Jordan ordered her Captain Morgan and Diet Coke, and Ryan stuck with just a bottle of water, while they waited for the proprietor's sons to return from the bay with fresh conch.

"I've been to Exuma before, but I never knew about this place."

"The best places are the ones the tourists haven't found yet. They catch the conch as the orders are placed. Can't get any fresher than that."

Jordan grinned. "I can't wait."

They were soon enjoying a conch salad and a cup of conch chowder. "You were right, Ryan. Best I've ever had."

As they continued eating, Ryan decided to explore Pritchard's paranoia with Jordan.

"So tell me, do you have any idea if someone would want to do you harm?"

"Well, this guy back in Chicago comes to mind."

"What was his name?"

"Loukas, Victor Loukas. His wife was terminal and received the placebo in one of the clinical trials we were administering. She died nine months later. When her husband found out that she had been given the placebo, he went crazy, threatened everybody involved and vowed revenge."

"I wouldn't read too much into that. He was upset. Vowing revenge was probably just a rash reaction. And coming after you here in Exuma, well, that seems a bit unlikely."

"You're probably right. I really never gave it any thought until you asked."

Jordan took the final bite of her salad. "Although he's mega-rich, developed half of the South Side of Chicago, and owns and occupies a high rise in the Loop that would make Donald Trump proud. The scary part is that he has ties to the mob. At least, that's the rumor. If he really wanted to come after me, I don't think an ocean could stop him. If he did it back in Chicago, he would be a suspect. Here, not a chance. Besides, everyone would focus on my uncle's death and assume it had something to do with Wall Street. It would be the perfect smoke screen."

Ryan's silence was his answer.

She held his eyes. "You think I'm being melodramatic?"

"I never said that."

She couldn't hide her tightening lips. "Now that I think about it, unless they were after my uncle, it has to be Loukas. There's no one else in my life it *could* be."

"No one?" he asked, the question dripping with innuendo.

"No, no one. Sayulita—the clinic—that's my main focus

now. That shouldn't make me any enemies. Or at least none that hate me enough to want to see me dead."

* * *

Back in the jeep, Ryan had an idea to take their minds off of the investigation. "I hope you brought your bathing suit."

"I'm wearing it under my sarong."

"Good, because I know an incredible beach, private and pristine as the first day of creation."

Jordan smiled, seeming to forget all her troubles for the moment. "How could I say no? Where is it?"

"Not far. It's on Deadman's Cay."

Jordan gave him an *Are-you-messing-with-me* look but said nothing.

The drive along the winding road, with its breathtaking ocean panoramas, had a soothing effect on both of them and their mood rose with each passing mile.

They had just hit a straightaway on the road to Rolleville when a dark blue, older-model sedan roared up behind them. The sedan was moving at twice the speed of Ryan's jeep and didn't slow down until it was a few inches from his rear bumper.

"Oh shit," Ryan muttered under his breath. Noting two dark-skinned male passengers in the sedan, he felt a jolt of adrenaline shoot through his body. *Hey, Pritchard, I think I found your Haitians.*

Jordan noticed Ryan's attention to the rearview mirror. She turned around to look at the trailing sedan, then back at Ryan. "What the hell's going on?"

Ryan had no time to respond. The sedan's engine growled louder, and even as Ryan sped up, they were still gaining ground. A sharp turn was coming up and Ryan downshifted, causing the jeep to buck, pressing them tautly against their lap-only seat belts. They managed to hold the road as they swung around the curve, but the sedan was undeterred and caught back up to them within a few seconds.

"Oh, god!" she exclaimed. "What are they doing? Get us out of here!"

Ryan did not react to Jordan's hysterics. His focus was on the rearview mirror and the road ahead. He was able to gain separation from the sedan around the curves, only to have the sedan catch right back up on each straightaway. A half-mile of straight road lay before them, and Ryan knew he couldn't outrun the other car.

Suddenly they felt the sedan crash into their bumper. The jeep lurched forward and Jordan screamed. Ryan wiped the perspiration out of his eyes and floored the accelerator as they raced down the narrow road surrounded by palm trees on one side and cliffs to the ocean floor below on the other. His hands tightened on the wheel as they barreled toward the next curve a few hundred yards ahead.

But the powerful sedan was too fast and slammed into them again, harder this time. The jeep bounced forward and to the side. Ryan managed to coax the vehicle back into a straight line without oversteering but their pursuers smashed into them again with a sickening thud. Jordan careened forward, throwing her hands up against the dash just in time to avoid bashing her head.

"Sonovabitch," Ryan snarled. The road ahead left no margin for error. There was no room to the left unless he wanted to drive his jeep up a never-ending row of palm trees; to the right was certain death, a sharp curve with a steep drop off the cliff to the ocean below, protected only by an old rusted-out guardrail that had no chance of keeping a speeding vehicle from taking the plunge.

He knew it was only a matter of time before the sedan would be in position to run them off the road. He swerved around a hairpin turn, the wheels of the jeep fighting to hold the road, spraying pebbles at the flimsy guardrail only inches away.

The blue sedan cranked it up soon after they emerged from the turn and hit them a fourth time, nearly spinning them out. The road was now climbing higher over the shoreline below. Through his peripheral vision, Ryan saw Jordan clutching the dashboard with her left hand and her seat belt with the right. She kept her focus straight ahead as if a glance at their pursuers would draw them in closer.

Suddenly a star appeared in the windshield, followed by another. As she bent forward to examine the markings, Jordan screamed, "Christ, they're shooting at us!"

His brows furrowed, Ryan hunched over and fought the wheel. He knew two sharp turns lay directly ahead. *I wonder if these guys know about these turns. Pritchard said they had only been on the island for a few weeks.* Ryan was afraid it would be his last chance.

"Hold on tight," he shouted, ramming the gas pedal to the floor.

After rounding the next curve at breakneck speed, Ryan yanked the emergency brake and spun the jeep into a perfect 180, a bold and delicate maneuver given the 200-foot drop lurking just off the shoulder-less road. He punched the gas and raced head-long toward their pursuers. The sedan driver's eyes bulged as he desperately swerved to avoid the madman in the jeep charging right at him.

At the last second, Ryan sideswiped the sedan, sending it through the guardrail and careening over the cliff. With the wheels still spinning and the engine racing, the sedan plummeted down to the jagged rocks below. A thunderous explosion sent a sickly plume of black smoke up into the placid tropical sky.

Jordan was breathless as they screeched to a halt. After she had managed to steady herself enough to speak, she sputtered, "Oh my god. Where did you learn to drive like that?"

His eyes cold and steely, a new Ryan Matthews seemed to emerge from his old skin like a molting snake. "FBI," he said. "Best damn training in the world."

CHAPTER 10

Ryan and Jordan peered down at the burning wreck. Oily black smoke billowed into the air as ravenous flames engulfed the twisted mass of metal. They stared, mesmerized by the spectacle, and knew beyond a doubt that no one could have survived such a holocaust. Ryan felt some of his anxiety begin to dissipate as they stood in silence.

Soon, Franklin and his rescue crew arrived, followed closely by Pritchard and Bradshaw. Gazing over the cliff, Pritchard said, "Looks like somebody came to a bad end." He paused. "Are you up to filling in the specifics for me? Of course, we can wait a while if you prefer." They both shook their heads and Ryan gave him the details of their harrowing adventure.

"Mon," Franklin said, as Ryan finished his story, "dat must have been some fancy driving. By da looks of the skid marks, your jeep did a U-turn and accelerated back toward da other vehicle at high speed, all within fifty yards."

Pritchard squinted at Ryan. "The Bureau?"

"I guess so. I thought I'd forgotten about that part of my life. But I can't explain it. Something just kicked in. It was like I was driving on autopilot."

The blackened mass of the sedan was still smoking as the tow truck dragged it back up the cliff face. Ryan and Jordan followed Pritchard and Bradshaw over to the area where rescue workers had covered two bodies with a tarp. Pritchard pulled back the cover.

"The bodies are burned beyond recognition, but based on their jewelry we have every reason to believe that these are the Haitian suspects."

Only now was Ryan struck full force by the impact of the chase, the deaths, and the implications involved. Shaken and weary, he asked, "Is it okay if we go, Everett? I could use a drink."

"Go ahead. I will be in touch with you folks later this afternoon."

Ryan and Jordan drove slowly back to his place. "Funny," Ryan said, shaking his head.

"What?"

"After something like that, all you want to do is ratchet your life down to a slower speed." His thoughts turned to Cindy, Jake, and Karly and he fought back tears as he relived his nightmare on the long drive home.

After a long pause, Jordan said, "I think when you face your own mortality, you realize the value of the simple things."

Ryan was still deep in thought and did not respond. They drove the rest of the way in silence.

* * *

At the house, Ryan didn't ask Jordan if she wanted a drink, he just went ahead and fixed them both a stiff Scotch. Jordan's with soda and his straight up. They retired to the living room sofa and sat quietly for a while. It was Jordan who spoke first.

"So you learned all that fancy driving in the FBI, huh?"

"You don't believe me?"

She grinned. "Lots of guys try hard to impress a lady. I didn't realize you were the genuine article."

He returned her grin. "I won't take that as an insult."

"Please don't." She took a hit on her drink. "So how did they recruit you?"

"Oh, the usual way, I suppose. They were there waiting when I graduated from Wake Forest."

"And you went right into the James Bond stuff?"

He had to smile at that. "No. I started out in the bioterror division. I guess it isn't often they have a chance at an athletic valedictorian with a bio and chemistry degree."

"How long did you last?"

"About two years. It got real boring."

"Bioterrorism? Boring?" she exclaimed in disbelief. "The two words don't seem to go together."

"It's boring when nothing ever happens. Most of my time was spent in training and running what-if scenarios. And that was the exciting part. In two years, I was only in the field twice and both of those turned out to be false alarms."

"So you embarked on another course."

"I figured if my goal was to save lives, I could do more good trying to save Americans who were dying every year from disease."

Jordan gazed at him as if trying to peer into his soul.

He glanced at her, understanding her intent. "You won't find it on my face. It's deep inside. I was passionate. I wanted to do it all. I—"

"I can see that," she interrupted.

"But it all came to an end when the plane carrying my family to Exuma crashed into the sea." Ryan paused and envisioned himself sitting with Cindy, Jake, and Karly around the dinner table back at their home in North Carolina. In his vision, they were all laughing about something, but he snapped back to reality before he could recall what it was. "Since that time my life has been devoid of passion and purpose."

She took his hand and waited, perhaps sensing his need for silence. After some time had passed, she said, "You haven't lost your purpose, Ryan. It's only hidden behind your pain."

He cast her a haunted look, wanting desperately to believe her.

"Don't you see, Ryan?" she implored. "It's only your fear of the pain that keeps you from finding your passion again." She squeezed his hand gently. "You were a brilliant researcher once. You still are. You owe it to yourself to get back in the game."

* * *

They were napping on separate couches when the doorbell rang. Rubbing his eyes, Ryan went to the door just as Jordan was waking up.

Pritchard was pacing on the front porch when Ryan opened the door.

"Everett, what's the latest?"

"Nothing new. All the suspects are deceased and we have no viable motive." Pritchard rubbed his chin and shook his head. "Furthermore, we are not even sure if the assassins' main target was Henry Carver, Jordan Carver, or the entire Carver family."

Ryan joined Pritchard out front and closed the door behind him. "If the target was not Jordan, then why did they come after us today?"

"I'm not sure. Could be they were just trying to tie up loose ends or throw us off the track."

"If that was their strategy, then it seems to have worked. Is there anything you do know?"

Pritchard squinted his eyes and frowned. "About the only thing we know for certain is that these men were professionals."

"And how do you know that?"

"The report from Interpol came in about an hour ago. They each had impressive wrap sheets. Duval was a key suspect in several bombings in Port-au-Prince a few years back, but the authorities did not have enough to hold him. Edmond and Sanon have been off the radar for the past four years, but Interpol lists their probable occupation as mercenaries."

"Mercenaries? Is that the politically correct way to say assassins these days?"

Before Pritchard could respond, the front door opened and Jordan walked out. "Did I hear someone mention assassins?"

Pritchard straightened up and responded in a serious official tone. "Yes, Dr. Carver. Ryan and I were discussing the background of the men who blew up your aunt and uncle's yacht and who attempted to deliver a similar fate to you and Ryan earlier today. As I've just informed Ryan, at this point all the suspects are dead and yet we have come up with no motive as to why professional hit men would travel to Exuma and come after you and your family. We are not even sure if these men were after your uncle, you, or both. Any ideas?"

"No idea. I have been in shock since the death of my aunt and uncle. We already discussed my uncle's background and the pension scandal that led to his retirement. While I suppose such an incident can lead to many adversaries, I am unaware of anyone who was so devastated and outraged that they would, or even could, plan an assassination three years after the fact on a small Bahamian island. Unless there is something my uncle was hiding from me, I cannot think of anyone who would go to such extremes to bring him harm."

"I followed up on your uncle's background and the pension scandal. I cannot disagree with what you say. So if your aunt and uncle had no known enemies, or at least no enemies willing or capable of such an elaborate undertaking, then the only possible conclusion is that your uncle developed a powerful enemy who you are not aware of."

Before Pritchard could continue, Jordan responded. "I guess anything is possible. But he has been retired for three years and sailing around the globe. Hard to imagine that someone would wait this long and then strike at him, and me, on Exuma."

"Then, as I was about to add, the enemy must be yours and your aunt and uncle were unfortunately sacrificed in their attempt to eliminate you. Are you aware of anyone who would want to do you harm?"

Jordan turned to Ryan before facing Pritchard again. "No. I

have been racking my brains over this and cannot think of anyone who would have a motive to do me harm."

Pritchard relaxed and reached into his jacket pocket, pulled out a passport, and handed it to Jordan. "Okay then. Here is your passport back. You are free to leave the island but we will need an official statement on the events of today before you leave."

"We will be in first thing tomorrow, Everett."

"Thanks, Ryan. I will see you tomorrow then. By the way, Dr. Carver, if you can think of anything that could assist in our investigation, please contact me at any time."

"Of course."

Pritchard shook hands with Jordan, then Ryan, offered his condolences to Jordan again and thanked them both for their cooperation. "I do not mean to alarm you any more than you already are, Dr. Carver, but these men were most likely hired assassins, which means the person who hired them is still out there. If that person's target was not your aunt or uncle, then you are still in danger and I caution you to proceed with great care."

As Pritchard pulled out of the driveway, Ryan asked, "Why didn't you mention this Victor Loukas character to Pritchard?"

"I thought about it for a second and then decided why bother. I can't imagine there is anything he could do from Exuma and I have no proof that he was involved."

"That's probably true, but it couldn't hurt to get it on the record in case Pritchard discovers a connection with one of these men and Loukas. Who knows what they might turn up as the investigation continues. Give it some thought and we can always notify Pritchard tomorrow morning."

"You make a good point. I just didn't want to cause that man any more pain if he was not involved. Let me think about it."

* * *

After dinner, Ryan and Jordan decided to enjoy what remained of their bottle of Silver Oak on the back deck. The beach and crashing surf were illuminated by a full moon and billions of stars shining in the pure night sky.

"I can see why you never came back to the states, Ryan. It is so beautiful here."

Ryan smiled. "That it is, but I have been thinking that I'm about due for a trip back."

"Well, you are certainly welcome to stay with me back in Chicago, but I am only going to be there for a few more weeks once I leave Exuma."

"Have you given that any thought yet?"

"I planned on being here for two weeks, so my flight back is still ten days away. But given the circumstances, I will probably head back early."

Ryan's smile disappeared. "Then what?"

"Then I pack up and relocate to my own version of paradise in Sayulita. And you're welcome to visit me there as well." Jordan hesitated, then smiled. "And we are still looking to fill positions on our maintenance staff, so if you still want that job, I may be able to make an exception despite your cleaning skills, being that you saved my life today."

Ryan raised his glass and smiled back at Jordan. "Be careful of what you offer, I may take you up on all of them." Ryan took the final swallow of wine from his glass, then grabbed the bottle and topped off Jordan's glass and poured the remainder into his. He took another sip. "I hate to bring up the subject, but have you given any thought to what you're going to do with your aunt and uncle's remains?"

"They loved life on the ocean. I thought I'd have them cremated and scatter their ashes out at sea."

He thought a moment and said, "I bet that's the way they would have wanted it."

"Oh I am sure it will piss off the vultures back in Manhattan. I've already picked up several messages from some of my uncle's old friends. They want to have an extravagant memorial service stateside. I am going to call them back tomorrow and tell them to do what they want—but not to wait for me. I have no interest in listening to a bunch of old millionaires eulogize my uncle."

"I'm sure we can make the arrangements needed in the morning. What about dealing with estate issues?"

"That was going to be my first call tomorrow. Their attorney is an old family friend and one of the vultures I just mentioned."

"Sounds like you've got it all worked out." Ryan took another taste of his wine and lit up a Marlboro. "Have you given any more thought of notifying Pritchard about Loukas?"

"I've been thinking about it. As you said, I guess it can't hurt. I'll tell Pritchard the whole story when we give our statements in the morning."

Ryan took another drag of his cigarette and dropped his shoulders. "I'm glad you came to that decision, Jordan. I know it's a long shot, but absent any other theories, it's about all we have to go on. And the possible link between Loukas and the Haitian assassins needs to be investigated."

Jordan shifted in her chair and took a drink of wine. "There's one other possibility. I've been reluctant to bring it up because you'll think I'm nuts. But the more I think about it, the more I feel it is a viable theory. Well, at least as viable as the Loukas theory."

"Okay, I'm curious. Let's hear it."

"The primary goal of my clinic is to cure people from their disease and, as a result, curb their dependency on the daily medications they need to stay alive. And this will take a lot of money out of the pockets of the big pharmaceutical companies."

Ryan chewed on that for a moment. "Jordan, I know you believe that your clinic is going to save a lot of lives—and I sure hope you're right—but the mega-billion-dollar pharma companies are not going to have you murdered just because you're selling experimental treatments. At this stage of your clinic, it doesn't make any sense to do so."

"I told you that you would think I'm nuts." Jordan grinned. "But I think you're being naive. Why would they wait until I was a real competitor? Wouldn't it make more sense to eliminate me before I hit the radar screens?"

Taken aback, Ryan cleared his throat. "Okay, even if you are right, unless you have some specific information such as a person or company who made threats or approached you in an aggressive manner, there is nothing to even investigate. I think it will be more productive to concentrate on Loukas."

"I don't have a name or a company in mind and hope I am wrong. What you said makes sense. I guess for now, we will focus on Loukas."

"Are you sure that someone like Loukas could keep tabs on you to the point where he would know you were coming here to Exuma and that you planned to cruise on your aunt and uncle's yacht? Seems as though it wouldn't be easy to uncover that kind of information."

She set her glass down and began to pace around the room.

"But I don't have any other suspects. Besides the pharmaceutical companies, the only lead I have is Loukas. I can remember the anger, the dark rage on his face when he learned the details of his wife's death. You had to be there, Ryan. You had to see the man."

Ryan took a drink before offering a response. "You mentioned that this Loukas was both loaded and connected. I guess anyone with enough cash and connections could arrange for the murder of just about anyone in the world. Let's discuss it with Pritchard tomorrow and get his feedback."

* * *

Jordan's eyes settled on Ryan as she exited the interview room at the George Town Police Station. "I gave Pritchard a step-by-step replay of everything that happened yesterday and then told him about Loukas."

"What was his response?"

"He didn't say much, just wrote down everything I told him even though he was recording our conversation. He said he would see what he could do and thanked me for my time."

"That sounds like Everett. Thorough and tight-lipped. I'm up next and will press him on the issue after I give my statement."

"Sounds good. I'm going to step out and make some overdue calls and then see about making the final arrangements for Aunt Jenny and Uncle Henry. Want to meet me at Rosey's for lunch when you're finished?"

"I'll see you then."

* * *

Ryan was into his second Kalik when Jordan strolled up and took a seat next to him on Rosey's deck overlooking Emerald Bay.

"I'm sorry I'm late. It took longer than I thought to make the arrangements. How did it go with Pritchard?"

Ryan shook his head. "Pritchard was no help at all. He told me the investigation was over. Orders from Nassau. Nothing more he could do unless new information fell in his lap."

"What about Loukas?"

"He said they did not have the resources to pursue such a lead. He suggested I contact my friends back at the FBI if we really wanted to pursue it and gave me a copy of the Interpol reports on the three dead Haitians."

"Ryan, I can't drag you in on this. This is *my* problem. You hardly know me. Besides, you've done too much already."

"Look. I still have connections with the Bureau. A guy I went through training with came down to the islands for a visit just last year. He's stationed in Chicago. Hopefully, I can get him to sidestep protocol and dig up some background on Loukas. You'll get nowhere on your own. It'll be a big runaround and it could be dangerous. If I'm in for a penny I might as well be in for a pound." He felt a rush of real purpose like he hadn't felt in years.

"I don't want to be an ingrate but I don't want to feel guilty about you risking your neck helping me, either."

He finished his beer. "Look, Jordan, all I have these days is my neck. I think there are much worse things than risking it once in a while. In fact, it's a gift to have something to risk my neck for."

She hesitated. "You're just angry because Pritchard gave you the cold shoulder. Take a few days and think about it. If you still feel the same way then we'll fly back to Chicago together and use your FBI contacts. Fair enough?"

"That's fair enough, but too late. I already booked our flights. Let's get some lunch and then head back to my place and pack. We have the first flight out tomorrow morning."

CHAPTER **11**

The American Airlines 757 gave a small shudder as it made a turn to port causing Ryan's stomach to churn. He reminded himself to relax as he released his vice-like grip on the armrests. He hadn't been on a plane in years—since before the accident. The simple tasks of the reservation process, keeping track of luggage, and going through customs in Miami had already aggravated him. He really wasn't looking forward to reacquainting himself with the hustle and bustle of life off the island.

Jordan sat to his right as he gazed left out the window. The big jet convulsed as it arced into its final approach. Over the dipped port wing, he saw a massive, featureless expanse that he presumed to be Lake Michigan, partially frozen and frosted by falling snow. The skyline of Chicago clung to its shore under a heavy gray sky. When the pilot announced the temperature in the Chicago area as ten degrees Fahrenheit, Ryan shivered.

After some fairly dramatic—or so it seemed to him—wobbling on the approach to the runway, the aircraft made a fairly smooth landing. The passengers uttered a shared sigh of relief and the hulking jet lumbered over to one of the terminal buildings.

After a twenty-minute wait for their luggage, Ryan and Jordan followed their porter outside and onto one of the busy airport access roads. Ryan's breath was taken away by the icy air and sharp, gusting wind. His skin hadn't felt anything under sixty degrees on Exuma. He shoved his hands deeper into his pockets, tucking his chin inside his collar while waiting for one of the many yellow cabs to open up. He was glad he hadn't thrown away the coat he brought to the island five years previous.

* * *

As Ryan unloaded their bags in the foyer of Jordan's upscale lakefront condo, he announced, "I've set up a meeting with my friend from the Bureau for ten tomorrow morning."

"Where at?"

"It's at the Dirksen Federal Building on Dearborn Street."

"Sounds good. That's not too far away." She paused, then added, "And for your gracious hospitality on the island, dinner's on me."

The smile she flashed made him skip a breath. Hidden in her eyes he could clearly see an invitation for something more. It took him a few seconds to register that she was waiting for a response.

"Great. That sounds . . . great." He struggled to come up with something coherent. "I'll bet you have a favorite place."

"Café Ba-Ba-Reeba. Spanish tapas. You'll love it."

* * *

They settled in close together at a cozy table in a quiet corner of the restaurant. Café Ba-Ba-Reeba was comfortably crowded. Although there were a dozen wait staff delivering tapas and sangria to scores of tables divided up in several smaller rooms, the place remained intimate.

"I thought a place called Café Ba-Ba-Reeba would be flashier."

"What, you expected flamenco dancers and singing waiters?"

"I guess I did." He perused the menu. "What do you recommend?"

"The baked goat cheese and beef brochette will knock your socks off."

He smiled over his wine glass. "Well, so far the sangria is great."

"Be careful. It may taste like fruit juice but it's strong."

After a couple of pitchers of the brandy-laced Spanish wine, some excellent spicy food, and fun conversation, Ryan began to harbor fleeting thoughts of romance. He had been attracted to Jordan since the moment they met. But with the death of her aunt and uncle, the brief time she spent as a suspect in their deaths, and then the life and death car chase throughout the island, the timing for a romantic interlude just never seemed right. Now, with an ocean separating them from those events, tonight felt like the right time to explore that possibility.

Back at Jordan's, she turned to him slyly and, with a smoky look, announced that she was going to slip into something comfortable. Ryan's heart picked up a beat as he watched her slink off to her bedroom. The drinks had left them buzzed, but that in itself was a double-edged sword. On the one hand, the alcohol lowered their inhibitions; on the other, following a full day of travel and a large meal, it had made them both sleepy.

He plopped down on the couch and turned on the TV to keep himself from dozing off. The minutes ticked by in red digital numbers on the cable box as Ryan struggled to keep his eyes open. After twenty minutes, he figured it had been long enough for any woman to get comfortable. Ryan staggered to his feet and tiptoed to Jordan's bedroom door. After two light raps with no response, he turned the knob as he called her name. She was curled up on her bed, wearing a sleek nighty that barely covered her backside. She had a content look on her face, her breasts rising and falling with her breathing.

Ryan shook his head. Smiling at what could have been, he pulled a comforter over her and retreated back to the living room, quietly closing the door behind him.

* * *

Jim Crawford was a youthful-looking man with even features, a poster boy for the Bureau. He greeted Ryan with a hearty slap on the back and introduced himself to Jordan, openly admiring her without making her feel as if she were on display. She sat in his office with her feet crossed at the ankles, waiting while the two friends went through their requisite exchange regarding Bureau training and the good old days.

When they had finished catching up and got down to business, Jordan leaned forward and added her own descriptions of their dilemma and answered questions that Crawford directed at her. After Ryan's narrative of the events of Jordan's five days in Exuma, the FBI man's opinion was that the theory of Loukas's involvement might be a good one, though he admitted to a complete lack of evidence to support the suspicion.

In effect, he told them what they already knew: it was nearly impossible to build a case worthy of an indictment against such a well-connected man. However, he did offer to investigate on his end to find out if any additional information was within the reach of the Bureau.

"What's first?" Jordan asked.

"I'll try to find out if Loukas has or has had any connections with these Haitians—or *any* Haitians, for that matter."

Jordan nodded at the FBI man. "That makes sense."

Ryan grinned. "That's why he gets paid the big bucks."

"Yeah, right," Crawford scoffed. "I finally bought my first boat recently. An eighteen-foot bowrider."

"Still going after those lake bass, Jim?"

"You know it," Crawford said. He was about to launch into a fishing story when Jordan stood up. She had had enough of the male bonding rituals for one morning.

She extended her hand. "Thanks for everything. We look forward to hearing about your findings on Loukas."

Ryan took her cue and rose to his feet. He reached into his jacket pocket and produced a small sheaf of papers, folded lengthwise and bound by a rubber band. "The chief in Exuma is a friend of mine. He gave me these before we left the island."

With a puzzled look, Crawford took the papers from Ryan.

"It's the Interpol report on the Haitians," Ryan explained.

"Ah, well done." Crawford gave the papers a cursory glance. "That's a start. It'll save me some leg work." They exchanged cell phone numbers, and Ryan and Jordan were on their way. When they reached the lobby, Ryan asked Jordan to wait for him and walked back to Crawford's office.

"Jim, you don't have anyone following us, do you?"

"Afraid not buddy, why do you ask?"

"It's probably nothing. I guess I'm just paranoid after what happened on Exuma, but I could swear I've seen the same person several times since landing at O'Hare."

"You have a description for me?"

"Big burly-looking guy with a hook nose. Probably 6'2", two hundred thirty pounds give or take, black wavy hair, maybe forty years old. Not the type of guy who blends in easy with a crowd."

Crawford jotted down the description. "Any identifying marks? Scars, tattoos?"

"He never got close enough for me to see, so no way I could say for sure."

"Okay. I'll enter that description into our database and see if we get any hits."

* * *

An hour later, they were eating deep-dish Chicago-style pizza in another of Jordan's favorite places when Ryan's cell phone rang. It was Jim Crawford. Jordan moved over closer to Ryan, and he held the phone so she could hear both sides of the conversation.

"I got Jordan here Jim, what did you find out?"

"Sure enough, we had a file on Loukas, and a thick one at that. He's a guy we keep tabs on. We know he has connections to organized crime but we've never dug up enough dirt to obtain an indictment," Crawford said. "Even so, I don't think he's your guy."

"Why not?" Ryan asked.

"He's been locked away in a drug rehab program for the past five weeks. Apparently he went off the deep end after the death of his wife and has been mired in painkillers and alcohol ever since."

"Damn, that doesn't sound promising."

"No, it doesn't. My sources tell me that drugs and alcohol have been his only focus for a good while and I couldn't find any info regarding his recent involvement in anything, legit or not. I think this angle is a dead end for you, buddy."

Ryan pulled the phone up to his ear and made a quarter turn away from Jordan.

"Sounds that way. Well, thanks for looking into this for us, Jim. Anything else?"

"I'm still waiting for the results on that other matter, but should have something before the end of the day."

CHAPTER **12**

Senator McNally entered his office and walked straight to his secretary's desk.

Marge O'Neil, a heavy-set middle-aged woman with a no-nonsense attitude, lowered her reading glasses as she looked up from her work. She was not intimidated by the senator, or anyone else for that matter, and always spoke her mind freely. Some on the senator's staff found her demeanor a tad brusque, but McNally valued her exceptional work ethic, the speed with which she could accomplish any task, and the fact that she challenged him on a regular basis. He didn't need any more yes-men (or -women).

"Good morning, Senator. How was your trip to Africa?"

"Very successful," he replied. "But I'm glad to be back in civilization."

"Don't gripe, sir. These trips around the world are going to help get you elected president someday."

The senator smiled. She certainly had a way with people. "That's the plan, Marge." He grabbed a fistful of messages from her desk and continued on to his private office, shutting the door behind him.

He'd barely sat down when Marge rang him.

"Yes?"

"Senator Dorn is on his way over," she said, "and Senator Nichols's office confirmed this morning."

"Thanks for seeing to that. Go ahead and set them up in the conference room, and let me know when they've arrived."

He hung up the phone and began preparing a few notes for the conference, the final in a series of six behind-closed-doors meetings over the past year that he'd arranged with the two senators to cobble together what would be his most important accomplishment to date: a comprehensive bill aimed at Social Security reform. He was deep in thought when his private line rang. Only a handful of people—a few top CEOs who happened to be big supporters, a couple of his special projects operatives, and the White House staff—had the number, so he knew it was serious business. He picked up on the second ring.

"Yes?"

He felt his heart beat harder in his chest and removed his handkerchief from his pocket to wipe the beads of sweat that were beginning to form on his forehead as he listened to the caller's message.

As soon as the person on the other end of the line had finished, the senator replied with as much cool as he could muster. "I'm glad you called. I appreciate the update. Keep your head, and focus on the objective. I'll do what I can on my end to clear the path, okay?"

Marge knocked on his door just as he was hanging up.

"The senators are here and waiting for you in the conference room," she said.

"Great," Senator McNally said. "I'll be right out."

* * *

Senator McNally entered the conference room, where he found Senators Jim Dorn and Allen Nichols waiting. Dorn and Nichols were older than McNally in chronological years, but only Dorn, enjoying his fourth term, had served longer in the Senate.

"Good morning, gentlemen," McNally said warmly. He held both men in high regard and rarely bothered to hide his affection for them. Dorn and Nichols returned his greeting, and McNally took a seat opposite them at the table.

"Let's get started," McNally said. "Gentlemen, we've been over this a half dozen times now, and it's time to finalize our bill. You know my position. I believe it's imperative that the bill we sponsor is actually capable of being passed, and this means we need to offer compromise so that both sides of the aisle can come to an agreement. You know my position is that the wage base on which Social Security is taxed must be increased and that the minimum age of eligibility must be raised. What we need to come to agreement on today is the amount of the wage base increase, the manner in which we will step up the minimum age requirement, and what we are going to offer up to the other side of the aisle to persuade them to pass the Social Security Reform Act."

Dorn, balding, perennially sour-faced, and twenty-three years McNally's senior, was the first to comment. "My thoughts haven't changed," he said dryly. He laced his wide fingers together and rested them on his sizeable belly. It was his trademark move, designed to put everyone on notice that he was about to lay down the law. He was plenty adept at making his case, if a bit predictable. "I don't believe there should be any wage cap on Social Security tax, and we should leave the current retirement age alone. And I have no reason to throw in a carrot to induce the other side to pass the damn bill. We all know that this needs to be done to protect Social Security, and we'll hang them out to dry if they don't support this bill."

Senator Nichols shook his head in disagreement. Lean and angular and sporting wire-rimmed glasses, he was in every way Dorn's opposite and strung together his sentences with quick precision. "My constituents will hang me out to dry if I co-sponsor a bill that has no cap on the Social Security wage base. I'm afraid that we are going to need to put a reasonable cap into the bill. I am open to a step-up raise in the minimum age requirements, and I agree with Senator Dorn that this bill is already bipartisan. There is no need to offer any carrots."

McNally was quick to counter. "Allen, ninety-five percent of the people who voted for you don't even earn enough to receive any relief from the current Social Security wage base cap. They'll applaud any initiative you make to protect their future Social Security that passes a larger proportion of the bill on to the wealthy. And Jim, if we don't begin to raise the minimum eligibility age, any gains made by raising the earnings cap will be offset—and then some—by an ever-growing population of people eligible for Social Security. You know this. I know this. Hell, anyone who has studied the problem to any degree knows this. So let's stop fucking around and put out a bill that makes at least a little bit of sense."

"Ed," Senator Dorn said, "you know I agree with you in principal, but even if we all get behind these initiatives, the other side is going to shoot it down."

Senator Nichols removed his glasses and searched them for dust and debris. "I agree. The other side is going to shoot it down if we go all the way on both of these provisions."

McNally scratched his head. "So you both agree with these provisions, yet it wasn't a minute ago you were both on your high horses saying the bill is what is needed to save Social Security, that it's already structured as a bipartisan bill, and that we'll hang the other side out to dry if they try to shoot it down. Now I agree that the other side will shoot it down as is. That's why we need to offer them a big carrot to accept the bill with these provisions."

Dorn rubbed his paunch. "And what are you suggesting that big carrot should be?"

"Gentlemen, as you know, the inheritance tax relief provision is set to expire soon. Their proposal to have it made permanent has been killed on the floor of Congress. Their big supporters are the ultra-wealthy, and this reinstatement of the inheritance tax will harm them the most; these constituents are pissing and moaning louder than anyone else to find a way to get inheritance relief reinstated. If we offer to include this in the bill, I assure you we can get our Social Security bill passed. And Allen, before you complain that your constituents will go berserk if you vote to extend inheritance tax relief, we know that this will never affect the majority of the people who voted for you. While they may not jump for joy about this provision, in the end they'll gladly accept the bill as progress."

"That may be, Ed," Senator Nichols said, "but providing tax relief to the wealthy is everything this party is against."

"This is Congress, Allen. Sometimes we have to compromise our principles for the greater good. Besides, the additional tax revenue we receive from reinstatement of the inheritance tax would just be squandered on some worthless social program or used to fund another war that doesn't need fighting. The economic fight is on our turf, and if Social Security reform is not passed now, it may be too late to fix it in a few years."

Senator Nichols laughed amicably. "You're a hard person to disagree with, Ed, especially when I agree with everything you say. Maybe with this additional provision, the bill could work."

"It has to work, or our country is going to be in big trouble. A trouble I'm afraid we will not be able to recover from."

Senator Dorn sighed. Like Nichols, he looked ready to give in. "I think we need to take a shot at this. Ed, if you'll fill in the fine points and send me a copy, I'll certainly review it with an open mind."

"I'll have a final draft of the bill to each of you by the end of the day. You can review it over the weekend, and if we're all in agreement, we'll move forward next week."

Marge stopped Senator McNally before he could sneak by her on the way back to his office. "How did the meeting go?"

"Good," he said. "I think I finally got them to sign on."

Although she relished keeping Senator McNally in line, at the moment his secretary was beaming with pride. "That's great news, sir. Congratulations."

"Thanks," the senator replied. "But even if we get the bill passed, it will only buy us another five years or so, unless . . ."

Marge cocked her head. "Unless what?"

It was tempting to fill her in, to unload on someone outside the bubble. But he could never share what he knew. "Never mind," he said, and retired to his office. Once inside, he locked the door. If Marge tried the door and found it locked, she'd know not to disturb him. She had always respected his boundaries, even during those moments when she no doubt felt he deserved another scolding.

He walked to his credenza and picked up a photo of two smiling elderly gentlemen, one of them wrapping his arm around the other's shoulder, standing on the deck of a beautiful luxury yacht. The gentleman on the right bore a striking resemblance to Senator McNally, albeit thirty years into the future. McNally set the photo down on his credenza and wiped away a tear that was trickling down his cheek.

CHAPTER **13**

William Craven answered his cell phone on the second ring.

"Good afternoon," the man on the other end of the line said. "What do you have for me?"

Craven sighed as he gazed out the window of his taxi. He hated giving his boss anything but successful reports. "Good news and bad," he finally answered. "Bad news first. Our friend is on the move, so we're still awaiting resolution. Good news is, we've hired someone local to finish the job. He knows the territory and assures me success is imminent."

"Good. No more screw-ups. In the meantime, I've got something else I need you to take care of."

Craven loosened his tie. "Hit me."

"Witherspoon is reporting positive results in Nigeria—*one hundred percent* positive. I've instructed the investment bankers to put together a deal to acquire GenClone. I want you to start preparing background reports on all key personnel."

"Done," Craven said. "Anything else?"

"No. I think you have more than enough to keep you busy."

CHAPTER 14

The news from Crawford was discouraging. By the time their pizza arrived, Ryan and Jordan had lost their appetites. None of the fun and good cheer of the previous evening at Café Ba-Ba-Reeba lingered. Thoughts of the Loukas dead end weighed on both of them. Ryan couldn't think of anything to offer but more speculation.

"Isn't there a chance that the Haitians were after your aunt and uncle for their own reasons?"

Jordan didn't answer. Moving her fork back and forth across her pizza, she seemed lost in thought.

With little enthusiasm, Ryan said, "Maybe the Haitians only went after you because they had messed things up and wanted to tie up the loose end."

Jordan continued her listless motions with her fork. "I don't know. That doesn't make sense," she muttered under her breath.

Ryan reached over and patted the back of her hand. She gave him a weak smile.

"Will you be going back to Exuma?" Jordan asked.

"If you don't mind, I'll stick around for a few days. I'm still concerned about your safety. Hell, I could have called Crawford from Exuma and faxed him the Interpol report. Even though Loukas seems to be a dead end, there is someone with deep pockets and a lot of power who may want you out of the picture and I've got nothing better to do right now. You can rely on Jim Crawford, but he is not authorized to arrange protection unless they can pinpoint a viable threat."

"I appreciate this, Ryan. You are welcome to stay as long as you want." She looked up from her plate. "I love having you around, but hate the thought of having you risk your neck for me."

"I know, but we already had that conversation. Case closed."

The waiter appeared with a take-out container. Jordan placed the uneaten half of the deep-dish pizza into the box and turned to Ryan, her eyes dull. "I'm not feeling too well. Would you mind taking this pizza while I use the ladies' room? We can eat it at home tonight."

Ryan stood, concerned. "Okay. I'll have the valet get the car. I'll meet you outside."

Stepping into the bitter cold outside the restaurant, Ryan presented the ticket to a young man with dark skin and a maroon smock just as a tall young white man with long hair pulled back in a ponytail and wearing a similar smock snapped it away from him. "I'll get it."

When the valet wheeled up with the jet-black BMW X5, Ryan smiled. The car was an exact match for Jordan: sleek, sexy, and sassy.

The pony-tailed kid hopped out of the car and hurried away to the next customer before Ryan could give him his tip. Standing by the SUV with the driver's side door ajar, Ryan spotted Jordan strolling toward him down the covered entryway. He admired her fabulous figure as she approached. Mesmerized, Ryan tossed the pizza box over to the passenger seat.

The explosion stopped Jordan mid-stride, the flash of light searing her retinas. When reality hit her, she moaned, "Oh my god!" Louder and in a panic, she wailed, "Ryan! Where are you?"

A shower of flaming debris from the BMW rained down around her. Her eyes darted back and forth as she searched for Ryan through the smoke. Then she spotted what looked like a twisted bundle of rags huddled on the pavement about ten feet from the mangled car.

She threw both hands to her mouth, the screams of a nearby woman reverberating in her head. Everything was moving at a tortured, dragging pace.

She turned, almost as if in a trance, to discover the source of the shrieking: the sounds were her own. She screamed Ryan's name, unable to move, her eyes riveted to the still form on the street.

CHAPTER **15**

Shaking her head as she slowly emerged from the haze of shock, Jordan finally gathered her courage and dashed over to peer down into Ryan's blackened face. A brave bystander from the other side of the street had grabbed him by the arms and dragged him away from the burning debris. She took a deep, ragged breath and placed her finger against his neck, searching for a pulse. A soft sigh escaped her lips as she released her finger. She had detected a weak flutter—a hopeful, yet frightening indication of Ryan's precarious condition.

When the paramedics arrived, she explained that she was a doctor and close friend of the victim, and they let her ride along to the hospital. She averted her eyes as the paramedics ripped his clothes off, revealing more charred skin. As a doctor, her first impulse was to jump right into the fray and administer first aid, but she knew they would not allow it. In fact, the uncontrollable trembling of her entire body rendered her useless to assist.

At the hospital, Ryan was rushed into the emergency room. Jordan was ordered to wait outside. Within fifteen minutes, two uniformed Chicago cops came in searching for the woman whom they had seen ride away with the ambulance. Though both looked to be in their early forties, the officers were a study in contrasts. One was short, nearly bald, and sported a pencil-thin mustache. The other was tall and thin with unkempt hair and great bushy eyebrows that hovered over his pale eyes like storefront awnings.

Jordan had little to offer them, as she knew no more about the explosion than any of the other bystanders. Still, they plowed dutifully onward with their mundane questions that, given Ryan's condition, increased her ire with every passing word.

"What's your relationship with the victim?" the short one asked.

She glared at her inquisitor. "Friend," she said.

"Whose car was it?"

"Mine," she said through tight teeth.

"Why did the car explode? Was it a bomb?"

"Look," she snapped, "what's the use of all these questions? My concern right now is with his status. I don't want to focus on anything else, especially answering a bunch of nonsense."

The tall cop did not take well to her outburst. "Look, lady. This is serious business and our questions are anything but nonsense. These days a bomb goes off and people want to know if terrorists are involved. Trust me, you'd rather deal with us than the FBI on this one. If you evade our questions, you're gonna wind up a prime suspect."

"I'm not evading anything. But you're asking me things I don't know. I already told you that I was walking out of the restaurant when I saw my car explode. That is *all I know*." She emphasized the last three words as though the cops were schoolchildren, all the while staring at the ER door.

"You know they're not gonna let you go in there," the taller officer said. "When they're ready, they'll come out and tell you what's going on. In the meantime, why don't you just cooperate and answer our questions, dumb as they may sound."

Jordan sighed and bowed her head. "Okay," she said, her voice lowered, "ask away."

The shorter cop licked his thumb and turned a page in his notebook. "Okay now, any idea who might want to see your friend Mr. Matthews hurt?"

"It's Dr. Ryan Matthews, and the answer is no—at least not

to my knowledge."

"Where does he live?"

"Exuma."

"Where's that? Someplace up north?"

"No. It's an island in the Bahamas."

The cop gave a nod and wrote it down. "So, who do you think might have reason to do something like this?"

"Oh, for Christ's sake." She ran a hand through her hair in frustration. "This isn't the first time I've been through this sort of thing."

The tall cop raised his impressive brows.

"I'm not sure, but I think they were after me, not him."

"Who are 'they'?"

Exasperated, Jordan spit out, "The drug lords, okay? The goddamned drug lords."

The cop looked confused. "So there's some kind of gang connection?"

Jordan was gritting her teeth and about to answer when Dr. Sidkey appeared. She dashed over to him.

"Is he okay?" she asked.

The doctor took her by the shoulders. "Relax. He's going to be all right. He's got a concussion and some second-degree burns to the arms and chest, but he's conscious and alert."

She felt her knees weaken and realized that the doctor was supporting her as she leaned against him.

Leading her to a nearby chair, the doctor made certain that she was stable before continuing. "He was lucky. Apparently, he was on the opposite side of the car from the explosion, and partially protected by the door"

"How long is he going to have to stay here?"

"Oh, I'd say about a week. Burns can be tricky. There's always the possibility of infection. We're hopeful that they will heal up without the need for skin grafts."

After gathering enough detail to satisfy her medical back-ground, she left Dr. Sidkey and found herself confronted by the tedious presence of the two police officers, who were by no means done questioning her. "Look," said the taller of the Mutt and Jeff duo, "you left us with a real provocative statement. You said the 'drug lords' did it. Is that some new gang?"

Jordan sighed and asked to sit down. The cops flanked her on the bench and she explained the whole story for them from Exuma up until the present. The shorter one wrote every detail in his notebook, asking once for the spelling of *pharmaceutical*. At the end of the interview, all they told her was that they would turn the information over to the Detective Bureau. If they knew anything more than that, they weren't about to share it. They said they would be in touch and then departed, leaving her alone on the hard bench in the fluorescent-lit hallway.

Jordan steeped for a moment in the realization that this was all really happening as tears welled in her eyes. After a few moments, she got up and went to the bathroom to freshen her makeup and attempted to pull herself back together.

When she came back out, she found Jim Crawford waiting for her in the corridor. She updated him on Ryan's condition before proceeding to explain everything that had happened. Crawford told her that he would follow up with the police to see if they had come up with any suspects. He cautioned her that, at present, this crime was not in the FBI's jurisdiction. That would only happen if the police suspected out-of-state or terrorist connections. Since the police weren't too fond of calling in the Feds, he would have to dig around on his own time.

Seeing her concern, Crawford gripped her arm. "Try not to worry. From what you tell me, ol' Ryan is gonna be fine. Meantime, I'll see what I can find out and arrange for your protection. Whatever you do, don't leave the hospital until I've made those arrangements."

* * *

Jordan awoke to the sound of laughing nurses down the hallway. She was huddled under her coat on a long wooden bench. Some kind soul had dropped a hospital blanket over her. She looked around, blinking under the fluorescent light. White-clad staff began to appear in the corridor as the day shift clocked in. In the distance, the clatter of trays and utensils suggested breakfast was being prepared. Wiping the sleep from her eyes and stretching out the painful kinks caused by her hard bed, Jordan got herself ready to tackle the day.

Now that the panic was over, she remembered why she hated hospitals. For one, she loathed the antiseptic smell that always had a way of clinging to you, even after you left. What really bothered her, though, was the inevitable insensitivity that accompanies the impossible task of taking care of such a large number of ailing people. She knew it was an odd opinion for a doctor to hold, but she hated the idea of doctors and nurses kidding with each other, gossiping, and chatting about their weekend plans or last night's date, when in every room, people were suffering. Some were near death, and none of them were laughing.

She went into the ladies' room, washed her face, and reapplied some lipstick. Taking the elevator to the cafeteria on the third floor, she had a breakfast of scrambled eggs, bacon, and toast.

As Jordan was finishing her second cup of the watery hospital brew, Dr. Sidkey entered the cafeteria. Sure enough, he was chatting lightly with a nurse, and both were laughing. He spotted her and walked over.

"Hi, there," he said. "Your friend is awake, but he's in a fair amount of pain. The good news is that he's out of ICU and in a private room on the fifth floor. He was just asking for you. That's a good sign. When they're hurting that bad they don't usually ask for anybody."

"Thanks for the update. Is there anything else I should know?"

"We're going to run an MRI on him this afternoon. He fought us on it. Says he wants to get out now, but it's way too early. He's survived a major explosion, and while there aren't any signs of internal injuries, we need the MRI to be sure."

She agreed and headed to Ryan's new room.

Much of his body was swathed in bandages, and a couple of smaller dressings covered the left side of his face. He turned from the window when he realized someone was there. She held his hand in hers. "I was so worried. How do you feel?"

"They tell me I'm still as handsome as ever."

Jordan grinned. "Yes, they're right. I'm glad you're not going to need skin grafts. That can be a long and painful procedure."

"Yeah," he said, "and they don't always work. I guess I'm lucky." Ryan reached for some ice chips in a glass by his bed, but she was one step ahead of him. She held the chips to his lips until they dissolved. "I don't know if it's the burns or these damn hospital rooms, but all I can feel is thirst."

"Hospital rooms are like that," she replied.

Something in his eyes told her that he was troubled and he hesitated to speak. She gave his hand a gentle squeeze. "What's on your mind? Something's bothering you."

"Well, yeah. It is." He didn't withdraw his hand, which she saw as a good sign. But as soon as he started talking, her face dropped. "Jordan, here's the deal. I'm here in Chicago with you because I want to help, but I don't like being a pawn. Something's going on and you're not telling me everything."

Her eyes shifted away from his. "You think I'm holding back on you?"

His eyes were exploring hers when she returned his gaze. "Yeah, I think you are."

She looked away again. A few awkward moments passed until at last she turned to him. "You're right. And I'm not being fair. I'm going to tell you everything."

CHAPTER **16**

Senator Edward McNally put the flask of bourbon back in his desk drawer and wiped his mouth with the back of his hand. His eyes lingered on the drawer. He liked his flask. It was a nostalgic throwback to a different era, when appearance and protocol hadn't been as important. He hadn't been born until the mid-sixties, of course, but he felt a connection to the old days. In his quieter moments, he sometimes longed for simpler times, even if he knew deep down that those times had never truly existed.

Alas, in the current political climate, image was everything—a fact he rarely needed to bring to the attention of his staff, most of whom were even younger and hipper than him. Like them, Senator McNally, though wistful where the past was concerned, perfectly understood the present and what it took to win political capital. He understood politics as equal parts stagecraft and message branding.

He heard a staccato clack of hard-soled shoes on the marble floor approaching his door. It was a Saturday, and quiet—just the way he wanted it. There would be nobody in the office. No secretary, no aides. He had given them all the day off.

He got up when he heard the hallway door open and greeted a stocky, bearded man at the door to his private office. Carl Wiley, like Senator McNally, was in his mid-forties, but the long, stressful hours had already weathered him. He looked a tad soft around the middle and tired around the eyes.

The senator felt a touch of sympathy for his colleague, as well as a bit of relief that politics hadn't had the same effect on him. "Carl, come on in. I've been waiting."

"Sorry I'm late, Ed. Got here as quick as I could."

Taking Wiley by the elbow, McNally ushered him into his private office. "How are things at the FDA, Carl?"

"As far as I'm concerned, great, since you helped me get appointed commissioner."

"Nice up here at the top, isn't it? Remember scrounging for power back in Philly? Kissing every ass in sight for a shot at the ring?"

"Yeah, I remember and I've got the scars to prove it."

"It's nice that you remember where you came from."

Something flashed in Wiley's eyes. Irritation? Maybe.

The senator wasn't too concerned. He sat back in his leather desk-chair. All around him hung framed photos of the last three campaigns. Each one featured a shot of himself, victorious.

"Well," he said, "what's the status report on my favorite projects at the FDA?"

Wiley sat down across from McNally. "Everything is on track, nice and steady."

McNally shifted in his chair. "What's this I'm hearing about a certain drug they're calling CTR 80? I heard it's on the fast track."

Wiley squirmed, failing to meet McNally's eyes. "It was, but I have my way of slowing things down. Hell, just last week we put the kibosh on Genomics's new cholesterol-lowering drug because they failed to get the proper signature on one of the consent forms. I'm sure your pharmaceutical boys were happy about that one."

"Indeed they were. So do I need to concern myself that the drug in question will make it out of phase three?"

"No way, Senator. Not a chance, at least not in this decade. We can tie their regulatory staff up for years."

"Good, good," the senator said. "I'm sure you've heard about the Social Security bill I'm authoring. I can't afford any distractions. The plan will only pass if I get help from people like you. You do your job, and everything's easier."

Wiley nodded wearily. Like everyone else in the business, he knew that getting anything done in D.C. was a Herculean task. Distractions, whether scandalous or simply bureaucratic, often killed promising legislation.

For his part, the senator knew his Social Security plan would either make or break him. Not everyone agreed in Washington that Social Security was in peril. In fact, predictably, the issue was fairly evenly divided on partisan lines. But few were privy to what Senator McNally knew. And even fewer were aware of the big picture. The potential solutions bandied about by experts—raising the retirement age, increasing the Social Security tax rate, or partially or fully privatizing Social Security—would amount to nothing if the senator failed to succeed behind closed doors, where the real work was being done to protect the American economy and the country's future. His bill was a stopgap—necessary but only a partial solution. If it passed and showed promising early returns, it would in all likelihood catapult him to the next level. But the real work—the labor of love for which he worked ceaselessly in utter secrecy—would never see the light of day. If it did, all bets were off.

CHAPTER 17

William Craven ran his hand over his head. His bare scalp picked up what little light was in the dim and dank working-class bar. The place smelled of stale beer and tobacco. Smoke drifted in cumulous layers throughout the joint. Behind the bar, an array of different-shaped bottles covered the lower portion of the dirty mirror. Photos of the owner and his Marine buddies on some far-off Pacific island papered the wall behind the cash register. Sitting alone on their barstools were the ubiquitous die-hard drunks, nursing their whiskeys and grumbling about their lots in life. Craven's dark tailored suit rendered him as out of place as a banker in a hobo camp. As he tossed back his Macallan on the rocks, the roar of a landing passenger jet pierced the brick walls of the seedy tavern.

He gestured to the waitress, a tall young blonde with upswept hair. A red tattoo in the shape of a heart with the name *Eddie V* stenciled through the middle of it peeked through the wisps of dyed hair on the back of her neck. When she arrived, he snarled at her. "That last one wasn't a double. Make sure the next one is."

She took his empty glass, barely hiding her disdain. "Yeah, I'll be sure to tell the bartenda'." Her New Jersey accent was tinged with sarcasm. She sashayed away as if she expected him to keep his eyes glued to her hips like most of the other guys.

But he didn't. He just glowered at the spot on the table where his drink had been.

While the waitress flirted with the bartender as he poured Craven's drink, a tall, burly man with a hooked nose and dark, wavy hair approached the booth. He sat down with a curt nod at Craven and looked for the waitress, who was now approaching with the double Scotch.

The burly man said, "I'll have a VO, rocks, honey."

"How was the flight?" Craven asked without a hint of sincerity.

"How comfortable can a coach seat be for a guy like me? Cheap bastard airline didn't even offer drinks."

Craven didn't attempt any more pretenses. He leaned forward, and in a controlled rage, growled between tight teeth. "Okay, enough bullshit. What the fuck happened?"

The burly guy wasn't about to take it. He, too, leaned in. "Look, Craven, you said to get rid of her. You didn't say how. I told you before, I do it my own way."

"Yeah, your way. You fucked up. I was told that if you wanted this kind of job done and done right, you go to Ed Sulari. Well, I went to Ed Sulari, and look what happened. We may be screwed now. Not only did you botch the job, but you managed to make a spectacle out of it. Hell, I think it made every paper in the country." He caught his breath. "That might have been our last shot at her before she gets herself a couple layers of security."

Sulari started to speak, but Craven interrupted.

"Tell me everything that happened from the minute she arrived," he demanded. "And I mean everything."

Sulari hesitated. "Look, it's gonna make the papers anyway. That's how we do it. Besides, if the cops think it's a mob hit, they don't work so hard to find out who done it. It's safer for us. The target was a respectable citizen. It's not like we were going to be able to follow her to a back alley at three in the morning and clip her as she scored some drugs. If we go up to someone like that, where they hang out, and—bada bing bada bang—give them two in the hat, we are going to get made. This way is cleaner. Trust me. I had the perfect setup using the kid from the valet service."

"What kid? I didn't know anything about a kid."

"The kid is a valet at one of the services in the city. So we decide to follow them around until they went to eat. The kid had the valet uniform, and most of the valets are foreigners who can't understand much English, so it was easy to manipulate the situation. After they go in the restaurant, the kid swipes their keys and places the bomb under the passenger seat. When they leave the restaurant, the kid's there to take the ticket, get the car, and activate the bomb. It's one of them pressure-activated jobs. I was watching across the street. Carver comes out a few minutes after the guy she's with has already gotten the car, and before she gets there, he flips his pizza box onto the passenger seat and *BOOM!*, the fuckin' thing explodes. Just bad luck is all it was. The trigger was too sensitive."

"Unbelievable," Craven muttered. "Okay, now go back to when she got off the plane and tell me everything she did up until that point."

"After they got off the plane, they went straight to her building. Twenty minutes later, they walk up the street and go to dinner. Some Spanish place, Barba something. Doesn't matta'. They walk to the restaurant. Couple hours later, they come out, they're kinda cozy. Then they go back to the apartment."

"Why didn't you make the hit then? They're probably boozed, their guard is down. Perfect time."

"How was I to know he wasn't packing? Or that he ain't private heat? You didn't tell me nothin' about him. He coulda had backup. I didn't know none of this stuff, so I was careful. Let me tell you, he didn't look like no slouch. He looked like somebody. So I was careful. That's how I work: careful."

"Where did they go after that?"

"Next morning they head downtown to the Federal Building."

"Did you follow them?"

"Sure."

"And?"

Sulari seemed annoyed by all the questions and in no rush to answer. The waitress came over and placed his drink on a napkin in front of him. He raised the glass to his lips while admiring her backside as she walked away. "Nice ass," he muttered, leering after her.

Craven ignored him. "So, what were they doing at the Federal Building?"

"I followed them until they walked into the FBI office and then I got the hell outta there."

Craven gritted his teeth. "Damn, the guy is hooked up—maybe officially, maybe just a friend—but he's connected."

"Looks like it."

"Is that what you meant when you said that he looked like somebody?"

Sulari cocked his head. "Yeah. Somebody you need to sweat. Somebody who could handle himself. Guys like that ain't so easy to take out. They always watchin' their back. And he had the look. Head always turning, hands close to his pocket, like he was some kind of cop or somethin'."

His eyes busy, Craven asked, "Okay, this kid. Who is he?"

"Local druggie. I've used him before. Strung out on heroin. He'll do anythin' for a buck. And I mean anythin'."

"Well, your druggie has gotta go, too."

"You didn't pay for him."

"I'm telling you, he's gotta go. I'll pay. If the cops get to him, he'll finger you. If they get to you, that puts them one step closer to me. No, he's a dead man."

Sulari leveled his gaze on the man in the suit. "You got it, but it's gonna cost you another ten large."

"I don't give a shit."

"You got it."

The two men sat in silence as the working-class bar churned along in its daily routine. Neither man wanted to show the other any sign of weakness. The silence was finally broken when Craven asked, "Have you checked out the guy with Carver?"

"What I could. I got a man with connections in the force. The Chicago P.D. don't seem to be too excited about him. They're not goin' to any special trouble to find out who tried to waste him."

"That's good. What else?"

"I got a connection down in the Bahamas, too. Our stranger's definitely American, but we don't know much else. It doesn't look like he's got nothin' to do with law enforcement down there."

Craven sat back in his seat, his mind whirling. "Any chance this guy is with the Company?"

"What company?"

Craven rolled his eyes. "The government—the Feds, CIA."

"Couldn't tell ya. But that's the kind of guy he looks like. Definitely."

"Or he could just be some schmuck who she met on the island."

Sulari shook his head in agreement. "I figured that, too. She's some sweet piece of tail. In a way, it's a shame."

Craven threw the big man an irritated look.

"What? I can't appreciate beauty? I'm just sayin', she's hot as shit, and it's a shame she's gotta get wasted. That may be the only reason the dude is protecting her."

The hoodlum was beginning to get on Craven's nerves. "It's not safe to think that way. Better to assume he's someone on the inside who could do her a lot of good."

Sulari finished his drink and gestured to the waitress for another one. His eyes explored her swaying hips as she approached. He flashed her a crooked smile and mumbled something about her ass before ordering his next drink. As Craven waited to regain Sulari's attention, he surveyed his surroundings. He noticed that many of the other men in the bar were huddled in conversation, too. But he knew they were talking about such banalities as tonight's bowling league competition, how the clandestine date with the bar girl down the street went, or maybe even plotting a holdup of the local convenience store. By a contrast too steep to measure, he and Sulari were talking about things that would affect the lives of millions of people, not to mention the fortunes of a select few. Yet, there he was in the same bar, drinking the same booze, and breathing in the same foul air. In this dump, the fates of the high and mighty were decided along with those of the plebian and insignificant. It gave him a sense of superiority. *What a waste of humanity these bums are.* As unsavory as his current assignment was, he would never count himself among these low-life scumbags.

The waitress now gone, Sulari was ready to talk. "Okay," Craven said with the authority of a corporate executive about to end a meeting. "So it's up to you to get rid of the kid. If you fail, things are not going to go well for you."

His words reached the thug like a hard slap in the face. Sulari leaned forward and grabbed Craven's arm. "Ya know, you may think you know me, but I don't think you know enough. I made my bones while you were going to frat parties. Sure, I do a little freelancing on the side, but I'm with the Outfit, and I think mine's bigger than yours. Don't *ever* threaten me again, suit."

For a long moment, their eyes locked. Craven's were unreadable, though a contemptuous sneer was beginning to form on his lips. All at once, his hand lashed out cobra-swift as he lunged across the table and seized Sulari's neck in a death grip. He squeezed harder, his face not changing as the thug's went ashen.

"Buddy, I was eliminating scum for God and country when you were still rolling bums in alleys for rent money. And my outfit could buy and sell your outfit down the river with the money we keep in petty cash."

Seconds before Sulari was about to pass out, Craven released his hold and then stared down two of the patrons at the bar watching the excitement until they feigned a lack of interest and turned back to their drinks.

Sulari sat gasping and wheezing, his eyes bulging. "Motherfucker," he mumbled, "no need for that commando crap. I was just tryin' to make a point."

"I'll make the points—you'll listen and follow orders."

"Yeah, sure," he mumbled, massaging his throat. "Jesus Christ." Sulari was trembling now, though doing his best not to show it. "I'll get it done."

Craven gave a mocking grin before getting back to business. "Yeah, you will."

For his part, Sulari regained his composure. "I'm gonna need ten large in my offshore account for the kid."

"We already agreed to that. I don't like to have to repeat myself." Craven reached for some peanuts in the bowl that sat before him. He munched on them nonchalantly as he discussed cold-blooded murder in a manner the other bar denizens would use to discuss tomorrow's weather. "You'll also need to find out more about this guy Carver's with. I want you to tail them and see what they're up to." Without saying a word, Craven could tell what the man sitting across from him was thinking. "And yes, I will pay you more. Listen, money is not the object. We have plenty. But I need results. Do I make myself clear?"

"Sure, I hear ya. There won't be any more problems."

Craven glared at him. "Good, because if you become a loose end like that kid, you're expendable, too."

Sulari sipped his drink and put on the best macho front he could. But the sweat on his upper lip gave him away. He didn't dare stand up until Craven dismissed him.

"Before we go, I have one more question. Did you get the guy's name? The news reports haven't released it yet."

"It's Matthews. Ryan Matthews."

Craven's mind went into overdrive as it processed the name. *It couldn't be. That's too much of a coincidence.* "Ryan Matthews?"

"That's right, so what?"

"I think I know . . . wait a minute. I have to check this out. Don't do anything until you hear back from me."

With a shrug, Sulari said, "You the man. I'll wait until I hear from you."

Outside, Craven brushed off the sleeves of his topcoat as he waited for a cab. *Ryan Matthews. The muthafuckin' Ghost of Christmas Past.*

CHAPTER 18

Jordan perched on the edge of Ryan's hospital bed and settled herself into a comfortable position. Ryan leaned back into his pillows. Her eyes avoided his as she said, "First of all, I need to confess that our meeting at Rosey's was no accident."

Ryan's brows shot up, his eyes widening.

"Though it's true that I was down there to visit my aunt and uncle, my ulterior motive was to meet you."

His spine went rigid. "What? Why? Why did you want to meet me?"

She squirmed, unable to hide her tension. "Let me start at the beginning. I was approached by a man several months back who worked in the drug industry. He said he'd heard of the clinic that I was opening and told me he had a cure for ovarian cancer. Nevertheless, he warned me that the drug was not now nor would it ever be FDA approved. I was skeptical, but intrigued. Through my own experience and research, I know that there are many drugs out there that offer real cures that are not FDA approved, so I took a closer look. The information he showed me was promising, and I was prepared to offer this as an alternative drug for my late-stage ovarian cancer patients. However, when I was told that it came with a five-million-dollar price tag and that my clinic's cut would be ten percent, I told him I wasn't interested. He kept calling and sweetening the offer, but I refused to reconsider."

She paused. "My refusal had nothing to do with the cut my clinic was offered. I was appalled at the exorbitant price being charged overall. It really pissed me off."

Ryan was disoriented, and this flood of new information wasn't helping. "I still don't understand. What does this have to do with me? Sure, I worked on an ovarian cancer cure several years ago, but it never panned out." Just uttering those words brought back a flash flood of memories: Cindy's initial diagnosis, the canceled drug trial, the fatal crash.

Jordan shifted, tucking one leg under her. Ryan moved over to accommodate her. "I'll get to all that, but first let me tell you more about these last-hope medical clinics based outside the United States. There are basically two types of clinics. The most common offer some homeopathic remedies using a mixture of herbs, minerals, spices, shark cartilage, apricot seeds, and other home-grown remedies. They pretty much agree to treat anyone, and the price is usually based on how much the patient can afford. Besides temporary placebo effects, patients rarely live longer by going to these places. Actually, a lot of them die much sooner than they would have if they'd just stayed with traditional medicine."

Ryan tilted his head. "That's what I've always thought of these places. I have to admit, I wasn't too impressed when you told me you were opening a clinic in Mexico offering non-FDA-approved treatments."

If Jordan was insulted by his remark, she didn't show it. "My clinic's not going to be anything like that. It falls into the second category. These clinics offer miracle drugs that are available only outside the States. The drugs offered are typically drugs in the pipeline at major multinational pharma companies all the way down to the micro-biotech firm still trying to get funding for clinical trials. From what I can tell, I don't think most give a damn if the drugs work or not. They're just interested in the money. They charge millions of dollars and make ridiculous claims that only someone in a desperate situation would believe." She paused as if she had just realized who she was talking to. "Listen,

I'm sure you know most of this stuff, but my clinic is going to be different. I just want you to understand how my clinic fits in and why I sought you out."

Ryan had been in medical research his entire career and there had always been stories of hucksters who prey on the wealthy when they're desperate and vulnerable. He wanted to believe that Jordan was different and kept an open mind as she continued.

"At my clinic we'll only be charging enough to generate a reasonable profit back to our investors. We offer treatment for under ten thousand dollars in most cases. And I'm planning to offer these same drugs to anyone who's able to make it down there, even if they *can't* afford it. While I am not able to sit here and say with one hundred percent confidence that every treatment we offer is a definitive cure for the disease it is meant to treat, I can tell you that we have thoroughly researched every treatment we will be offering and believe it will give our patients a better shot at survival than anything else on the market."

Ryan admired her passion and was pleased to hear that she wasn't all about the bottom line. He knew many people in the medical field who didn't give a damn about anything other than lining their pockets. Over time, greed took priority over the Hippocratic oath. Still, there was no way to know for sure what Jordan's true motives were, and he hoped his feelings for her weren't somehow blinding him.

Jordan was on a roll now. "I review all the data and testing results of every drug that we offer. Unless there's strong evidence to support the claims of the drug and a reasonable explanation as to why it's not FDA approved, I won't offer it in my clinic. So far, I have nine drugs that we'll be offering when the clinic opens that will treat everything from cancer to diabetes to Alzheimer's disease, and we're hopeful that our patients will live a longer and higher quality of life as a result of these drugs."

Ryan shifted. The pain was growing, and despite his interest in her story, he was having a hard time concentrating on her words.

Reading the discomfort on his face, Jordan asked, "Can I get you something? Or have the nurse get you something?"

Glancing at his IV, he grimaced. "I think my pain dispenser is empty."

"I'll get the nurse."

"No need. I'll be the obnoxious patient and ring for her."

The nurse was not the Nurse Ratched type but a man's fantasy version—a cute redhead with a voluptuous body and caring demeanor. She marched into the room within seconds, saw him eying the IV bag and said with a winsome smile, "I'll check your records and refill it right away." The redhead glanced at Jordan. "Is there anything else I can do for you?"

Ryan smiled and let his eyes rest on her long enough for both women to notice. "No thank you."

When the nurse left the room, Jordan rolled her eyes.

Ryan grinned. "What? She's a nice kid. Gave me a back rub this morning."

The bit of jealousy that Jordan revealed did much to alleviate his flagging spirits. He started to smile but thought better of it. *Better stay on track. Something deeper is going on.*

Pushing his feelings aside, Ryan was once again all business. "The way I see it, if a drug can't get past the FDA, it doesn't work. It's that simple. The FDA has top scientists and investigators, and if they don't approve a drug, it's because the clinical trial results didn't show it to be safe and effective."

A frown clouded Jordan's face. "That's complete bullshit, Ryan! That's what they *want* you to believe. Ever since the Vioxx fiasco, those bureaucratic pencil pushers at the FDA are too scared to approve any novel drugs. The higher-ups got their asses handed to them for approving Vioxx, and you better believe they won't make that mistake again anytime soon. While they're busy covering their asses, hundreds of promising new drugs are getting shot down."

He wondered if her resentment was blurring her judgment. "I don't think they're capricious about giving or withholding approval. I'm sure they need to have a good reason for not approving a new drug. Otherwise, the drug companies would go ballistic."

Jordan pounced on his naivety. "Sure they do. But it doesn't have to be because of the data. New drug submissions to the FDA are often hundreds of thousands of pages long. There's a lot of room for mistakes. Any number of procedural mistakes might happen, and the FDA often throws the baby out with the bathwater. They hide behind their bureaucratic rules to keep from having to make a rational decision."

Ryan stared at the foot of the bed. "I agree that there are bureaucratic snafus that delay approvals, but companies don't abandon good drugs just because they have to go back and repeat some procedural issues. If it's a good drug, it will eventually make it to the market."

Jordan shook her head in frustration. "That's only if the company is persistent, has the resources, and can't find a more lucrative way to market the drug. I'm almost certain now that the people after me have a high stake in these other clinics and fear that they'll lose hundreds of millions of dollars a year if the patients they're recruiting and charging millions can get the same drugs at my clinic for a fraction of the cost. They even have one of these clinics a few miles from mine. I didn't know about it until I was approached. They tried to get me to join their little fraternity, and I refused. Now they want me out of the way." She paused as if to steel her emotions. "They *need* me out of the way."

Ryan shook his head in disbelief. "Jordan, you should have told me all this earlier. If you had, I might not be in this bed now. Still, I don't understand why you wanted to come down to Exuma and meet me in the first place."

"Ryan, I had no idea it would get this crazy. I hated not telling you, but I needed to make sure you were not somehow involved with them."

That caught him by surprise, and it stung. "Involved?" He had to restrain himself from shouting. "How would I be involved, and why in the world would you ever even consider that as a possibility?"

"As I was researching this supposed ovarian cancer cure, I traced its origins back to Tricopatin, and back to your former employer, Fisher Singer Worldwide. I found out that FSW bought your company and that you were assigned the lead position on the Tricopatin project. I was surprised to learn that the project was canceled midway through human trials. From everything I reviewed, Tricopatin looked promising. I came to find you to learn what went wrong and to find out if the drug *was* a potential cure. If it was, I hoped to convince you to come work with me at the clinic so we could offer your wonder drug to my patients for a reasonable price."

Jordan watched as Ryan squeezed his rubber bubble device on the IV for a fresh shot of morphine. A few seconds later, he felt the drug course through his veins. He sighed and returned his attention to her.

"I can assure you that Tricopatin doesn't cure cancer. For years I believed that it would." His body sagged and his voice grew rough. "And I even staked Cindy's life on it." Anger swept over him, and his voice rose. "I can't *believe* those bastards are pushing Tricopatin as a cure!"

"Well," Jordan ventured, trying to defuse his reaction, "maybe they have more information now, you know? Maybe they discovered something you missed."

"No! I reviewed the trial data myself." Ryan was adamant. "The trials were not shut down because of some bureaucratic red-tape issue. In fact, the FDA was more than accommodating in allowing us to advance the drug to human trials. The trials were halted because tests revealed that, for some inexplicable reason, Tricopatin made the cancer grow faster than in the placebo group."

Jordan looked forlorn as she listened to him describe the failure.

"We thought there might be a way to alter the drug to produce desirable results, but shortly after the trial was canceled, I

left FSW, and then Cindy, Jake, and Karly's plane went down, and
I . . ." He paused to get a grip on his emotions. "At that point I lost
my desire to continue my research. None of it seemed important
anymore. If the drug you were offered was a copycat version of
Tricopatin, I think your first assessment was correct. These guys
are a bunch of charlatans offering false hopes with no chance of
a cure."

They both fell silent as a sense of gloom settled over the little
room.

Ryan opened his mouth to continue just as the cute redhead
breezed in.

"It's time to change the dressing on your burns. And you
really should be resting." The last statement was aimed at Jordan
with a pointed look.

Jordan rubbed her eyes and stood up to leave. "I'll be back
tonight," she said to Ryan as she leaned over the bed and kissed
him on the cheek. "Maybe I can sneak you in a treat." She said it
just loud enough to make certain the redhead heard.

CHAPTER **19**

Jordan's revelations had given Ryan a lot to mull over, but sleep was beckoning. With the sedatives pumping into his veins, his eyelids grew heavier as his body relaxed into the bed. He closed his eyes and awaited a dreamless slumber.

Instead of the welcome sleep, he found himself five years in the past. Back when it all started to go wrong. . . .

* * *

It was a normal Thursday morning, and Ryan was running late for a 9:00 a.m. meeting with his lab director. He had done FDA paperwork until 3:30 that morning and had woken up late. Cindy was rushing Karly and Jake to finish their breakfast and get out the door in time to catch the school bus when the phone rang. Ryan answered.

"Hello, Ryan, this is Albert Seymour."

The hair on the back of Ryan's neck stood up. "Hello, Dr. Seymour."

"Ryan, I need to see you and Cindy in my office today to discuss Cindy's latest test results."

A chill ran through his body. "Albert! What is it?" he blurted, not about to let the doctor get away with a cryptic reply.

Dr. Seymour hesitated. "I shouldn't discuss this over the

phone, but . . ." He took a deep breath. "The biopsy that we took from Cindy yesterday confirms the abnormal CA-125 blood test results that we saw last week."

Ryan's heart dropped to the pit of his stomach, and his legs began to wobble. He wished he weren't a scientist—all of this would have sounded like mumbo jumbo, and he wouldn't have understood the implications of the doctor's words. "What stage?"

"I'd like to run some additional tests," Dr. Seymour said.

Ryan knew he was hedging, and the doctor's attempt at sugarcoating what he had to say was infuriating.

"Damn it, Albert! You don't need more tests. I know what a biopsy is. What stage is it?"

"Stage four."

Ryan hung up the phone in a fog of grief. The shock on his face held Cindy's attention and she knew without asking. After the kids were out the door, they clutched each other and cried.

It was a veritable death sentence. A mere six weeks earlier, Ryan had been celebrating the greatest success of his career. His company had completed pre-clinical testing on Tricopatin, a drug with the potential to become a revolutionary cure for ovarian cancer. Today he would need to rely on his raw courage to carry them through the next hours.

Later that morning at Dr. Seymour's office, they heard the whole story. After a third test reconfirmed the diagnosis, Cindy Matthews—at the age of thirty-four—was given less than two years to live. Ryan's familiarity with the clinical details, as well as his own family's connection with ovarian cancer, made him no stranger to this killer. On Cindy's side, her mother had died of the cancer at forty-two. This family history fueled Ryan's drive to find a cure. His own daughter Karly was no doubt at an increased risk, too. He was determined to defeat this beast.

Cindy's chance for survival was now reduced to a miracle cure, a cure Ryan hoped he had developed in Tricopatin. But it would be several years, if ever, before the FDA approved the drug. Although pre-clinical test results were promising, all that meant was that it could cure lab rats. Human clinical trials had not even begun yet, and even if they had, final approval would still be years away. Time was not on their side.

Ryan's firm, Immugene, was small and cash-strapped. It had neither the resources nor the bureaucratic connections to rush the drug through human trials and achieve government approval. But with the desperation of a protective husband and father whose family is threatened, Ryan promised Cindy he would find a way to cure her. It wasn't something he said rashly to make her feel better. He'd never been more determined about anything in his life. He refused to let this disease take her away from him.

When word of Immugene's success with Tricopatin's pre-clinical tests reached the market, several large pharmaceutical companies took notice, and the acquisition offers began to pour in—some of them from major players. It wasn't Ryan's plan to sell out. Ryan, along with his best friend and business partner Eric Maynard, started Immugene with venture capital. The two men shared big dreams. Their business plan involved surviving on the venture capital until they could bring a major drug to human testing. The plan from there was to take the company public and raise the vast amounts of money needed to advance through clinical trials. If the drug proved successful, Immugene would be worth several hundred million dollars, and Ryan and Eric would be multi-millionaires. But now, with Cindy's diagnosis, Ryan was running out of options. Immugene did not have enough time to go public, and Cindy's only chance for survival was for her to receive Tricopatin within the next six months.

A month earlier, pharmaceutical industry leader Fisher Singer Worldwide had made an enticing offer to purchase Immugene for $150 million plus. The "plus" would come in the form of negotiations on stock options, compensation packages for retained Immugene employees, and severance packages for the employees who were let go once the acquisition was complete.

Even though Ryan theoretically held absolute authority over sale or acquisition, he was receiving pressure to accept the offer from the venture capital firm that funded the operation. Their original investment in Immugene of $30 million would now be worth four times that. In addition, stock options from FSW could produce substantial gains for them down the road. Because Immugene had only one product that had passed pre-clinical testing and three others in the early developmental stages, and considering that only one out of a thousand drugs in pre-clinical testing ever reach the market, the offer seemed too good to be true.

Still, Ryan hadn't given the offer much consideration because, once the acquisition was made, he would lose all control of Tricopatin. Believing in the revolutionary potential of his drug, he wasn't willing to make this exchange.

But now that he was fighting a losing battle against time, Ryan was willing to discuss all options with any viable suitor. Besides, FSW's offer far surpassed the seven other written offers he had received. With several hundred pharmaceutical products on the market, facilities in all fifty states and in sixty-one foreign countries, over 125,000 employees, and annual sales in excess of $75 billion, the company had the capacity to move Tricopatin to human trials faster than anyone else.

Three days after Dr. Seymour's diagnosis, Ryan was on a plane to New Jersey to meet with the CEO of FSW. The sale was negotiated within a grueling forty-eight hours, and Immugene was acquired and absorbed into the pharmaceutical giant twenty-eight days later.

Immugene investors received $150 million and an additional three million stock options priced at the current stock price of FSW. The options would vest upon successful phase two testing of Tricopatin. Based on the company's historic stock-appreciation rate and projected time line to complete phase two testing, the stock options held a potential additional value in excess of $250 million. Out of the proceeds paid to Immugene, Ryan would receive $5 million in cash and one million stock options.

The company would keep Ryan on board as an executive vice president and assign him as the chief scientist on the Tricopatin project. He would also continue to be involved in the research on several other new drugs under development. Eric Maynard was also retained, and would receive $750,000 and an additional fifty thousand stock options. Although Ryan and Eric were partners at Immugene, Ryan was the majority partner and the individual responsible for the development of Tricopatin. Eric assisted Ryan but focused the bulk of his efforts on the business side of the company. As part of the deal, Ryan negotiated a $350,000 annual salary for himself and $225,000 for Eric.

Ryan arranged for the Tricopatin project to be run out of Fisher's research facilities in Research Triangle Park in Durham, North Carolina, less than twenty minutes from his house. The most important negotiation of all for Ryan involved FSW's agreement to fast-track Tricopatin and begin human testing within six months. His executive position and previous familiarity with Tricopatin also enabled him to obtain assurances from the CEO—off the record, of course—that Cindy would be enrolled in the clinical trial and would receive the Tricopatin injections and not the placebo.

One hundred and sixty-seven days after the finalization of the sale of Immugene to Fisher Singer Worldwide, Inc., human clinical trials for Tricopatin began. One hundred patients with late-stage ovarian cancer were selected to participate. Fifty of the patients were scheduled to receive nine injections of Tricopatin over a course of three months, or one dose every ten days. The remaining fifty patients received the same regimen using a sugar and water placebo. None of the patients, except Cindy Matthews, knew whether they were receiving Tricopatin or the placebo.

One week after the third injection, most patients reported feeling better, including many of those taking the placebo. At first, the test results did not show any significant progress. After six weeks of the trial and four injections per patient, most patients continued to report feeling better, and unofficial preliminary results indicated that the cancer was diminishing in some of the patients. Following the sixth injection, FSW petitioned the FDA to do an interim review of the test results in hopes of fast-tracking the drug to market if the final results of the trial turned out to be as promising as the interim results.

Ten weeks into the trial, and the day after all of the test patients received their seventh injection, the FDA ordered FSW to halt the clinical trial of Tricopatin. Their findings suggested that Tricopatin was not making the cancer diminish. In fact, evidence indicated that the drug was actually accelerating the cancer's growth.

Upon receiving this news, Ryan sunk into a quagmire of outrage and devastation. The outrage was directed at the FDA for canceling a promising clinical trial over three-quarters of the way through. The devastation came because he knew that his wife, the love of his life, would soon be gone.

Three days later and without a word to Cindy, Ryan flew to Washington and met with the FDA to review the test results. He was shocked to see that the placebo group's cancer had not advanced as far as that of the Tricopatin group. Ryan argued that during the pre-clinical studies, interim testing was not performed, and all of the animal subjects were 100 percent cured at the end of the trial. He went on to contend that the true effects of the drug would be revealed after a patient completed the entire series of injections.

The FDA officials rejected his argument and told him that if FSW had not petitioned for an interim review, the trial would still be going on. But given the results of the interim review, they could not, legally or ethically, allow FSW to continue to inject the patients with a drug that caused their cancer to grow. With that, the Tricopatin study was officially terminated.

It was on the short flight back to Durham that Ryan decided that, although it was the longest of long shots, Cindy still had a chance for survival if they went ahead with the final two injections as scheduled. The next day, Ryan removed enough of the Tricopatin from the lab's vault to complete Cindy's treatment. Five days later, he gave Cindy the eighth injection.

Cindy's rebound made his heart soar. Soon she was feeling better than she had in months. Her energy level was high, and she regained much of her strength and vitality. The Matthews were feeling hopeful leading up to their meeting with Dr. Seymour to review the latest test results.

The CA-125 blood test showed that the cancer was continuing to grow with no signs of remission. Dr. Seymour reminded them that most patients with advanced stages of cancer were on chemotherapy, and that was the main reason they were in poor health and had no strength or energy near the end of their lives. He went on to explain that cancer at an advanced level can cause endorphins to be released, which could explain the temporary strength and energy boost that Cindy had been experiencing. Dr. Seymour gave her six more months, at best.

The next morning, Ryan found Jason Handley, FSW's eastern division human resources director, along with the head of security, waiting for him in his office.

"Good morning, Ryan. I have something to ask you."

In an attempt at nonchalance, he replied, "What's up, Jason?"

"Dr. Matthews, the FDA has completed a post-study audit of our trial on Tricopatin, and we cannot account for two missing vials of the drug. Our security records indicate that you were the last person to access the vault. We are also aware that your wife was a participant in the clinical trial and that she had two treatments remaining when the FDA canceled the trial." A pause followed, pregnant with accusation. "Do you deny stealing the two vials of Tricopatin?"

"No, I don't deny it," he fired back. "In fact, I have already injected Cindy with both of them." Despite the implications of his admission, Ryan was in no mood to play games with Handley or anybody else from the company. He was the one who had invented Tricopatin, and if it could possibly save his wife's life, they had no right to stop him from using it. Damn the consequences. Damn the company. They could all go to hell.

Handley rose from his seat; the security man followed.

Handley's voice was firm. "Dr. Matthews, I have no choice but to terminate your employment for theft of classified and restricted company property. Mr. Craven will assist you in gathering your personal belongings and then escort you from the premises."

Nine days later, Ryan injected Cindy with the final dose of serum. He'd had to lie to Handley about that last dose in order to ward off a security sweep, and counted on Handley, and anyone else above him, to not know the dosage schedule that Ryan himself had established. But despite completion of her treatment under the prescribed time lines, Cindy's follow-up test results showed the cancer advancing. All hopes for a miraculous recovery withered away.

It was a melancholic time. Ryan and Cindy took long walks in the woods. They talked about the fun they had had at the last New Year's Eve party, the last vacation with the kids at the beach, their family ski vacation to Wintergreen. At other times they said little or nothing. Often they wound up in each other's arms, nursing their hurt, their lost future, and the thought of the kids growing up without their mother. Cindy had extracted several promises from him about the kids' upbringing and their future, and Ryan paid close attention to her wishes. They sealed all promises and commitments with a kiss, which both considered sacred.

One afternoon on one of their walks, Cindy said, "I've been thinking how nice it would be to take the kids to the islands. We've always considered that part of the world a piece of paradise." Her eyes warmed. "And I still think of our honeymoon on Exuma." Taking a shaky breath, she clasped his hand to hers as tears welled up in her eyes. "I didn't know until now—this moment—that those were the highlights of my life."

Ryan staved off his own emotions. He wanted to appear strong, encouraging. "And the kids won't mind missing school, either," he said.

The next week, Ryan caught a flight to Nassau, followed by a puddle jumper to Exuma. The plan was for him to find the spot closest to paradise, a place worthy of spending one's last days.

God forbid she should spend them in a hospital bed immersed in institutional sterility and surrounded by a host of white-clad strangers.

Ryan followed a rental agent from ramshackle bungalows to virtual palaces. On the third day he found what he was looking for: a simple stucco cottage snuggled between bunches of coconut palms and bougainvillea. Out back, the turquoise ocean spread out to the horizon and sparkled like a jewel. The surf crashed ashore in an endless procession of sugar-frosted waves. Ryan was certain this was the place. He sent for Cindy, the kids, and the caretaker they had hired after Cindy's diagnosis. He settled into his new paradise and waited for his family.

The last thing he heard before he bolted upright were the words from the black box recorder on his family's downed flight: *Mayday, Mayday, Mayday!*

CHAPTER 20

Eric Maynard picked up the morning paper off the front porch of his home in North Raleigh. The twittering birds were muted by the buzz of leaf blowers as the Mexican gardeners hurried about the sprawling grounds.

Back inside, Eric glanced upward. A cathedral ceiling soared to the second level. His wife, Laura, was descending the staircase while putting on earrings.

"Hi, honey," he said. "Aren't you going to have some break-fast?"

"No time," she replied, giving him a peck on the cheek before stepping out the door.

He headed to the kitchen where Maria, the family's house-maid, was preparing coffee, shirred eggs, Canadian bacon, and toast. He was on his second cup of coffee when he spotted the article in the paper. It was on the third page, below the fold—a follow-up story to the car bombing in Chicago that had been all over the news last weekend. He set his cup down when he read the name of the victim: Dr. Ryan Matthews.

Ryan Matthews. He finally ventures back to the States, and this is what happens to him. He couldn't help choking up at the thought of his old friend almost being killed. He hadn't seen Ryan since the memorial service for Cindy, Jake, and Karly. On the few occa-sions Eric attempted to reach out to him in Exuma, Ryan always clammed up. Eric pressed forward with his life, figuring they would reconnect once Ryan had rebounded from his tragic loss. Despite their lack of communication over the past five years, Eric still considered Ryan to be one of his best friends. After reading the article, Eric picked up the phone.

"Ryan, is that you buddy?" he asked as soon as he'd been connected to Ryan's room.

"Uh, hello?" Ryan's groggy voice betrayed a healthy dose of painkillers still in his bloodstream, but he seemed to recognize the voice on the other line. "Eric, is that you?"

"Yeah, it's me."

"How're you doing?"

"Better question is, how are *you* doing? I just picked up the Raleigh paper and there you were. They picked up the story from the AP and added a piece about your ties to the local community. Evidently you're alive. So, how the hell are you?"

"I'm healing up. In fact, I should be out of here today. It's been six days and I'm leaving one way or the other. In fact, your timing's great. I was planning on giving you a call later today to let you know I'm flying into RDU tomorrow."

"Great! I know Laura will be thrilled to see you too. So what brought you to Chicago in the first place? And what the hell happened?"

"It's a long story buddy, but I'll fill you in on all the details when we get together."

"Okay. Sounds good. Call me when you get in. We've got a lot of catching up to do."

"Will do. It's been too long. Say, Eric, are you still with FSW?"

"Sure am. I'm in charge of the facility in RTP now. I'll give you all the details when you get here."

"Sounds good. I'll give you a call once my flight is confirmed. If you have the time, I'll come by FSW after I land. That is, if I'm not still banned from the building."

"I think I can sneak you in. After all, I'm the man in charge at RTP now and the corporate security director hasn't been down for an interrogation in almost a year."

Ryan couldn't tell if Eric was joking or serious so he responded cautiously. "If my visit is going to cause you any trouble we can always meet somewhere else."

"No worries. I'll work on rearranging my schedule and free up some time for you tomorrow."

* * *

Ryan felt surprisingly good and was just wondering about Jordan when she appeared at the door with Jim Crawford in tow. She leaned down and gave him a quick kiss on the cheek. "I hear they're springing you today."

"That's what they said. All the tests results are negative and they said if I can live with the pain, then I am free to go. Of course, since I have no insurance company they have to justify their services to a cash buyer, so to speak. I'm sure they would like me to stay around a few more weeks at four grand a night."

"That's the Matthews I know," Crawford joked. "Always bitching about something."

Before Ryan could retort, Jordan jumped in. "Jim has been a big help."

"What have you been up to, Jim?"

"Well, as I told you the other day, no hits on that ID you gave me last week in our database." Crawford glanced over at Jordan. "And I assumed you didn't want to alarm Jordan with details of someone possibly following you, but now that she is beyond alarmed, I gave her and all the law enforcement patrols working the hospital the description of the guy. However, no one matching that description has turned up so far. Now that you are feeling better, I want you to sit down with a sketch artist so we have something better to work with."

"I'd be happy to. What else? Any good news?"

"Since you and Jordan are American citizens who were recently attacked on foreign soil and are now being pursued within the U.S. by the same person or persons who mean to do you harm, your case now falls under federal jurisdiction."

Ryan smirked. "It's been over a decade since I was in the Bureau, Jim. Remind me how that's going to help us out."

Crawford smiled back at Ryan and hesitated. "First of all, I'm authorized to provide both of you with federal protection." His smile faded. "And I strongly advise that you take me up on that offer."

"And what about the investigation?"

"We've taken the case over from Chicago P.D. We're still checking out the car for any clues and I should have a detailed forensics report in the morning. We have also drafted a short list of perps with a penchant for bombing."

"How short of a list?"

"Not as short as we would like. But, as you know, the best sources are on the street, and I've put word out to my snitches along with the description of the guy you thought might be following you."

"Sounds like a long road lies ahead, Jim."

"As you know, it can either be a very long road or we could catch a break and have things under control before the day's out. Anyway, let me know your plans and I will make any arrangements possible for your protection."

Crawford stepped out to make a few phone calls and arrange for the sketch artist to come over to the hospital to meet with Ryan.

"I'll meet with the sketch artist today, but I'm not sticking around in protective custody and waiting for the FBI to solve this crime," Ryan said to Jordan. "I'm flying out to Raleigh tomorrow. I need to find out more about the Tricopatin derivative that's being sold on the black market. My buddy Eric Maynard is running the show at FSW, and I'm hoping he can provide some insight. He was my college roommate and my partner at Immugene. We worked on Tricopatin together for several years. If anyone can shed some light on this, it'll be him."

An awkward silence followed, disturbed only by the distant

murmur of the hospital cafeteria cart making its morning rounds. Jordan seemed at a loss.

"Jordan, this is a very dangerous situation and I think you should stay in Chicago and let Jim continue to protect you."

"My clinic is scheduled to open for business in two weeks. Jim has been great, but I'm not waiting around for the FBI to solve a crime that they don't have a clue about. Protective custody could last for weeks or even months and I'm leaving for Mexico in ten days one way or the other."

"Jordan, I understand, but . . ."

Before Ryan could continue with his objection, Jordan interrupted. "As you know, I am convinced that my clinic is the reason behind these attacks. So if you are going to Raleigh to see what you can discover about a once-promising drug that is banned by the FDA, and that same drug is now being sold in a clinic similar to mine, then I think you're probably barking up the right tree. I'm coming with you."

* * *

Ryan was upbeat the next morning; despite the pain he was still experiencing from his burn wounds, he was still cheery on the flight to Raleigh. Jordan seemed more content as well. They rented a car at the airport and set out for the regional headquarters of Fisher Singer Worldwide in Research Triangle Park, Ryan's old stomping grounds.

As they pulled into the parking lot of the FSW headquarters and strode into the lobby, Jordan admired the opulent surroundings. "Très ritzy."

A security guard directed them to the executive offices via a private elevator. When the door opened, Eric emerged from plush surroundings with a huge smile on his face. The two old friends shook hands and then Ryan introduced Jordan.

"It's a pleasure meeting you," she said, stepping forward to shake his hand.

Eric cleared his throat awkwardly as he returned the hand-shake. "Yes, nice to meet you. Jordan, was it?"

She smiled. "Haven't we met somewhere before? You seem oddly familiar."

"I doubt it," Eric said. "I think I would have remembered you."

Jordan blushed, but as she did, she tilted her head and narrowed her gaze, revealing a hint of skepticism. "Ryan has told me all about you."

"Hopefully only the good stuff," Eric said, forcing a laugh.

After everyone was seated in Eric's office, Ryan went on to recount everything that had happened since Jordan arrived on Exuma—well, almost everything. While it was an extensive and graphic account of the attempts on their lives, it said nothing of the growing relationship between Ryan and Jordan.

Eric listened, looking distraught at all the right places in the story. Jordan took over and told Eric about her experience with the mysterious stranger who had offered her a drug that he claimed would cure ovarian cancer. She went on to relate the stranger's warning that the wonder cure would not be receiving FDA approval anytime soon, if ever. When Jordan finished, Ryan turned grim. "The roots of this drug seem to reach back to FSW. It sounds like Tricopatin."

Eric seemed uneasy, like someone at a high-stakes poker table with a bad hand, but remained silent as Ryan filled his old friend in on the rest of the story.

As Ryan was finishing, Eric's secretary brought in coffee and pastries, causing a momentary distraction. She poured the coffee for them and exited before Eric spoke. "That's some story, but I'm not involved with Tricopatin anymore. I really don't know anything about it."

Ryan had been watching his friend's facial expressions as he talked. He sensed an underlying current of unease. Putting on a smile to alleviate the tension, Ryan said, "Come on, Eric, you never could lie, especially to me. I can see it in your face. You know something about this."

"That's not it, Ryan. You've been out of the loop for a while. New rules around here don't allow us to say anything—and I mean anything—about any drug, whether it's new and in development or old. That's the truth." He looked furtively about, leaned toward them, and almost in a whisper, said, "You remember how ruthless these SOBs are."

Although Eric had plausible reasons for not wanting to discuss the matter, Ryan wanted to call his hand. *I may have been out of the game a long time, but I haven't lost my common sense.* "We both know the damn drug doesn't work. If FSW is peddling this junk outside the U.S. as a cure for ovarian cancer, there's no way I'm going to stand by and allow them to bilk people out of their savings and shorten their already doomed lives. Hell, I feel like an accomplice just thinking that they may be selling my worthless drug for millions of dollars a pop."

Eric was pumping his knee in a nervous twitch. In poker, they call this a "tell"—the subconscious communicating something that the conscious wants to repress. "I have a conference call I need to be on in a couple of hours; let's go for an early lunch," he said. "We can talk old times."

Ryan's initial reaction was to grow angry, but then he realized that his friend wanted to move the conversation to neutral grounds, where they wouldn't be monitored.

Soon they were out on the street. Ryan climbed into the passenger seat of Eric's Mercedes CL600 while Jordan followed in the rental car.

"Nice wheels."

"Five hundred and ten horses and zero to sixty in 4.5 seconds. Can't beat it."

"They must be treating you well at FSW."

"No complaints, except my travel schedule. This company never takes a breather."

Ryan thought about pressing the issue at hand as they headed for the restaurant, but decided to wait until the three of them sat down for lunch.

Once they were all seated and had ordered drinks, Eric said, "I meant it when I said I can't talk about company business."

Ryan had no intention of letting him off that easy. "Eric, I'm not some cub reporter looking for a story here. I'm the one who invented the damn drug and if FSW or anyone else is selling this useless drug, I need to know about it. You owe me that much, buddy."

"Look, you're way off base. Several months after the FDA canceled the trial, the brass decided to take another look at Trico. They sent it back to the lab, and our scientists discovered what they believed to be the reason behind the drug's failure. The drug was then transferred to one of our subsidiaries. Fisher is not even directly involved with Tricopatin anymore. We receive royalties on each sale and have retained full rights to market and sell the drug in the states in the event of a future FDA approval. The drug being sold outside of the U.S. is a new and improved version. From what I have been told, the results are showing that it does indeed work. This is not, as you put it, a useless drug. And nobody is being ripped off in any way."

Ryan was skeptical. "What changes did they make? What did they find out?"

"I don't know. I wasn't part of the research team that made the discoveries." His eyes avoided Ryan's.

Eric's answer did not have even a whisper of truth to it. "You were not part of the team?" Ryan's voice rose. "*You* were not part of the team? Hell, you devoted years of your life to the drug. Why in the hell would you, of all people, not be part of the team?"

Sheepish, Eric said, "I honestly don't know. Maybe they wanted fresh eyes on the problem rather than using people who might taint their ideas or discoveries. Besides, you were the mind behind Tricopatin; I was nothing more than your glorified assistant. That's why you got the big bucks."

This explanation still didn't ring true to Ryan, and he leaned closer to the table as he opened his mouth for his next response.

Jordan's sudden pressure on his shirt sleeve calmed Ryan

down. He tried, against his more basic impulses, to be diplomatic, settling back in his seat. "Okay, well, whether you were on the team or not, you have to know what the alterations were."

"You know I can't tell you any information about that. I wouldn't make it through the week at FSW if I did."

Desperation was creeping into Ryan's voice. "Come on, Eric. You know I have to know. This drug was my life. This is for me. Nobody else will ever have to know."

Eric's resolve increased in proportion to Ryan's efforts to make him crack. "Ryan, I *can't* get into it. Not now. You'd be shocked at how fast they can find and plug leaks."

Ryan took a deep breath. "I don't understand. If they think the drug works now, why aren't they going through another FDA trial?"

"Think about it, Ryan. The company spent almost two hundred million to buy Immugene in order to get their hands on Trico and sank another thirty to forty million in fast-tracking it into a phase two study. At the end of the day, they had zero to show for it. I'm not sure of all the details, but as I hear it, instead of writing off this quarter-of-a-billion-dollar disaster, they throw a few more million at the problem just to see if there is a simple fix. Amazingly, they think they can find a quick fix, but of course nothing's for sure. We all thought the original Trico was the answer. So instead of blowing another fifty million on a human trial, they take the drug outside the U.S. and try to recoup some of their investment while they get a sense of whether another FDA trial will pay off down the road."

"So they're experimenting with human lives?"

"Isn't that exactly what's done in an FDA clinical trial?" Eric snapped back.

At this point, Jordan could not hold her tongue any longer. "Yes, but the participants in a clinical trial are not paying five million to get an unproven treatment."

Eric grew defensive. "No, but half of the clinical trial patients are giving up traditional life-sustaining treatment to be given a sugar pill that has zero chance of curing them. The placebo group's chance of survival is zilch. They're the real guinea pigs."

"I don't disagree with that," she conceded, "but how can you charge five million dollars for an unproven drug? Or any drug for that matter?"

"This isn't just about science; this is a business, and these guys are in business to make money. Selling promising drugs outside the U.S. allows us to generate profits and determine if the drugs are worth the time and expense to put through the FDA approval process. Hell, these people are going to die anyway. Why not give them a fighting chance, get some research done for free, and generate a profit at the same time?"

Ryan shook his head. "You and the boys at FSW have it all figured out, don't you? But if that's all true, why was Jordan told that the drug would never be FDA approved?"

"I have no idea. Sounds like a marketing-exclusivity pitch to me. Listen, these sales guys make huge commissions on these drug sales. I'm sure they'll say just about anything to close a deal." He stopped and took a swig of his drink. "And before I receive an earful on that, listen. I don't make the rules, but if you want to be in the big leagues, you have to play by theirs."

Jordan jumped back into the conversation, scorn lacing her words. "Do the rules include eliminating the competition?"

Eric bristled. "That's not my end of the business, but I'm sure the less competition, the better, as far as the company's concerned."

"So murder is an acceptable way to eliminate the competition?" Jordan's eyes held an equal measure of fear and revulsion.

"Oh, god, of course not! I didn't mean it like that," Eric countered. "I have concerns myself, after hearing your story, but you need to understand that these clinics outside the U.S. are set up as foreign corporations, with no paper trail back to the big pharma companies. There can be numerous partners in these ventures; hell, I hear the top sales people are making an easy seven-figure income. If they thought you were cutting into their commission, I guess anything is possible."

"But you—" Jordan was interrupted by a look from Ryan.

Ryan held out his hand and clasped Eric's. For now, their discussion was over. "Hey, look, it's been great to see you again. Sorry for the Spanish Inquisition, but I hope you understand. You know I don't give a damn about the big-league rules. But, if the company is marketing my drug as a cure for ovarian cancer and charging five million bucks, they better be damn sure it works. God knows it didn't help Cindy."

Eric looked uneasy. "You know how terrible I feel about Cindy, but even her doctor agreed that participation in the trial was her only shot at long-term survival."

"I know, I know, and I pushed her into that trial. And if FSW found a way to reformulate Trico into an actual cure, then I will know that my work was not done in vain. If so, I can live with that; even if the bastards are charging an incredible fee for a drug that we know costs next to nothing to produce. But if I find out they're fucking with people's lives by shooting worthless shit into the bodies of the sick and desperate, I will take them down."

"Please step cautiously, Ryan. There's a lot of money involved, and as you've found out, this could get dangerous." Eric's remark contained a somber tone of finality.

After Eric left to go back to work, Ryan asked, "Do you still know how to get in touch with the rep who wanted you to push Trico at your clinic?"

Jordan pulled out her cell phone and began scrolling down a long list of saved contacts. "I think I may have the number stored in my phone. Just a second. Yep. Here it is. His name is Jerry Cottle."

CHAPTER 21

On the drive back to the hotel, the afternoon clouds, shaded a dark battleship gray, hung so low over the Carolina countryside that the treetops seemed to be holding them up. The weather matched Ryan's mood. Though Eric's revelations were disturbing, what their conversation revealed about Eric's character was even more troubling. He knew that Eric was more gifted as a businessman and leader than as a research scientist, but couldn't bring himself to believe that he would be involved with a company that was bilking the desperate out of their fortunes. Ryan still wanted to believe the best of his old friend, even if the industry Eric worked in had become unethical.

Ryan realized he was coming at the situation from too personal a perspective, considering what had happened to his family. He thought about what Eric had said: "I don't make the rules, but if you want to be in the big leagues, you have to play by theirs." *It's the big leagues, all right, the big leagues of heartless exploitation and corruption.*

Yet when Ryan calmed down and thought about it, Eric was doing no more than what any loyal team player would do. In fact, he might not even agree with a lot of the decisions his company made; even as executive vice president, he was in no position to change the course of the entire ship.

The issue of Tricopatin was paramount. Ryan was curious

about what FSW had done to his creation. Eric had been evasive, which made Ryan even more suspicious. What changes had they made and what exactly had they learned? Was this linked in any way to the people trying to eliminate Jordan? These were the questions that chased each other around in his mind. He hated not having the answers.

On the other hand, Ryan was somewhat encouraged. When he left the pharmaceutical world, the FDA had declared that his supposed wonder drug had only helped people die faster. Now, it seemed, the shrewd weasels at FSW were selling it for millions. But, if Eric *had* told the truth—if the drug did hold the promise of a cure—perhaps all of his research had not been in vain. It was a tantalizing, if unlikely, possibility.

As he was mulling this over, Jordan apparently had been doing some serious thinking of her own. She reached over, turned off the car stereo just as the latest Zac Brown Band hit finished playing, and said, "You're the former FBI guy. But when trying to solve any crime, don't they always say to follow the money?"

"And where do you think that leads us?"

"As your friend said, sales people earning seven-figure commissions would have a lot of incentive to eliminate the competition."

Ryan had been thinking the same thing. "When you come right down to it, that's the only thing that makes any sense. Money is the clearest motive for anyone wanting to . . . harm you." He tiptoed around the word "kill."

"There has to be a way to find out more—maybe this Jerry Cottle can shed some light on the situation," Jordan suggested.

After parking in the hotel's lot, Ryan smiled at her as he opened his door. "I have a plan."

The plan required that they register in the hotel under a shared false name. Once in the hotel room, Ryan went straight to work. He picked up the phone and dialed. "Good afternoon. May I speak to Jerry Cottle, please?"

After a pause, the other party replied, "This is Jerry. How

can I assist you?"

"My name is Lawrence Calk. I got your name from a good friend who heard about your service. Look, my wife has ovarian cancer. The doctors have painted a bleak picture, but they haven't said the word 'terminal' yet. I figure they don't want us to start looking for a miracle cure."

"Yes," Cottle said. "I'm sure you're right."

"My wife and I are rational people, and we listened to everything they had to say and we both concluded that she probably *is* terminal. According to the research we've done on the side, we think she has maybe six months to live. I . . . I . . . ." Ryan let some emotion creep into his voice for authenticity. It wasn't difficult: all he had to do was remember the events surrounding Cindy's stage IV diagnosis.

Cottle was quick to express sympathy and to let the caller know that he had heard the same sad story on numerous occasions. He assured his caller that there was still hope.

"Sorry," Ryan sniffed. "This is hard for me. I heard that you had a connection to a clinic out of the country that may be able to help her." He injected desperation into his voice. "I know this treatment is expensive, but I don't care. I can't put a price tag on my wife. So what's the next step?"

He listened as Cottle went into his sales pitch, clearly eager to reel in the fish that had unexpectedly jumped out of the ocean and flopped down at his feet. Ryan glanced at Jordan, who was sitting up on the edge of the bed, all ears. Cottle finally got around to mentioning the $5 million dollars, paid in three equal installments: one-third up front, one-third at the end of treatment, and the final one-third to be held in escrow and released once the cancer was in complete remission.

"Whew!" Ryan let out a forced cry. "I knew it would cost a lot. I just didn't realize how much. It might not be easy to come up with that."

Cottle plunged in with the remainder of his pitch. "I understand. Unfortunately I am not at liberty to negotiate on the price.

If this is something you cannot afford . . ."

Ryan cut him off. "No. I have the money. If we decide to do this, I would just need time to liquidate some of my holdings."

"I understand. We deal with this situation frequently. There is nothing due until you have visited our facilities and signed on for treatment. And then only one-third of the total is due at the start of treatment. When you decide to move forward, will that be an issue?"

"No, I can come up with the initial payment in fairly short order. But if we decide to move forward, I would need a month or so to free up the remainder."

"That will not be a problem." With the client pre-qualified, Cottle continued his song and dance. "I sense that you are hesitant and I'm sure you're worried about dealing with a foreign company as well as concerned about what results might be achieved. So let me give you the facts. We have a drug that has cured stage four ovarian cancer on numerous occasions and all those who have received the treatment remain in full remission. When you meet with the clinic director, view our five-star facilities, and hear the testimonials from other patients, I am sure you will realize that this is the only real option you have."

Ryan hesitated. "You know, Mr. Cottle, you're right. We really don't have another option. If your cure doesn't save my wife, I'll lose her."

"That's the unfortunate fact, Mr. Calk."

"Still, I'm not the kind of man who can make such a big decision so quickly. Let me talk to my wife, and I'll call you back." He hung up. Jordan's mouth opened, but Ryan spoke before she could say anything. "If I said yes too quickly, he might get suspicious. We need to string him along. When I call him tomorrow and tell him we've decided to move forward, he'll have no reason to doubt me."

Jordan grinned. "You're one sneaky bastard, Mr. Calk."

* * *

The next day, slipping back into the role of the desperate Lawrence Calk, Ryan telephoned Jerry Cottle.

"My wife and I have talked this over, and we've come to a decision. I'd like to take my wife directly to your clinic in Mexico. I can't afford to lose more time. The clock is against us now."

Cottle let him finish without saying another word. Ryan knew the crafty salesman was clamming up now that the sale had been made.

"I want to view the clinic and speak with a doctor. If everything still sounds good, I'll need a day or two to liquidate some of our stockholdings and then we'll make payment arrangements. How does that work for you?"

Not wanting to blow a big deal and a huge commission, but still concerned with letting a patient go alone without his escort, Cottle responded, "Well, usually I make the flight arrangements and travel with the patient down to the clinic. I like to spend the day showing them around, introducing them to our professional staff, and making sure that all of their questions are answered. Unfortunately, I have two appointments in the next two days that I must attend. Where was it you said you lived?"

"We live in Virginia, but are currently in Durham, North Carolina. My wife was being evaluated at Duke."

"I'm out in California and won't be able to meet you for another three days. Can you wait until then?"

Ryan knew that once Cottle saw Jordan the jig would be up. "Now that we've made our decision, we're not going to be able to sleep tonight as it is. We just don't feel like we have the luxury of wasting any more time. Can you just make the arrangements for us without actually accompanying us down there? We're anxious to at least get a look at the place."

Cottle hesitated. "Sure. Give me an hour, and I'll call you back to confirm. Where can I reach you?"

Ryan gave him the phone number for their hotel and said they would be awaiting his call.

Forty-five minutes later, the phone rang. Cottle confirmed

that everything was set and dictated the agenda to Ryan. He informed Ryan that, if the clinic met their expectations, treatment would begin as soon as the funds came through.

Ryan hung up and turned to Jordan. "We're on. We leave for Puerto Vallarta tomorrow. Cottle said we'd be talking to a Dr. Saul Pohmer when we get there. He wanted to book the flight and have a car waiting for us at the airport, but I told him we'd rather make our own travel arrangements. We don't want to blow our cover."

"So what's the plan when we get to Mexico?"

"I have some ideas that I'm working through, but don't expect a detailed plan." His smile was full of mischief. "I've convinced myself that plans limit creativity. I'd prefer to jump in and see what comes to mind."

"A natural-born innovator, huh? I can see why you were a good researcher."

He ran a hand through his hair and frowned. "The jury's still out on that. All I know is that I've got to find out this supposed new formula for Tricopatin and make sure it is not the exact same poison that I fed to my wife and the other guinea pigs during the clinical trial."

"Then maybe we can find out why people are trying to kill me," Jordan added.

CHAPTER **22**

Despite their enjoyment of being alone together, Ryan and Jordan had no intention of lying low in a hotel room. They decided to visit a few of Ryan's old haunts, beginning with Charlie's Pub, a local college dive on Durham's famed Ninth Street, a few blocks from Duke's East Campus. The stench of stale beer and cigarette smoke filled the air. Every television in the bar was surrounded by rowdy Duke basketball fans cheering on their beloved Blue Devils.

Attempting to be heard over the hoopla, Jordan shouted, "So this is where you used to hang out?"

"I don't remember it being this loud and obnoxious. I guess my age is showing. Let's head to the bar in the back room. It should be a little tamer."

The back room was just as Ryan remembered. A smattering of middle-aged patrons were nursing their cocktails, while a couple of forty-something adolescents poured twenties into the video poker machine.

Ryan ordered a couple of beers, handed one to Jordan and joked, "This place hasn't changed in twenty years. I could swear those same two guys were playing that damn poker machine the last time I was here. I guess they still think their ship's just about to come in."

After another round of drinks was delivered, Ryan laid out

some strategies for their pending visit to the New Hope Cancer Alternatives clinic in Puerto Vallarta. When the drunks at the poker machine began shouting obscenities at the blasted game, Ryan and Jordan decided they needed a change of scenery. As they perused Ninth Street, searching for a more relaxing atmosphere, the name on one door caught their attention. The G Loft, with its high leather-backed chairs, suede couches, Buddha statues, dim lighting, and soft jazz playing in the background, seemed out of place in a college town. And it was exactly what they were looking for.

After a couple of martinis, they ordered a bottle of wine and decided to explore the secluded loft. They found an empty couch and nestled into each other's arms, enjoying their wine, the soft music, and the pleasure of each other's touch.

When the last couple left the room, Ryan and Jordan found themselves alone. In harmony, they turned towards one another and set down their wine glasses. Without a word, Ryan caressed her cheek and slowly pressed his lips against hers. Soon they were lost in a passionate embrace. It all felt so natural. Only the sound of feet mounting the stairway ended what promised to be a true display of their affections.

Back at the hotel, they wasted no time. Their coats dropping to the floor, Ryan pushed the door closed and brushed his lips across Jordan's. She responded passionately, and soon they were lost in each other.

Moments later, Jordan pulled away. Ryan took on a look of surprise and disappointment. But his eyes were soon wide and filled with desire when she surprised him again by lifting her blouse over her head, still buttoned. He breathed in deep as he saw her full, luscious breasts heaving in a black lace bra.

Soon, the fire that had been smoldering beneath the surface over the past two weeks consumed them. They melted into each other's arms as the rest of their clothes fell to the floor. Ryan slowly pressed her onto the bed. Jordan wrapped her feet around his ankles and gave herself to him completely.

Neither spoke a word as they yielded to the impulses they'd painfully denied themselves until now. The intensity was almost impossible to bear, and the release of Jordan's climaxes came as if she were riding waves higher and higher. Ryan managed somehow to hold himself in check as he brought her to the crest once again. With a determined effort, Jordan pulled herself away from the seductive enticement of the next wave until they both felt the eruption of release, collapsing together in a tangle of arms and legs.

CHAPTER 23

Ryan gazed out the window at the cumulus clouds floating past the port wing. They had connected to an Aeroméxico 757 in Mexico City and were now bound for their final destination, Puerto Vallarta.

The night before had changed everything. Today they had the sated, easy look of lovers. Ryan thought about the implications. In a sense, he still felt like he had betrayed Cindy. He knew that was irrational, yet he couldn't keep the feeling from lingering. The sheer intensity of their joining provoked in him a desperate yearning to be whole again. This had not been the case with Cindy. With Cindy he felt complete. Without her, a void was ever present, and his life had been empty and devoid of any real meaning, until now.

One irritating thought swirled relentlessly around his head like a pesky mosquito: maybe Jordan only needed him as her protector. His heart told him otherwise—he couldn't believe that Jordan was that type of woman. Still, Ryan knew he wasn't a genius when it came to women. In fact, he was sure that what he did not understand about them could fill volumes. But he was also pretty sure that no one could fake the magic they had shared last night.

The big jet landed on the tarmac with a slight bump and taxied over to where buses were waiting to take them to the terminal.

They departed the aircraft and squinted at the bright Mexican sun. They breezed through customs, and, in under an hour, they were in the rented SUV heading towards Sayulita. As they picked up the coast road, the aqua blue of the Pacific glistened through the palms. Having been cooped up in a plane for the better part of the day, they opted for open windows over air-conditioning, and the breeze felt refreshing. The road first went through the cluttered highway towns that lined Banderas Bay north of Puerto Vallarta, then wound through the foothills along the coast. After passing a local bus, their progress was brisk. For a brief moment, the smell and feel of the tropics put Ryan back in exile on Exuma. But a glance at Jordan behind the wheel, her mane of dark hair whipping back in the wind, let him know that, in so many ways, he was in a whole new world.

Thirty-five minutes outside of Puerto Vallarta, Jordan pulled over to the side of the road. Over the canopy of tropical trees they could see the serene blue waters of the magnificent Pacific Ocean. The mountains of the Sierra Madre rose stately behind them.

Jordan turned toward Ryan. "I fell in love with this place when I came here in college, on spring break. I did my undergrad at Northwestern and my entire sorority made the trip. I've been coming back for vacations ever since. Three years ago I decided that I would not spend the rest of my career running clinical trials. After watching so many hopeful patients wither away, I committed myself to doing something that could actually help people in desperate situations live. With my uncle's financial backing and his high-powered connections, I put together an exploratory committee of experts and began formulating a plan to make this clinic a reality."

"What did these experts do for you?"

"The goal was to discover drugs that offered enhanced benefits or even real cures for people stricken with terminal diseases. I had it on good authority that such drugs existed, but had yet to pass FDA scrutiny."

"Sounds like you and my friend Eric have been drinking the

same Kool-Aid. I just can't believe that drugs exist that actually provide benefits to terminal patients beyond traditional medicine and yet cannot get approved for use in the United States."

"Maybe I am drinking the same Kool-Aid as Eric, but sounds to me like you're drinking the Kool-Aid being served up by the FDA. I'm not saying all of these drugs are perfect. Many of them come with the potential for some pretty nasty side effects. But there is a big difference in approving a drug designed to treat something like insomnia with harmful side effects as opposed to approving a drug to treat terminal patients. If a new drug offers the patient a real chance at a cure, however small that chance may be, isn't that a better alternative than just accepting fate and waiting to die?"

Ryan didn't respond. He rubbed his chin and stared out at a distant yacht rocking peacefully up and down in the brilliant blue waters of the Pacific. His thoughts turned to Cindy as he debated the implications of Jordan's question. He could not deny that this very issue was one that had haunted him for the past five years. *Is it better to give a terminal patient an experimental drug that could save their life knowing it could have potential devastating side effects, or let them live out their remaining days with traditional treatments that have proven to extend life for many months or even years?*

"Listen, Ryan. I'm sorry. I know this is a touchy subject for you. I didn't mean . . ."

Before she could finish, Ryan cut her off. "Jordan, there is no need to apologize. You're right. Hell, I came to the same conclusion over five years ago and took a similar action. Just because it did not work out in that one particular instance doesn't mean that other terminal patients shouldn't be given every chance to survive."

Jordan's eyes welled up and she reached over and gave him a big hug. As they held each other, Jordan whispered, "I'm so happy to hear you say that. I can't begin to tell you how wonderful that makes me feel."

Jordan kissed Ryan's lips, then released him from her hug

and got out of the SUV. She wiped the tears from her eyes with a tissue as she stepped over the guardrail and headed to a point overlooking the ocean. Ryan gave her a minute and then joined her.

"So tell me, what did your committee of experts discover?"

"I can't get into all the details due to confidentiality agreements, but based on what they came up with and my own follow-up research, all of the pieces of the puzzle started to come together and the clinic went from a dream to a real possibility. And when it came time to take the next step, I knew this was the spot." Gazing out at the ocean, Jordan paused. "At the time, I had no idea a similar clinic existed in this area. It isn't like they advertised on billboards. I only found out after the call from Cottle. Turns out, the NHCA clinic is just around the corner on this hillside overlooking the Four Seasons Resort in Punta de Mita. My clinic is ten miles straight ahead in Sayulita, just before the hotel. How about a tour before we check into our room?"

"That sounds like a plan."

When they pulled up to Jordan's clinic, Ryan did a double take. Back in the States or the Caribbean the building might have been mistaken for a hotel. Coconut palms dotted the terrain, and jungle vegetation crawled over the white stucco walls.

Ryan quipped, "When can I get a reservation?"

"It was a hotel at one time. Fortunately, most of our renovations were internal. We didn't have to do much to the grounds. Come on, I'll show you around."

They were halfway down the first-floor corridor on their way to the administration office when a middle-aged woman in a starched white lab coat approached them. The photo ID card hanging from her upper pocket read Francine Chambers. Auburn hair draped her shoulders in ringlets.

Francine gave Jordan a big hug, and the two of them spent a few moments discussing the events of the past few weeks. Both of their eyes filled with tears as Francine expressed her sympathy over the tragic deaths of Jordan's aunt and uncle.

Wiping the tears from her eyes, Jordan apologized. "I'm sorry for carrying on, Ryan. This is Francine Chambers. She's a dear friend of mine. We used to work together in Chicago, and she'll be assisting me with the clinic." She turned to the woman and said, "Francine, I want you to meet my friend Dr. Ryan Matthews." Smiling at Ryan, Jordan continued, "Ryan is a brilliant research scientist. I'm trying to impress him so he'll decide to come work with us at the clinic."

Francine looked at him with knowing brown eyes, then asked Jordan, "Is your house ready yet, or are you staying at the hotel?"

Jordan informed her that the house she had rented would not be ready for another week and that they'd be at the hotel for the next few days.

Francine started off down the hall and said over her shoulder, "We got two more bookings today, so this puts us near capacity come opening day."

"That's wonderful, Francine. Is everything still on schedule?"

"We have the final inspection set for next week, and I've been assured by the government official that there'll be no problems."

As Francine hurried off, Jordan continued down the corridor with Ryan. "Given this was a former hotel, the room structure turned out to be convenient. The windows face the prevailing winds, and the whole place can be cooled without air-conditioning, although we do have it."

"How many rooms?"

"Forty-two semi-private and fourteen private. We have six doctors on staff and more on standby. At last count, we had forty-four nurses on board who are in training to care for the unique group of patients who'll be staying at the clinic. We also have a four-person administrative staff that works in the two offices up front."

On the second floor, they toured the now-vacant lab, and Jordan showed Ryan the rendition of the planned finished product. "We have the budget to acquire the latest and greatest medical-testing equipment and that is exactly what I plan to do once we move into phase two of the program."

Ryan knew Jordan was fishing—and that he'd be better off not taking the bait. But he couldn't help himself. "Phase two?"

Jordan threw him a hopeful glance. "Phase two involves the research lab. Development is just about to get underway. We'll be looking to hire someone to head up the department." She delivered the line he'd been waiting for. "You'd make the perfect candidate."

"Let's see what we can find out about Tricopatin. We may find out that it's still a flop and these guys at NHCA are just a bunch of hucksters."

Jordan shrugged, clearly not surprised. "They very well may be hucksters, but that doesn't negate the fact that you invented a drug that cured ovarian cancer in rats." Jordan took Ryan by the hand. "And I'm sure with more time, you would have figured out the manipulations needed to make it work on humans."

Ryan smiled. Jordan's confidence in him and praise of his abilities brought up feelings and emotions that he had not felt since he reviewed the test results of Cindy's cancer following her final injection of Tricopatin. Ever since that day, the day he discovered his miracle cure was a complete bust, he had been void of confidence in his abilities as a scientist.

* * *

The hotel was draped in pink-and-white stucco and sat nestled in lush vegetation, dominated by fern palms and coconut trees. Rain-forest greenery was worked into the landscape, lending the grounds a manicured, yet natural, look.

After checking in, Ryan and Jordan wandered through the open-air lobby to admire the panoramic view of the ocean, which sparkled in the sun through the shrubbery surrounding the veranda. A soft breeze blew in off the water, and a wind

destinations. Of course, at the cost of $5 million dollars, this luxury came with a steep price tag that nobody but the ultra-wealthy could afford.

Pohmer informed his new prospects that while most of the patients at the clinic had been diagnosed with terminal cancer, the clinic also catered to patients with milder problems who preferred to heal in a resort-like atmosphere.

As they entered the lab facilities, Pohmer pointed with pride to a vial encased in a glass showcase and labeled *Serapectin*. Several other drugs were also displayed, but Serapectin was clearly the featured drug. "This," he said, pointing to the drug, "is our pride and joy. One injection every ten days for ninety days, and your cancer will be cured."

Ryan, struggling to remain in ignorant-patient mode, let an appropriate amount of awe creep into his voice. "That's amazing."

"That's right, it is. We've successfully treated over one hundred and seventy patients for ovarian cancer."

One shot every ten days for ninety days, sounds familiar. I would love to speak to these patients. That is, if they're still breathing.

Jordan's face lit up. "Darling, what do you think?"

"It all sounds promising. Would it be possible to speak with some of your former patients, Dr. Pohmer?"

"We get that question a lot. I wish I could allow you to, but all patient records are confidential. Nevertheless, we do have a portfolio of thank-you letters that we have received, and I would be happy to share those with you."

"That'd be great. I'm sure they'll provide us with some encouragement." Looking back at Jordan, Ryan said, "I think this is what we've been looking for, honey. Let's get your treatments started right away." The nod from Jordan was Pohmer's cue.

"That'll be fine. We'll get you started with evaluations first thing Monday morning. Of course, we are going to have to run our own series of tests. We'll need your complete medical history and all your records sent down from your physician in the States."

"Of course," Ryan said. "The release has been completed. As

soon as we place the call, they'll be sent right over."

"There is also the matter of diet, physical therapy, and strength training which will be necessary to enhance your treatment."

"Will my wife be required to stay here for the entire ninety days?" Ryan was doing his best to sound concerned.

"I would plan on a full four months. Although the treatment phase is ninety days, we don't advise going home until our follow-up testing confirms the cancer is in full remission. Based on experience, it can take up to thirty days after the treatment is complete for the patient to test cancer-free. And we keep our patients under the strictest supervision to help maintain their health during the course of treatment. Of course, you are free to visit anytime. You'll find that most of our patients, even though they are ill, like it here. We do our best to pamper them."

Ryan and Jordan smiled at him as if he were their savior. Pohmer seemed to revel a moment in that role before speaking again.

"Of course there's still the matter of—"

"Ah, yes," Ryan interrupted, "the money. I will have the initial payment wired to the hospital's account on Monday."

"That's good. I'll have you talk to our business manager, Mr. Valadez, before you leave. Is there anything else you'd like to see?"

"I don't think so," Jordan said. "We'll be back in the morning."

* * *

About a half-hour later, while Ryan was giving Valadez some fairly inventive details on the Calks' imaginary lives, Pohmer stuck his head in the door. He made sure everything was all set, handed Ryan the portfolio of thank-you letters, and said goodbye, explaining that he was off to make his rounds.

As they had planned two days earlier in the back room of

Charlie's Pub in Durham, Jordan took this opportunity to feign sickness and excuse herself to the bathroom.

The business manager's office was down a hallway off the main entrance. During the facility tour, they had used the elevators to travel between the various floors, but given the elevators' location in the main reception area, they would be useless for what Ryan and Jordan had in mind.

Jordan used the stairwell to gain access to each level of the clinic. She made notes of bathroom locations and other possible places to hide in case the need arose. She returned to the business manager's office where Ryan was reading the doctor's portfolio. When she reappeared, he asked with a convincing look of concern, "Do you feel okay, darling? You took so long."

She put her hand to her stomach. "Sorry, I just had some nausea. I'm feeling better now, though."

Valadez inquired whether he could do anything for her. When Jordan declined, he thanked them for visiting the clinic, reassured them that they were making the right decision, and escorted them out to the valet, who had their vehicle waiting for them.

Ryan handed a ten-dollar bill to the valet, then hopped into the driver's seat of their rented SUV.

"Gracias Señor."

"De nada. How late does the valet service run?"

"Ocho."

Ryan closed the door and pulled out of the facility as Jordan breathed a sigh of relief.

"Did you see anything interesting on your bathroom break?" Ryan asked.

"It shouldn't be too difficult to sneak in unnoticed. This place has more in common with a resort than a medical facility. I found a rear staircase past the administrative offices that accesses all the floors. The challenge will be getting into the labs. It looks like they're only accessible with a key card."

"That won't be a problem," Ryan said with a grin. He

reached into his pocket and pulled out a key card with a photo ID of a lab technician named Cesar Hernandez. "I swiped this from a jacket hanging on a chair in the lab as Pohmer was going on about Serapectin."

"Nice work, Mr. Calk." Jordan squeezed Ryan's shoulder. "With their open-door policy and resort-style setting, two well-dressed Americans should be able to stroll right in without drawing any attention."

"I was thinking the same thing. And I didn't notice any video surveillance cameras except at the reception desk at the front entrance. As long as we avoid that area, we should be fine, unless they have hidden cameras."

"And why would you think they don't?"

"This isn't a Las Vegas casino. Cameras are meant to deter crime and they're most effective when placed in plain sight. But we still need to be extremely cautious. There will be some nasty consequences if we get nabbed with a stolen key card or found in a place we shouldn't be. I'm sure that industrial espionage is as serious a crime in Mexico as it is in the States."

"Hard to imagine a nastier consequence than getting blown up or run off a cliff."

"Point well taken."

* * *

That evening, Ryan and Jordan arrived at the NHCA parking lot a few minutes after eight o'clock and waited for their opportunity. After forty-five minutes, they noticed a black four-door sedan with tinted windows pull in. The car parked in an open spot three rows over from where Ryan and Jordan were waiting. Four well-dressed Americans, appearing to be in their mid-sixties, exited the vehicle and started for the entrance.

Ryan and Jordan jumped out of their SUV and followed several feet behind the group as they entered the facility. As the couples were checking in with the lone attendant on duty, Ryan and Jordan disappeared down the hallway, out of sight of the reception area. They took the staircase leading to the now-vacant third floor where the lab was located. They decided to hide out in the women's bathroom until they were able to figure out if security personnel were patrolling the floor and, if so, how often.

After thirty minutes of Zen-like silence, they heard footsteps approaching their bathroom hideout. As the door opened, Ryan and Jordan lifted their legs out of sight from under the stalls.

The guard didn't bother turning on the lights and left as quickly as he had entered. After waiting patiently through three passes, they were certain that his schedule was to make a pass once an hour. It was now a quarter past midnight, and the building was quiet. As soon as the guard had made his fourth pass, they slipped out of the women's room and, using the key card, gained access to the lab. Since they couldn't turn on the lights, they were both grateful for the pen lights that Ryan had had the foresight to bring.

They surveyed the lab. It was an enormous, mostly rectangular room. The far corner of the lab was cut at a ninety-degree angle where the clinic's drugs were proudly displayed behind a glass trophy case. From their visit with Dr. Pohmer earlier that day, Ryan was familiar with the lab's five rows that ran the length of the room. Each of the rows was lined with countertop-height lab stations and each of the countertops was filled with computers, high-tech electronics, test tubes, beakers, and burettes. The work space was designed so that technicians could work on either side of the rows and swivel chairs were scattered throughout the lab. There were four stations in each of the first three rows. The back two rows had two stations each. The lab's entrance was in the middle of the room. Directly back from the entry door, located past the first three rows, was a reception-style desk with twelve large file cabinets lined up against the wall behind it. This is where Ryan and Jordan decided to begin their search for more information on the wonder drug.

As Ryan expected, the file cabinets were locked. But these were not high-security locks and he was able to jimmy them open using a letter opener he found on the reception desk.

They began searching through each file in every drawer. The search was monotonous as many of the files contained scientific data that had to be reviewed thoroughly to determine if the information was possibly relevant.

As Jordan read through the last file in the third cabinet, something caught her eye. "Ryan, I found a file that references Tricopatin."

Ryan immediately grabbed the file from Jordan. Sure enough the file referenced FSW's Tricopatin drug, now known as Serapectin. He dug deeper into the file but couldn't find any reference to changes in the formula. The file contained a brief history of the drug, the failed FDA trial, and the dosing procedures for Serapectin. That was it.

Just as he put the file back in the cabinet and closed the drawer, the entry door opened and a flashlight swept the lab. They dropped to the floor just in time to avoid being spotted.

The guard left just as quickly as he had come in and Ryan whispered, "Come on, we've got another hour, keep searching."

They set to work with a new fervor. They continued to find evidence of the wonder drug in use, but they could not locate patient records, test results, documents that revealed the formula, or any reference to where the drugs were being stored.

They abandoned the file cabinets and began searching through the cabinets under the various lab stations. Some were unlocked and others were locked up with a mechanism no more sophisticated than the file cabinets'. The locks were easy to bust open, but each took a few minutes and the clock was ticking. They were deep into their search, checking every vial and test tube they found, when the guard returned.

Both ducked and held their breath. The flashlight beam swept the lab but instead of leaving this time, the guard entered. Ryan and Jordan exchanged a look as the guard's footsteps drew closer. When he entered the next aisle of counters and began to round the corner, both scurried as quietly as possible to the abutting aisle. When their shoes scuffed on the tiled floor, the guard called out, "*Hola . . . Quién está ahí?*"

They froze before Ryan reached up and knocked over a set of test tubes into the aisle adjacent to where he and Jordan were crouching. As the guard raced to the site of the broken glass, Ryan swung around the counter and, attacking from the rear, took the guard around the neck, applying pressure until he drifted into unconsciousness. Ryan had gone over a decade without using his FBI training; since meeting Jordan, he literally hadn't been able to live without it.

After dropping the guard to the floor, Ryan raced over to the door and flicked on the lights. He yanked power cords from the back of a couple computers and bound the unconscious guard's feet and hands. After fashioning a gag from the guard's own necktie, Ryan got to his feet. "We don't need to worry about him now, but we need to find what we're looking for before someone comes looking for him."

Glancing around the office for any place they hadn't already checked, Jordan said, "Maybe we're looking in the wrong area. What about the vial in the display case?"

"How do we know it isn't just a labeled test tube filled with colored water?"

"What do we have to lose? Besides, we're running out of time."

They fell into a full sprint towards the far corner of the lab where the wonder drug was on display. Ryan picked up a chair, heaved it through the glass, and grabbed the vial of Serapectin. "Now for the accounting office."

"After the racket you made?" Jordan said, aghast. "Don't you think we're pushing our luck? Let's get out of here before we end up in a Mexican prison."

"Not so fast. We need to locate any possible leads if we're ever going to find out who's been trying to kill you. This may be our only chance. Besides, we need to see if we can get our hands on a complete patient list. I want to see if any of these people are really still alive. That will tell us if this crap works or not."

Against her better judgment, Jordan agreed, and they headed off toward the accounting office. Using the letter opener to jimmy the lock, Ryan slipped in with Jordan behind him. The office had a glass partition, and everything inside lay exposed to the main corridor. Once inside, Ryan booted up the computer.

Drawing on her experience as a clinic operator, Jordan had some ideas as to where the information might be stored and under what titles. The sales reports told a story all by themselves: the clinic employed eight salesmen, with Jerry Cottle being the top earner at $7 million dollars in the last year alone. Even the low-end guys made over a million a year.

After printing off the sales reports, Jordan located the file in the hard drive that contained a patient list. Although the list did not include any medical information, it did provide names, addresses, and phone numbers, along with billing and payment details. A quick scan of the printed list revealed that patients paid anywhere from several hundred thousand dollars to $5 million for their treatments. A long list of patients had paid $5 million dollars, and it was this information that drew Ryan's attention. *These must be the suckers that paid for Tricopatin, or Serapectin, or whatever it is they're calling it these days.*

There was no security in sight aside from a lone clerk nodding off to sleep at the front desk. They held their breath as they headed out the door, prepared to run if alarms went off. Moments later, they were in the SUV on their way back to the hotel.

CHAPTER **25**

Gus Witherspoon returned the small stack of results to the clinic's chief of staff and turned to leave.

"You barely looked at these!" the doctor protested.

Gus was already halfway out the door. "I've seen enough."

The doctor chased after him, following him outside. "What about the patients? What about their families? What do we say to them?"

Gus stopped in his tracks. He gazed down at his boots, which were covered in dust. The dust, a fine powder that covered everything here in the bush, reminded him where he'd come from—and where he was going.

"Tell them we're going home."

The doctor, an angular man in his fifties, grabbed Gus by the shoulder and turned him around. "We come in here, throw together a clinic in record time, tell these people we're here to save them, and then leave? Just like that?"

"Just like that."

"I won't do it!" the doctor said, flicking spittle as he shouted, his face only inches from Gus's.

Gus removed the doctor's hand from his shoulder. "Doctor," he said, "you knew what you were getting into when we hired you. If you didn't have the stomach for this kind of work, you shouldn't have come. But it's too late now. You've chosen your lot."

The doctor's face turned red. "You sold me a bill of goods. You sold these people a bill of goods!"

A pair of security guards, normally employed to keep unruly villagers out, emerged from the clinic entrance and walked stiffly toward the doctor.

Gus motioned to them. "Please take a jeep and escort the doctor and his things back to town. He can catch a bus from there."

The doctor protested, his voice rising even louder than before, but the guards strong-armed him away.

Nothing, least of all an irate employee, surprised Gus anymore. Life was a series of choices. He'd already made his. Shit happened, of course. Villagers got sick and died. Drug trials went south. Doctors fumed. It was, simply, the nature of things. The average person was sickened by such a zero-sum game. The average person, in fact, was squeamish and self-righteous. But the average person would never change the world. Gus, because he was willing to do what no one else had the courage to do, just might.

As for the doctor, he would be kept close, without his knowledge of course, in case he took his indignation back home and decided to talk. It was his choice. But hopefully it wouldn't come to that. The powers that be had plenty of persuasive tools at their disposal, including other high-paying jobs that were worth even the most principled man's silence. Or, if push came to shove, there was always a more permanent solution.

Gus removed his cell phone and made a call transmitted halfway around the world.

"This is Craven."

"William, it's Gus. I need to speak to the man in charge."

"He's in a meeting."

"How long?"

"Can't say. Usual shit. Can I help?"

"Tell him the MS 4200 trial's a bust."

There was a pause before Craven replied, "You know what to do?"

"Shut it down, wipe it away, and make like it never happened. I know the drill."

"No leaks."

Gus bristled. Sometimes Craven reveled a little too much in his role as the corporation's top bruiser. "Don't worry, tough guy. If anyone threatens to talk, we'll send 'em straight to you."

Craven hung up the phone and made a quick mental note. Stedman and the others in the FSW boardroom would be distressed to learn of the early demise of MS 4200. But it was better the drug fail now, in its early stages of testing, than later, after the corporation had invested millions.

In any case, there were other concerns that ranked higher on Craven's priority list. A certain doctor and her lover were causing trouble south of the border, and it was Craven's job to make the duo disappear before anyone was the wiser.

CHAPTER 26

By the time Jordan awoke, Ryan had been making calls for over an hour. A room-service tray and an empty coffee cup lay on the bedside table. She parted the mane of hair that made a silken tent over her face and peeked out. She looked impish and adorable, and Ryan couldn't resist the impulse to lean over and kiss her.

With a smile, she scrunched deeper into the sheets. "What are you doing?"

"Trying to find an old friend of mine, Dave Butters. We went to undergrad together. He used to work for Kalliburton Labs, and over the years, I sent him business whenever I had a chance. Last I heard, he was managing their lab outside of Raleigh. I'm hoping he's still there. If anyone can tell us what's in this vial, he can."

She stretched. "The Big Vial Caper," she quipped. "I still can't believe we pulled it off."

"Well, we did. Now we have to find out what's going on with this drug."

"You think they are making it all up?"

"All they need to do is lie. It's making the drug cure cancer that's the hard part."

Jordan sat up in bed. "You're right. Of all the desperate people who come down here looking for a cure, how many would bother or even be able to check out the stats the clinic's touting? This is their last chance at life, and they're willing to believe in miracles. I guess you can write whatever you want in a file."

"Exactly. And as Dr. Pohmer said, all the patients' records are confidential, so no one is able to verify the accuracy of their claims. Those thank-you letters contained all the standard stuff you'd expect from a terminal patient who was suddenly cured. But without knowing for sure whether they're from real patients, the letters don't mean much." He reached for the coffeepot. "It's still hot—want some?"

"Please."

He fixed it the way she liked it—a medium amount of cream with two lumps of cane sugar—and handed it to her. She smiled.

"What's the big smile for?"

"For you. I love that you know how I take my coffee."

"No big deal," he said with a shrug.

"Yeah, actually it is."

While he wouldn't admit it, he cherished her sentiment. Not knowing how to respond, he started dialing another international number on the hotel phone.

Jordan excused herself and got out of bed. When she returned, looking rejuvenated, Ryan announced, "I tracked him down. He's still with Kalliburton and said he'd be happy to look at it. He said he could derive the exact formula of the vial's contents in a couple of hours once it was in his hands. If we can get it there by Monday, he agreed to go to his lab even though they're closed for President's Day. I called down to the concierge, and they said they could have UPS pick up the package within the hour."

"That's great! What do we do until then? And what are we going to do after we get the results?"

"Well, it will be at least forty-eight hours before we get the results back. I called the airline and tried to get a return flight out today, but they're booked up solid until Tuesday. I say we enjoy some time in paradise and try to forget about all of this for a few hours. After that, if the results come back and show that the vial is indeed Serapectin, and that Serapectin is just a modified version of Tricopatin, we need to track down some of the patients to find

"Damn," Ryan said. "We can leave our luggage, but we need our passports."

Scanning the area, he noticed a flower-shop van parked at the curb. He told Jordan to grab the SUV and meet him in the rear of the hotel, then dashed over to the driver as he was removing a magnificent display of roses from the rear of the van.

"These flowers are for my friend," Ryan said.

The driver glanced at the card. "Señorita Campbell?"

"Si, si, mi amiga. Listen," he said, "let me give her a real surprise. Let me deliver them for you."

The driver struggled with the translation, but seemed to get the gist of what Ryan was saying. "But, señor. Trouble for me. I . . ."

Ryan handed him a U.S. fifty-dollar bill. This was an impressive amount in a country where the daily wages of a delivery driver couldn't buy lunch for one at the resort hotel he was parked next to. The man handed him the flowers. Ryan pointed to the uniform shirt the driver was wearing. The delivery man looked at the fifty and decided to forfeit the shirt.

Ryan put on the uniform, handed his shirt to the driver, and grabbed a baseball cap sitting on the van's dashboard, tugging it down low over his head. "Wait here until I come back."

The driver nodded.

Five minutes later he opened the passenger door of the SUV, startling Jordan. "Let's roll."

* * *

The Mexican desert lay vast and desolate before them, a foreboding place. The towns and gas stations were few and far between. They hoped to make Cuernavaca before midnight, and after a short layover, Mexico City by late morning.

It was late afternoon when Ryan, who had taken over behind the wheel at the last gas station, noticed a blue pickup truck behind them. Jordan noticed his attention on the rearview mirror and turned around to see the lone vehicle on the barren stretch of highway about a hundred yards back. "You worried?"

"Not yet. But I'm keeping an eye on it. This part of Mexico is like the Wild West. Bandits have free reign here."

Ryan kept a heavy foot on the pedal, but the truck continued to gain on them.

"I'm beginning to get a bad feeling about this," Jordan said.

"If the truck was interested in passing us, it would have done so by now," Ryan admitted.

"Do you think it has anything to do with the people at the clinic?"

"I doubt it, but you never know. Right now our problem isn't who they are as much as what they plan to do."

"Any chance you can outrun them?"

"No. I've had the pedal to the floor for the past two minutes. Time for Plan B."

Barely slowing down, Ryan heaved his shoulders into a hard right turn off the hardtop and onto a dusty side road. The truck followed right behind them. Within seconds, the SUV was churning up a rooster tail of thick dust into the blue sky. The pickup disappeared from the rearview mirror, but Ryan knew it was still there.

"We're going to wind up in the middle of the desert!" Jordan shouted.

"Hold on tight," he warned. "Real tight."

He slammed down on the brakes as hard as he could, almost standing on the pedal. The trailing truck's tires locked, but it was too late. It crashed violently into the rear of the SUV.

The silence of the desert was broken by the clash of metal and glass. Jordan and Ryan jolted forward from the collision, but their seat belts kept them relatively unscathed. Ryan drew a deep breath and stepped on the gas. He was relieved that the impact had only mangled the rear of the SUV and the vehicle was still mobile. The pickup, on the other hand, was immobilized, smoke pouring from under the hood. They didn't linger to investigate. Ryan did a U-turn and passed the cloud of smoke and steam that shrouded the mangled truck.

Back on the paved road, they sped away toward Mexico City, neither saying a word.

It was just past midnight when they reached Cuernavaca. They pulled up to the first decent-looking hotel and went straight to bed.

* * *

In the morning, they were off again and reached Mexico City by lunchtime. Ryan said, "I hope the Puerto Vallarta police didn't bother to send a description of us up here. I'm counting on Mexican bureaucratic inefficiency to carry the day."

Jordan frowned. "Let's just hope your stereotyping is accurate."

Ryan and Jordan held their breath as they approached the security checkpoint. Ryan got through without incident and waited for Jordan. Sweat beaded on his forehead as he saw her being asked to step aside. He watched in panic as a security guard asked her to empty her purse on a side table. This attracted two more security agents. Ryan's mind was whirling.

A female agent went through the contents of Jordan's bag before triumphantly holding up a nail file. As the security agent asked Jordan to sign a form and then allowed her to pass, Ryan felt his heart rate return to normal. Jordan had handled it all with a cool aplomb that betrayed no sign of guilt or anxiety. His admiration for her climbed yet again.

The next flight that would get them back to Raleigh was several hours off, so they laid low, their faces buried in books they had purchased after going through security, until their flight was announced.

* * *

After an evening flight to Dallas and a red-eye to Raleigh, they debarked the plane with the stiff, slow gait of zombies. But Ryan perked up as they drove out of the airport. "Let's go over to Kalliburton and get a firsthand report from Dave. It's in Mebane, thirty-five miles up the road."

They were approaching Mebane when they heard the news over the car radio: a bizarre, one-car accident on Saturday night on Orange Factory Road in Durham was now being investigated as a possible homicide; the intensity of the fire that charred the car and its driver was not consistent with a typical car fire. According to the city's fire marshal, additional accelerants had been used to spark the inferno.

Ryan and Jordan wore identical masks of horror as the radio announcer reported the victim's name: David Butters.

CHAPTER **28**

William Craven did not tolerate mistakes from his subordinates. The former Green Beret had no patience for losing. Likewise, he hated apologizing, or begging for more time, or promising something he couldn't deliver. As the head of security for pharmaceutical giant Fisher Singer Worldwide, he knew he was ultimately responsible for these unfortunate recent developments. Thus, with a foul taste in his mouth, he approached his boss.

Jacob Stedman's emotionless eyes bore into Craven as the underling gave his report. Before he was able to finish, Stedman raised his hand. "I've heard enough. We need to call a meeting with the senator."

"I was going to suggest that, sir."

The hint of a sarcastic smile played around the edges of Stedman's mouth. "Sure you were. You don't know what the hot seat is until you've dealt with the senator. Go through the appropriate channels and ask him to bring his puppet along for the briefing. It's time to validate his commitment to our cause. We need to ensure that he is aware of this situation and assure him that we are doing everything in our power to rectify it. What we have here is not only the prospect of losing money but also the potential of a national scandal and serious legal ramifications. Believe me, the senator's not going to let that happen. The last thing in the world I want to do is to call a meeting with him over this. But we have no choice."

Craven chose his words with care. "But sir, with all due respect, you have more pull than some senator from—"

"Don't kid yourself. He will do whatever he has to in order to protect himself and his interests. If he feels he has been deceived, he won't hesitate to act. He has the power to make either one of us disappear, if it comes to it. At this stage, full disclosure is our best course of action."

Craven had been involved in the Phoenix program in Vietnam, and he knew something about making people disappear. He still thought of himself as a soldier, superior to the civilian types who surrounded him. No one would ever mistake him for a cheap hood; his bearing marked him as a warrior and a professional. The use of force when the going got tough had never let him down, and he believed it was the reason he had survived this long in his dangerous profession. Other more subtle methods meant little to him. His job was to get in and get out clean.

* * *

In Washington, FDA Commissioner Carl Wiley, collar turned up against the wind and rain, was pacing on the sidewalk when he spotted Senator McNally's stretch limo cruising toward him. It slid to a stop, and Wiley climbed into the backseat next to McNally. The limo was a warm refuge from the cold rain blanketing the Capitol.

McNally noted the commissioner's jitters. "Relax, Carl, the most they can do is kill you."

This did nothing to put Wiley at ease, even with the senator's accompanying grin. As the limo pulled away from the curb, he said, "I don't know these guys, Ed. They're your people."

"They're nobody's people. FSW is an equal-opportunity corporation that buys guys like us by the dozen. And they'll eliminate anyone who gets in their way. Something big is up. I don't have all the details, but I'm pretty sure the shit's about to hit the fan."

Wiley had never seen Senator McNally look anything but confident. The urgency in his voice sent shivers down Wiley's spine. "But what does this all have to do with me? Why do they want me there?"

McNally ignored the questions, poured himself a glass of Bulleit Bourbon from the limo bar, and offered one to Wiley. After a healthy belt, McNally said, "I know you thought this was the usual penny-ante shit you're used to. Grease a palm here, pick up an envelope there." Buoyed by the drink, he said, "No, pal. You're playing in the big leagues now, and the big boys play to win. Otherwise, someone pays, and pays dearly."

Wiley had started out as a director for the Philadelphia Department of Public Health. From there, he was nominated for a national job in public health before taking his current position as commissioner of the FDA. He was not accustomed to the hard-fought political wars. He was a scientist and felt above the fray. Of course, he learned the game when he came to Washington and was shocked by the callous disregard for humanity and the raw lust for power. In this club, power came before saving lives, whether in the public-health sector or the private sector. When he got the FDA job, an old veteran of the political wars told him, "You'll be lucky if you're not in the bag in your first year."

And he was right. Wiley hadn't been in Washington more than a couple of months before he learned that all good intentions fell by the wayside of expediency. It all came back to campaign financing. Nothing, he learned, was ever accomplished without money. The best-intentioned politician in the world couldn't achieve squat without getting reelected, and he couldn't do that unless he got in bed with money interests. It was unavoidable.

As they cruised down the JFK Expressway towards Balti-more, McNally continued. "This is no small-change shakedown. You've been getting big money. They probably want to make sure you're committed to the team. Let me give you some background since your head is on the chopping block, too."

Wiley winced and helped himself to a refill. The senator

cleared his throat as if he were on the Senate floor, and Wiley knew he was in for a speech, something the dashing senator was adept at delivering.

"These days the pharmaceutical industry is a hell of a lot more cutthroat than any other industry, including big steel, big oil, or Detroit. Combined, these guys spend tens of billions of dollars per year on research and development. While they each come up with a blockbuster drug every now and again, oftentimes they come up empty as a result of the fine work of your organization." He gave Wiley a smirk. "And billions more go down the drain. Not to mention the hundreds of millions these companies have to hold in contingency each year to fight the countless lawsuits they have to defend. The big problem started in 1996 when the National Institutes of Health announced that they'd mapped out the human genome. This breakthrough meant that, for the first time, the cause of major diseases could be traced to specific genetic defects. And, as I'm sure you're aware, if you know the cause, you can theoretically develop a cure."

As the senator paused to refill his drink, Wiley took the opportunity to interject. "I don't understand how that could be a problem for the pharmaceutical industry."

"This was a totally different science than the previous big-pharma, trial-and-error, drug-development machine. The smaller biotech firms are now in a much better position to capitalize on these new classes of bio-drugs. This caused Big Pharma to realize that their empires could soon come crumbling down unless—"

"I get all that," Wiley interrupted, "but the big pharma companies have been gaining access to these drugs by acquiring biotech firms. Let's face it, I'm paid to keep these biotech firms mired in red tape. A well-timed non-approval letter from my organization can devalue a company ninety percent overnight. I've saved your buddies billions already."

McNally all but ignored him. As they traveled past the tranquil farmlands along the New Jersey Turnpike, followed soon after by the industrial wasteland on the marshes of northern New

Jersey, the commissioner sensed that he had hitched his wagon to the wrong star. McNally was right; he was small-time, shaking down whomever he had to in order to fill the campaign coffers. It seemed like an easy, lucrative gig, until he realized how high the stakes were.

McNally adjusted himself in his seat and continued. "A few years back, FSW set up an offshore corporation owned by several blind trusts. As I hear it, the corporate ownership structure is untraceable. FSW has the best attorneys in the world working for them. Anyway, this corporation, New Hope Cancer Alternatives, set up alternative medical clinics in various locations around the world, hired the best sales force money could buy, and proceeded to peddle these unapproved drugs as miracle cures to the ultra-wealthy at obscene prices. I've heard they generate a profit in excess of a billion dollars per year. It is amazing what someone with fifty million in the bank who has run out of hope will believe. But, who wouldn't spend everything they have to hang on to life? What parents wouldn't give everything they had to save their child? You see where I'm going with this?"

Wiley understood.

McNally was just finishing his filibuster as they crossed into Manhattan. Even though it was the tail end of the after-work commute, the going was slow. Wiley gazed at the broad Hudson glittering in the still-bright sunshine. A barge was pushing a tanker upriver to the unloading terminals on the north shore. But his mind wasn't on the river scene. Instead, he was far away.

He heard McNally murmur, almost to himself, "My father came to this town in the sixties. He brought with him three kids, a Harvard degree, and little else. And look what he went on to accomplish."

Wiley discounted the obvious—that McNally's father had gotten ahead by nefarious schemes and underhanded dealings. For politicians and gangsters alike, the coin of the realm was power. All that counted were results.

"Yeah, my old man learned politics the old-fashioned way,

in a smoke-filled room with powerful men—none of this preening for TV cameras that we do today. And back in the day, he had to fight off those bastards on the other side of the aisle when they had all the money and power."

"Yeah, but he hung in there and won most of his battles," said Wiley. "I always admired him for that. He was one tough old bird."

"And he had to be, because we're in a tough business. The strong survive. The weak die off." McNally stared out the window. "I plan to be around a while. But to get where we're going takes money."

"Constituents think working for them in Washington is a privilege," Wiley said, his tone self-righteous, his confidence at its peak thanks to the alcohol. "Truth is, you try to do something good for the people, but you're powerless without money."

He sounds as if he believes his self-serving spiel, McNally thought. *Maybe Wiley is sincere after all. Or maybe he's just one hell of an actor.*

CHAPTER 29

Sulari knew he had to make the hit on Tommy Kruger. It had been ten days since Craven ordered the hit and the car bomb investigation had finally started to cool down. The kid was a loose end—he had to go. While Sulari wasn't about to cross Craven's orders, he was damn sure going to do it his own way. The bomb had been far too messy and brought on unwanted attention. He would not make the same mistake again. A traditional hit was out of the question. The two events had to appear unrelated. The kid was a junkie, and no one would give a damn about him when he was gone, unless the cops tied his death back to the car bomb.

Sulari pulled up across from Tommy's beat-up tenement building. He checked his pockets again, making sure he had brought what he needed, before getting out of the car and crossing the street. He entered the building through a badly dented metal door and had to grit his teeth to avoid gagging from the smell of urine and garbage in the hallway. He heard a couple of crackheads, a male and a female, screaming at each other in the first-floor apartment. Something small and furry scurried beneath his feet as he climbed the creaky stairs. He instinctively wanted to take out his piece and blast the damn thing, but it wasn't worth it. On the third floor—Tommy's floor—he found a bum passed out in the hallway next to a pool of vomit. *I'd be doing humanity a favor by taking all these junkies out right now*, Sulari thought as he stepped over the man. *A big fucking favor.*

He came up to Tommy's door and rapped three times. He waited ten seconds before he hammered the door with the side of his fist, shaking the door on its hinges. Still no answer. He could have forced the door but that wasn't part of the plan. Instead, he picked the cheap lock with a small pick he carried in his pocket.

He found Tommy hiding in the closet. When Sulari opened the door, Tommy's eyes bulged. "Shit."

"Surprised to see me, asshole?"

Tommy's face was drawn and pale except for the dark circles around his sunken eyes. "I . . . uh . . . thought you were someone else."

"Someone you owe money to, maybe?"

"Uhhhhh. Well, yeah."

Sulari grabbed him by his dirty T-shirt and yanked him out of the closet, shoving him onto the couch.

"I need you for another job."

"Look, man, I can't talk about it now. I need . . ."

"A fix."

"Yeah, I could really use one."

"I don't care about your junkie problems. I need to talk business."

The kid ran his hand through his mangy mop of hair and swiped his sleeve across his nose. "I can't focus, man. I'm in a bad way."

Sulari shot Tommy an evil stare. "I can fix you up, kid. I move smack as a sideline."

The bedraggled young man's eyes showed a dim glimmer of life. "You've got some H?"

"Yep. Want some?"

Tommy's breathing became faster paced. "I owe you one, man."

Sulari pulled a rubber cord from his coat pocket and began tying it around the young man's track-marked arm.

None of this was happening fast enough for the desperate

junkie. "Shit, man, let's go. I'm dyin' here."

"Then you're gonna do my job?"

"Whatever you want, just hurry."

Sulari cooked the dope in a blackened spoon and loaded one of Tommy's dirty syringes like a seasoned expert. Just seconds after the injection, Tommy let out a big sigh as all the tension eased from his body. He slumped back on the couch, and his eyes rolled back in ecstasy. Sulari waited about a minute before feeling for a pulse. He found none—the kid was dead.

He wiped the spoon and syringe clean of fingerprints and placed them on the floor next to the kid's bed. He knew the "hot shot" he had given Tommy would elicit no suspicions in anyone's mind. *The kid finally did more than he could handle*, he imagined them saying. *It was bound to happen sooner or later*. Another druggie dead of an overdose—who cares? No investigation required.

He slipped out of the apartment, careful to lock the door behind him.

At the downstairs landing, two cops in uniform blocked his way, one tall, the other short. After an adrenaline spike, Sulari regained his cool, figuring they must be there for the domestic disturbance he had overheard as he entered the building. Nevertheless, he also knew the cops would be suspicious seeing such a well-dressed guy in this part of town.

"Hold up a minute, pal," the tall cop said. "What are you doing here?"

Sulari squinted. They hadn't drawn their weapons, and he was certain they knew nothing about Tommy's murder. Still, they might frisk him. Damn cops; he hated them all.

The short cop glanced at his partner, then turned and faced Sulari. "Let's see some ID, buddy."

Sulari shrugged. With a mighty burst, he slammed himself between them and out the door. As he pounded down the street with the cops in chase, he knew they would not shoot unless he gave them reason. He hadn't drawn his own weapon, and it was against the Chicago Police Department's rules of engagement to open fire on an unarmed suspect. If they did shoot, it would have to be in the back, which gave him an even greater sense of confidence that they would not fire at him as long as he kept running.

But Sulari was not in great shape and the extra fifty pounds he was carrying was beginning to work against him. After only a block he was running out of steam. Even if he did manage to somehow outrun them, they'd call in backup, and he'd be finished for sure. Fleeing the neighborhood wasn't an option because his car was parked across from Tommy's apartment; left there, it would raise suspicions once Tommy was found.

The dingy street was all but deserted. *The damn druggies are all passed out. Too bad, I could lose these coppers in a crowd or take a hostage. But there ain't a fucking soul around.*

But Sulari made good use of his lead, and his mind was working faster than his legs. He knew the cops had no idea who he was, and they certainly wouldn't expect him to strike first. *I'll make the desolation of these streets work for me.*

As he came up to a blind corner, he sneaked a peek back. He was thirty feet ahead of them and they hadn't drawn their weapons. Sulari whipped his Glock 9mm out of his jacket pocket and screwed on the silencer in one fluid motion. When the two cops came flying around the corner, they were clearly not prepared for their suspect to be standing still with a gun in his hand.

He shot both of them at close range before either knew what hit them. He put one slug apiece into their heads for insurance. Sulari calmly unscrewed the silencer with a rag and walked away, leaving the cops face down on the sidewalk, their blood flowing over the curb into the gutter.

A few minutes later, he was in his car and heading for safe haven. As his heart calmed down from the rush of the chase, he rolled over the situation in his mind. The two cops were shot about a block and a half away from Tommy's. Tommy was dead from an overdose, with no signs of a struggle. Even if the two crime scenes were connected, there was no evidence to link the killings to him.

Sulari didn't want to screw around with Craven. Guys like Craven would kill anyone for any reason if it advanced their interests. Craven was a merciless killer with an endless supply of resources who would not stop until the job was done.

No, Sulari surmised, *this job was done. I'll get my money, and this will be my last deal with that asshole.*

CHAPTER 30

Carl Wiley was visibly shaking as the limo pulled up in front of a midtown Manhattan building. Built in the post-jazz era of large, dark stones, it boasted towers and turrets, projecting a strong influence of Gothic architecture. Impressive as it was, the old building was overwhelmed in the shadows of the modern skyscrapers that loomed nearby.

Senator McNally gazed up at the old relic. "You know," he said, still waxing nostalgic, "that's what's so great about this town. You drive down almost any street in Manhattan and find buildings from the nineteenth century, towers like the Empire State Building right out of the twenties and thirties, and the newest glass and steel monsters, all standing side by side. This town is America's museum."

Wiley was not in the mood for a discussion on New York, its unique architecture, or its place in the American tradition, so he simply nodded in agreement. The limo pulled up right in front of a No Parking sign. A pair of NYPD officers approached as they exited the vehicle. The younger one snarled, "Hey, can't you read the sign?"

The older one, having recognized McNally, elbowed his partner. "Good evening, Senator. Nice to see you again."

The senator looked at him with bleary eyes. "Is that you, Callahan?"

The old cop beamed. "Yes, sir, it's me."

"How's your family?"

"Fine, sir, thank you for asking."

"Say hello to the chief for me, will you?"

"Yes, sir, I will. You can count on that."

Wiley looked on in amazement. Even though he was the head of a powerful federal agency, he did not have the connections of an experienced senator, let alone relationships with people as low on the totem pole as a beat cop. Impressed, he whispered, "You know everybody, don't you?"

McNally grinned. "Not really. His name was on his tag. I must have run into him somewhere. He's old; he must have a family. Did I say something that suggested I knew him?"

Wiley didn't answer, but what he'd just seen confirmed what he already knew: he would never be the savvy politician that McNally was.

McNally got on his cell phone, and within a minute, two security guards came out of the doorway to escort them to the meeting. The structure housed one of the most exclusive and expensive gourmet restaurants in the city, but the public knew little about the rest of the goings-on within the old building.

Wiley sensed McNally staring at him as they descended several levels in a velvet-walled elevator. Nothing hinted that they were about to enter the lion's den.

Once they reached their floor, they passed through a set of locked doors guarded by a pair of security guards, and emerged in the inner sanctum of power. Wiley's jaw dropped.

McNally grinned. "Carl, your mouth is open."

Priceless Oriental rugs were scattered throughout the magnificent room. The walls were paneled in the finest Brazilian cherry. Fine art adorned the walls, and the open spaces were leafy and green. Enough exotic vegetation lined the room to give one the impression of being in a South American rain forest.

McNally pointed out an imposing plant with leafy arms that reached all the way up to the ceiling. "That thing's from South

America. I forget the name, but it's a man-eater."

"What?"

"It can grab you, suck you up, and eat you."

The last stop was the boardroom. The mammoth table had been shined to a high luster, and the high-backed leather chairs that surrounded it were individual works of art clearly not meant to accommodate the asses of mid-level managers. Off to the side, a shiny brass-railed bar stretched the length of the room, backed by an impressive array of bottles from all over the world. Two bartenders in starched whites stood ready to serve their distinguished clientele.

Wiley was happy to see that he and McNally were the first to arrive. After they ordered their drinks, McNally quietly filled Wiley in on Mr. Jacob Stedman. Born with a silver spoon in his mouth, as the senator put it, Stedman wouldn't rest until that spoon turned to gold. He was part of a business family with roots a mile deep in American industry. His position at FSW had been ordained since childhood, and he had been groomed for it from his earliest days. As the CEO of the world's leading pharmaceutical company, he was a well-respected man and considered by many in the corporate world to be the cream of the crop as a result of his success at the helm of FSW.

The senator had barely finished filling Wiley in when Jacob Stedman strode into the room, followed closely by two subordinates. Stedman looked the part: silver-haired, square-chinned, cold-eyed. He appeared to be in his late fifties or early sixties. His associates, too, played their parts well. One was clearly a lackey, there to keep his mouth shut unless asked for technical information. Perhaps his job was to take notes. The other, well dressed but menacing, looked every bit as Machiavellian as Stedman. He introduced himself as William Craven before heading to the bar.

The lackey followed Stedman to the table, where they beckoned the senator and Wiley to join them. The bartenders gave the new arrivals their drinks and left the room, securing the doors behind them.

Stedman took a quick sip of his drink before getting down to business. "Senator," he said, "we have a problem that must be dealt with. You're aware of Dr. Ryan Matthews and the tragedy he suffered five years ago."

The senator nodded. Wiley did not give any assent; he knew nothing about it.

Stedman continued, "After that we left him alone, keeping an eye on him from time to time. Each report came back that he had turned into a drunk island-dweller and represented no threat to our operations."

"And?"

"About a year ago, we learned that a Dr. Jordan Carver out of Chicago was constructing a medical clinic in Sayulita, Mexico, just a few miles away from our clinic in Punta de Mita. At first, we had no real concern. These clinics are all over, and none of them compare in quality to our operations. In fact, they cater their so-called 'natural' medications to anyone who can afford them. But they can't successfully market their product to someone about to take their last breath."

The senator nodded knowingly.

"About nine months ago, we learned that Dr. Carver had gained access to several of our drugs, the same ones we offer at NHCA."

Wiley spoke up for the first time. "How can that be?"

Before Stedman had a chance to answer, the senator asked, "When were you going to tell me this?"

Craven walked over from the bar and took a seat next to Stedman. "You're being told now. And we don't know how she did it. When we found out, our biggest concern was not that she had these drugs, but that she was going to sell them for a fraction of our price. We approached her about joining up. We offered her everything under the sun, but she refused. After that, we tried to get the permits pulled for her clinic, but it became apparent that, at the time, she had influential investors backing her, and we were unsuccessful."

"What do you mean 'at the time'?" Wiley asked.

Craven ignored the question. "After all else failed, we concluded that Carver had to be eliminated. We wanted to keep it clean and off U.S. soil which is why we decided to take care of the problem on her next trip to Mexico."

Wiley felt the hair on the back of his neck rise. He wanted to leave before he heard another word. He finally grasped the senator's warnings. He was in deep.

"Then we found out she planned to visit her aunt and uncle in Exuma," Craven continued. "Her uncle happened to be Henry Carver, who was also her big investor. We decided this would be the perfect opportunity to not only take her out, but to eliminate any prospect of old Henry Carver continuing his niece's efforts in her memory. The plan was—"

The senator motioned for Craven to stop. "Let me save you the trouble," he said. "I already know about the failed attempts on Dr. Carver's life. I know about the explosion in Exuma and the one in Chicago. I know about the two Haitians who went over a cliff and burned to a crisp. I know Dr. Carver has befriended Matthews. I know they broke into your clinic in Punta de Mita last Saturday night. I know that the FBI has opened an investigation into the attempted murders and that they have cobbled together enough evidence to give themselves jurisdiction—looks like your former employee has made use of his contacts at the Bureau. I also know that an old friend of Matthews's, David Butters, was incinerated in his car in North Carolina, and that one of your associates was successful in intercepting that package yesterday morning outside the offices of Kalliburton."

Wiley's jaw dropped. If the senator was worried about going up against the big boys, he didn't look it. It was Stedman and Craven who were sweating bullets now.

"Here's what I wish you would have known," Senator McNally continued. "Six months ago, an informal investigation was opened against Carver and her new clinic in Mexico. It appears that some of the drug formulas she plans to dispense at her clinic are being obtained through some not-so-legal means. With a little nudging, I could have gotten her charged with corporate espionage, patent infringement, and a whole host of other charges. But you had to go and start this war with her and Matthews and now they are out collecting evidence that could bring us all down."

Stedman's face went pale. "Senator," he said, "I had no idea. If we had known—"

The senator cut him off. "Let's not forget, gentlemen, that we're on the same team. If one of us goes down, the rest will surely follow. If you have a problem outside of your normal course of business, you come to me first." He placed his hands on the table and leaned toward Stedman and Craven. "Now, you need to stop making headlines and leave Jordan Carver to me."

Craven frowned. "What about Matthews?"

The senator straightened. "Do whatever you have to do. Just keep it off the evening news."

CHAPTER 31

Jordan plopped down on the hotel bed and kicked off her shoes. "Do you believe in coincidence?" she asked.

Ryan sat beside her and removed his own shoes. "Not in this case, hell no! My friend tries to do us a favor, and before he can deliver, he's incinerated? No! He was murdered. And I feel like shit for getting him involved."

Her voice soft, Jordan said, "It's not your fault, Ryan."

He buried his face in his hands, and she rubbed the back of his neck until he got to his feet and started pacing. "It is my fault. I knew we were up against someone well connected and should have been more cautious."

They became quiet for a while, and as Jordan drifted off to sleep, Ryan relived their frustrating day. . . .

* * *

Ryan and Jordan approached the receptionist at Kalliburton Labs, a twenty-something bleached blonde wearing too much makeup in a failed attempt to hide her swollen eyes; it was obvious she'd been crying. She greeted them with a slow Southern drawl and a tragic half smile. With grief heavy in Ryan's own voice, he asked to see the person in charge.

The receptionist picked up her phone, dialed a few numbers

and moments later a man appeared through an interior doorway. Hello, I'm Tag Donaghan." His voice was sullen. "How may I help you?"

"Hi, Tag. I'm Ryan Matthews and this is Jordan Carver."

They exchanged handshakes before Ryan continued. "Dave Butters was an old friend of mine. I'm still shell-shocked."

"We all feel terrible." Donaghan dropped his head and rubbed the bridge of his nose. "Dave was not only our leader, but a good friend."

Ryan swallowed hard. "I spoke to Dave on Saturday from Mexico. I had a serum that was in urgent need of analysis and he agreed to come in on the holiday to get the package. I don't mean to be callous at such a time, but the contents of that package are irreplaceable. I'm wondering if you can find out where it is?"

"I'll see what I can do. Wait here. I'll check the mailroom."

Ten minutes later, he returned empty-handed. "There is no record of any package arriving from Mexico today or over the holiday weekend and your name is not anywhere in our system. I also checked Dave's office to make certain a mailroom employee didn't deliver it there first thing this morning."

"That's strange," Ryan said, disappointed, but not shocked. "This would have been a UPS delivery. What's the normal procedure for logging in such a package?"

"During business hours, it would be delivered to Reception and Misty here would log it in both manually and in our computer system and then call the mailroom to have it delivered. If a package arrives after-hours or on a weekend or holiday, the delivery drivers all know to leave the package in our drop box. Then first thing the next business morning, one of the mailroom staff logs in all the packages and makes the rounds."

Ryan gazed up towards the ceiling trying to think of his next step, all the while realizing that his friend had been murdered because of him. "Thanks for trying."

Ryan wrote down Jordan's cell phone number and handed it to Donaghan.

"If the package does show up, will you please give me a call?"

"Will do."

Back in the car, Ryan called UPS.

"Hi, my name is Ryan Matthews. I have a tracking number for a package sent to a Mr. Dave Butters at Kalliburton Labs in Mebane, North Carolina. I need the status of the delivery."

"Yes, sir, just a moment, please," came the customer service representative's reply. As Ryan rattled off the tracking number he heard the representative punching her keyboard, and within seconds, she had the information. "It looks like it was delivered to David Butters this past Monday at 10:44 a.m."

Ryan turned to Jordan, even though she couldn't hear what was being said. "That's not possible."

"Sir?"

"Dave Butters was killed in a car accident on Saturday night."

"Oh god, I'm so sorry to hear that. But according to our records, David Butters at Kalliburton Labs signed for the package. There's only one Kalliburton Labs in Mebane, North Carolina. My records show that they're a major account, and we deliver there all the time."

"The company tells me that it never arrived. Could you give me the name and contact info for the delivery driver?"

"I'm sorry, sir, but that's against company policy. But I can give you the street address for the local office."

It was better than nothing.

At the UPS office in Durham, Ryan spoke to the supervisor who simply restated the company's privacy policy. Ryan was getting close to losing his temper when Jordan intervened.

She brushed her hair back and licked her lips. "I appreciate your company policy, and we're not looking to cause anyone any trouble. It's just that we need to find out what happened to this package. It contained sensitive medical data and the person we sent it to is now dead and the package is missing."

"Oh jeez, I'm sorry. I wish I could help, but I can't give out the driver's name or address. I could lose my job."

Jordan gave him a sad puppy-dog look but didn't say a word.

He fidgeted in his chair and scratched his head before speaking again. "But, the driver will be back to work on Thursday. He worked the weekend and holiday and is off today and tomorrow. If you want to come back then, eight a.m., you can speak with him personally."

Jordan gave the supervisor a big smile, thanked him for the information, and then she and Ryan headed for police head-quarters to try to get more information about Butters's accident. Predictably enough, the police would not provide them with anything beyond what had already been reported in the news. They merely confirmed that, because of the intensity of the flames and the lack of any other vehicle at the scene, the accident was under investigation.

Ryan and Jordan phoned Jim Crawford in Chicago to give him an update on their latest adventures. Crawford was a typical Bureau man, calm and cool, but Ryan heard the concern in his old friend's response.

"Look, you guys, I want you to come in. You need Bureau protection."

Ryan shook his head, as if his friend could see him over the phone. "Thanks, Jim, but we have too much to do. I have to find out what's going on."

Crawford knew enough about Ryan Matthews to drop the Bureau-protection plea. "It's your call, Ryan, even though I don't agree with it. But lay low—no credit card purchases or paper trails, switch hotels, switch rental cars, and ditch the cell phone and replace it with a prepaid cell that can't be traced. I'll be there with my people in the morning. Where can we meet?"

Ryan complied. "I'll call you back with our new number, and then you can call us when you arrive. We'll figure out where to meet then." After disconnecting, Ryan contemplated his next move before announcing, "I'm going to call Eric Maynard and let him know what's happened."

"Why?"

"Let's just say I'm curious to get his reaction."

He placed the call, listened carefully, and hung up. "His voice mail said that he would be out of the office all day, but that he'll be back tomorrow morning."

"Why didn't you leave him a message?"

"I want to hear his immediate reaction. Besides, Eric knew Dave as well as I did. It's not a message to leave on his voice mail."

Fifteen minutes after purchasing a prepaid cell phone and phoning Crawford with the number, they pulled up in front of a stylish three-bedroom ranch in Chapel Hill. The house had a spacious front lawn and a back yard full of Carolina spruce. It was now late afternoon and the big trees shadowed the house. With a heavy heart, Ryan rang the doorbell.

A tall, graceful woman opened the door. Upon recognizing him, she collapsed into Ryan's arms. "Oh Ryan, Dave's gone. He's gone."

Ryan murmured into her hair, "I know, Mandy. I know and I'm so damned sorry."

When Mandy finally realized that Ryan wasn't alone, she did her best to pull herself together. "Come on in. I didn't mean to leave you on the porch."

As they entered the quiet house, Mandy said, "The kids are at my mother's. I'm bad for them right now. I can't look at them without seeing Dave and breaking down."

"I understand." Ryan noticed Mandy casting glances at Jordan. "This is Jordan Carver. Jordan, this is Mandy Butters. We've been friends since college."

Mandy sniffed. "Yeah, we were the four musketeers in those days." She stopped to run her eyes over the room. Family photos—including one of Dave tossing their youngest son into the air—were lined up along the mantle. Her eyes lingered a moment before she finally said, "Sit down. Would you like some coffee?"

"Only if you let me help you fix it," Jordan said. Mandy smiled and the two women disappeared into the kitchen. Ryan sat down and tried to relax but the photos beckoned him. He got up and walked over to the mantle and looked at a photo of him and Cindy with Eric and Dave sitting on a picnic table at Eno River State Park. A sudden chill came over him and Ryan felt his heart freefall. By the time Mandy reappeared with a tray of coffee, he was in a funk.

The tray shook in her hands as she set it down on the table, splashing coffee into the saucers. "I'm sorry," she said.

"No worries," Jordan responded. "Let me do that for you."

Ryan joined Mandy who was now sitting on the couch and put his arm around her shoulder as Jordan served the coffee and then sat in the chair opposite them. Ryan wished he was there only to console Mandy, but he had some questions. "Did Dave mention anything about a UPS package?"

"He did say something about a package you were sending him. What was in it?"

"It contained something important, a new drug to test. But the package seems to have gone missing. I'm sorry to have to ask, but could you tell me what happened before the crash? Did Dave mention my call or the package to anyone? Did you notice anything suspicious?"

Mandy reached for a tissue and blew her nose. Her eyes were still watery. "Dave was so excited to get your call on Saturday. We talked about getting together when you came up. He said your package was going to arrive from Mexico on President's Day, so he was going to go to the office on Monday to pick it up. Later that day he called me after his round of golf. He said he was going to have a couple of beers with his golf partners and then head on home. That's the last time I heard from him." Her voice wavered. "Ryan, they say it may not have been an accident." Anguish twisted her face. "I don't understand why anyone would do anything to harm Dave. He was such a good man. He didn't make enemies. I just don't understand."

Ryan pulled her close to him as Mandy took several deep breaths. *She's a strong woman. Dave was a lucky man to have had her.*

Glancing at his watch, Ryan saw it was nearing five o'clock. He excused himself to make a call. Moving to a nearby room, he phoned the receptionist at Kalliburton Labs. "When I was there earlier today, I forgot to ask you something. Do you know the name of the UPS driver who services your office?"

Her reply was immediate. "There are two."

"Okay. I need the one who delivers on the weekends."

"Oh, he's a real Don Juan." Ryan could hear the hint of laughter in her sweet Southern voice. "His name's Mike, Mike Sperry."

"Do you know how to get in touch with him?"

"He wishes, but no."

Ryan had to smile at that one. "Thanks anyway, and have a nice day."

* * *

Ryan and Jordan checked into a motel in Chapel Hill, paying cash and giving a phony name, then got busy on the telephone. They called all seven Michael Sperrys in the Raleigh-Durham-Chapel Hill-area phone book. The first five either weren't home or were not a match, but with the sixth call, they knew they had the right one.

"Who is this?" Mrs. Sperry snarled.

Jordan happened to make the call, and the response from the Lothario's wife was nothing short of hostile. "My name is Dr. Jordan Carver, ma'am. I'm looking for Mike Sperry to check on a package delivery."

"Oh, that's rich," Mrs. Sperry spat back. "I thought I'd heard it all."

"Ma'am?"

"I wish the bum was home so I could watch his face when he talks to you. Doctor! Ha!" she fumed.

"Ma'am, I've never met your husband. I can properly identify myself to you in person. All I'm interested in is a package that your husband delivered. It's vital, and evidently it didn't show up at its destination."

The woman's voice took on a more conciliatory tone. "So, you don't know my husband?"

"No, ma'am. All I'm interested in is the package. It's critical that we track it down. The contents are very important to the healthcare field. Can you help me?"

"I'd like to, but I don't know when he's coming home. He has the day off tomorrow. Can you call back in the morning?"

"How about I just drop by the house tomorrow morning?"

"That's fine with me. The earlier the better. I'm sure he'll sleep all day otherwise."

Jordan took down the Sperrys' address and hung up.

* * *

Ryan and Jordan had a late dinner at a Chinese restaurant. As they sat waiting for the check, Ryan had a thought. "One thing is obvious about the package."

Jordan's eyes widened. "Go on."

"It's this delivery guy. The lab has no record of receiving a package and UPS has a delivery confirmation signed by Dave. This guy is either in cahoots with the bad guys or he's been paid off."

She considered this for a moment. "From the descriptions of him given by the receptionist and confirmed by his wife, he doesn't seem like a sterling character."

* * *

Still frustrated after reminiscing over the day, Ryan flicked on the TV in search of news about their case. The TV roared to life in the middle of a loud commercial touting the benefits of "a single pill, taken once a day. . . ." Ryan stabbed at the remote control, searching wildly before finding the mute button, but not before Jordan stirred to life. He looked over at her, embarrassed. "Sorry about that."

Curling up again, she muttered, "Come to bed. We've got a long day tomorrow."

He pulled the covers over her and kissed her on the cheek. "I'll be right there," he said. "Go back to sleep." He knew that sleep would not come easily for him that night.

CHAPTER **32**

After Wiley and the senator had left, Stedman dismissed his assistant, and he and Craven were alone at one end of the table.

Craven found himself on the receiving end of a steely gaze from Stedman.

"The senator's insistence that he handle Carver puts us in a difficult position," Stedman said. "Dr. Carver knows too much."

"I agree," Craven said. "That's why I hired our friends in South Africa to finish the job. They've already left Johannesburg and should be touching down early tomorrow."

"You what?"

"It's time to bring in the heavy artillery. The senator is blowing smoke. He obviously has someone inside our operation—someone who's keeping tabs on our progress. But if he had any real clout, he would have stopped us by now. Besides, we can't sit back and assume that some federal agency with a three-letter abbreviation is investigating Carver's clinic in Mexico. And even if this is in the works, it will be a long road before they can make a case against her. She'll be off to Mexico in no time and outside of U.S. jurisdiction. Hope is not a strategy. She and Matthews are a clear threat. Hell, while we were trying to find them up here, they were breaking into our clinic in Mexico. We've taken them too lightly, and it's time to stack the deck in our favor."

"Let's set aside for the moment the issue of whether or not I agree with you," Stedman said after a long pause. "My question is, why didn't you consult me first?"

Craven let the question hang in the air. "Because I thought I was hired for my independent thinking and my expertise in this field. Am I wrong?"

Stedman jumped on the question. "There is an enormous difference between *thinking* independently and *acting* independently. This sort of decision can't be made without my consent, much less without my knowledge."

Undeterred, Craven tried to strengthen his case. "Matthews is ex-Bureau, and it's probable that he has the Feds on our trail."

"What about the senator?" Stedman countered. "He has now made his wishes known. I fail to see how deliberately going against him strengthens our position."

Craven bit his tongue. He had already considered all of Stedman's misgivings and had worked his way through them with ease. Now he had to wait for his boss to catch up. "Think about it, sir. The damage is already done. We've already got a body count that made the headlines. If all of this was an unforgivable act, the senator wouldn't be issuing toothless warnings. If he were going to go against us, he would've already done so."

"Be that as it may, he has now drawn a line in the sand. I don't relish the prospect of crossing it."

"But what other choice do we have?" As Craven asked the question, he saw a flash of recognition on Stedman's face. Yes, they were in a bind. Yes, killing Dr. Carver would quite likely put their relationship with the senator in jeopardy. But the alternative—to let her and Matthews keep digging until they found enough evidence to bury them all—was unthinkable.

"Fine," his boss said, his jaw clenched. "We'll call her death *unavoidable*."

"Collateral damage," Craven said, "when we take out Matthews."

"That's right," Stedman said, bristling at the interruption. "After we eliminate the doctor, we'll pump a few million dollars into the good senator's campaign coffers. I can't see him getting too ruffled if the problem is eliminated, even if it is not done exactly as he had planned."

As they were about to adjourn, Craven's cell phone began to vibrate. Lifting the phone from his coat pocket, he looked at Stedman. "This may be important, I should take it." After getting the nod from Stedman, Craven answered.

It was Sulari. "It's done. I put him to sleep with a hot shot of dope. But I had problems. Two cops busted in while I was getting away. I had to handle them."

Craven suddenly wished Sulari were in the same room—and within strangling distance. He paused a moment to compose himself. "Dead?"

"As doornails."

"Are we in trouble?" The question was a deliberate fake-out. There was little danger of anyone tracing Sulari's miscues back to FSW. But the thug had just signed his own death warrant. He, too, would have to be erased. He had been put in charge of dousing a small brush fire, but instead had set the forest—in this case the Chicago P.D.—ablaze.

"I doubt it. The kid's dead in his room from an OD. The two cops went down a couple of blocks away, both shot. There's no tie in between the two. Depending on how many visitors the kid has, they probably won't find him for a week. Nobody will notice a foul smell in the hellhole he was living in. And nobody saw me except a couple of druggies who couldn't ID their own mothers."

"I see." Craven's tone was inscrutable.

"Listen, I'm gonna lay low for a few months just to be safe. You know how the Chicago cops are about their own. You'd think the president had been assassinated. But I need more green since the job involved more than I was contracted for. There'll be a lot of heat, and I need the extra dough to make myself scarce."

Craven, his hand over the phone's mouthpiece, waited a moment before getting back on. "Okay, but it's too risky to send a wire right now. I'll bring the cash. Where are you?"

"No way. I know about your 'no loose ends' policy. The money goes into my offshore account as agreed, or else."

"Or else what?"

"I rat you out. I know how to do it without messing things up for myself. In fact, I've done it before. My advice to you when dealing with the Outfit is to pay up. It'll be much cheaper in the long run."

Craven sensed a challenge. He liked challenges, because he always came out on top. "Why are you taking this attitude?"

"Because I can smell a weasel a mile away. I knew I was taking a chance with a suit like you. That's why I demanded a wire transfer to begin with."

"I'm going to need more time to do this wire transfer."

"Bullshit," Sulari grumbled. "Don't stall me."

Craven enjoyed letting Sulari dig himself a hole. But as amusing as Sulari's tough-guy act was, Craven knew he had to be careful. Keeping his patience, he calmly responded, "Look, give me forty-eight hours, that's all."

"And that's all you'll get. If it's not there, I do my thing and you hotshots go down, big time."

"I said I'd get it to you within forty-eight hours, and I will."

The line went dead, and Craven stared at his phone for a second before slipping it back into his pocket. He turned to Stedman, who had no doubt sensed the seriousness of the call. "We have another problem."

CHAPTER 33

It had been three weeks since Ryan first met Jordan at Rosey's.
Since the death of Jordan's aunt and uncle, someone had
orchestrated multiple attempts on their lives. In the past two
weeks Ryan and Jordan had flown from the Bahamas to Chicago;
and from there, after a six-day stay in the hospital courtesy of
an assassin's car bomb, to Raleigh-Durham, North Carolina.
Afterwards, they had taken off to Puerto Vallarta, Mexico, then
traveled by car to the New Hope Cancer Alternatives Clinic in
Punta de Mita, as well as to Jordan's clinic a few miles down
the road in Sayulita, Mexico, before returning to Puerto Vallarta,
escaping back to Raleigh-Durham via Mexico City.

After all they had been through, they still had no idea who
was trying to kill them. All of their leads had been extinguished
except one. Their remaining lead was thin at best, but since it was
all they had left, they decided to follow it through as soon as they
had readied themselves for the day.

A half-hour later, Ryan and Jordan were at the UPS driver's
house. It was a rundown bungalow in North Durham in bad need
of a fresh coat of paint and a day of yard work. Mike Sperry answered the door in droopy boxer shorts and a wrinkled T-shirt.

"My wife said you'd be stopping by." He gave Jordan a
quick look up and down, his sleepy eyes widening. "Uh, what
was it you wanted?"

Ryan jumped in first, unconsciously puffing himself up. "I believe you were scheduled to deliver a package to Kalliburton Labs last Monday, President's Day. Who did you deliver the package to?"

Sperry, still groggy, didn't give his answer too much thought. "Yeah, I wondered why they were taking a delivery on a holiday. That's never happened there before. I thought it was a little weird, but I just do my job. There was only one car in the parking lot. A guy was waiting for me at the front door."

"Did he have ID?" Jordan asked.

Sperry scratched his head. "No, I don't think so."

"You gave a package to a man without making him identify himself?"

The UPS driver bristled. "Look," he snarled, "my job is to deliver the damn packages. I'm no detective. If a guy is waiting there for it, who am I to question him? President's Day is supposed to be a milk run, but I had thirty-seven damned deliveries to make. We only require a signature. I don't check IDs. Look, my wife said she thought this was important, but I really don't appreciate you coming by my house to harass me."

He made as if to close the door, but Jordan flashed him a smile that seemed to soften his suspicions. "I know this is a little aggressive on our part, interrupting you in the middle of whatever you were doing. Just believe me that this is important and a matter of life and death."

"Okay," Sperry grumbled, "what do you want to know about it?"

"Can you describe this guy?" Ryan asked, his voice calmer than before, though his irritation with the delivery man was growing.

Sperry hesitated, reluctant to answer. "I don't know, executive type, a shiny suit. I thought that was funny. Most of those guys wear white lab coats, but being that it was a holiday, I figured he was going to some fancy affair later in the day."

Ryan kept up the questions to keep the delivery man talking. "Was he short or tall? Black or white?"

"Uh," he mumbled, scratching his stubble. "Let's see. White guy, a little less than six feet, medium build, brown hair with a touch of gray."

"How about his car?"

"Uh, not sure."

Jordan jumped back in. "Mr. Sperry, think about it. You said there was only one car in the parking lot, so you obviously noticed it."

"Let me think. It might have been a foreign job; it was black, looked brand-new, maybe a BMW or Mercedes. I can't remember." A fearful look descended upon his face, as if it had just dawned on him that he was in over his head. "Look, you guys, unless you show me a badge or something, I don't even know why I'm talking to you." He backed up and reached for the door handle.

"Wait, we only—" Ryan's protest was cut short by the slam of the door.

Back in the rental car and out on the highway, they got a call from Crawford on Ryan's cell phone. "Hey, folks, we're here. Where can we meet?"

"There's a Starbucks near the airport," Ryan answered. "Take U.S. 70 West about a half-mile, and you'll see it on the right."

"Can you meet in thirty minutes?"

"We'll be there."

* * *

Ryan and Jordan told Crawford everything that had happened up to that point. They left nothing out, including their exploits in Mexico.

Crawford thought for a moment before saying, "First we have to find out what really happened to your friend Butters. I had a copy of the police report faxed to me—the story has more holes in it than a screen door."

"And the UPS delivery at Kalliburton Labs?"

"We can check out the security cameras, see what they tell us. But for now we have to stash you folks somewhere safe. It's obvious that some powerful people are after the both of you."

Ryan was quick to answer. "I don't think that's necessary, at least not yet."

Crawford shook his head. "I disagree. There have been at least three attempts on your life. Your luck is going to run out. I have a friend with a place on Lake Gastin. It's available, secluded, and will keep you out of any further danger until we have a chance to figure this out. That is, provided you stay put."

Ryan exchanged a glance with Jordan. "Okay," he said, "but how long do you think we'll have to hide out?"

"Give me forty-eight hours to see what we can dig up. I know I can't keep you down for the duration. But I think it's critical that you guys disappear for a while."

* * *

Once they reached the cabin, Ryan dialed Eric's number from the prepaid cell phone. This time he was able to reach Eric right away. "It's Ryan. We need to talk, in person, tonight."

Eric was silent.

"Eric. It's critical."

"Okay. But not tonight. Tomorrow. Twelve o'clock."

"Fine. Where at?"

"Where we used to take the girls on the weekends."

"You mean En—"

Before he could finish, Eric cut him off. "Yes, you know where I mean, no need to say it over the phone. I'll see you there tomorrow."

After dinner, Ryan and Jordan took turns calling the patients on the list they had stolen from the NHCA clinic in Punta de Mita. The plan was to use a cover story, telling patients or their mourning spouses that they were with a law firm initiating a class-action lawsuit against NHCA. They would explain that the suit was over deceptive trade practices—that NHCA had lied to desperate patients and bilked them out of millions.

The evening was filled with frustration. Call after call ended with a transfer to voice mail. After almost five hours, Ryan and Jordan had left messages for the 173 patients on their list who had paid NHCA $5 million each for their treatment.

"They're all dead by now," Ryan groaned after leaving his final message.

"In that case, we should start receiving return calls from their families soon."

Just before midnight as Ryan and Jordan were snuggling in bed, Ryan received a call from Crawford. "We've been at it all day. Not much to go on yet, but we've got all available resources monitoring the situation. Something should break soon."

"What about the surveillance videos from Kalliburton?"

"They didn't reveal much. Just the UPS driver. The person receiving the package was not in the frame except for his outstretched arm reaching for the package. The only other potential piece of evidence revealed was the right rear fender of a car in the parking lot, but the camera didn't catch the license plate."

"I'd still like to take a look."

Crawford hesitated. "Not a good idea. There's nothing significant and I prefer to keep you hidden up at the lake."

"Listen, Jim. You know I can't sit here and do nothing. I'm coming in tomorrow morning regardless. Hopefully you will show me the video."

"Okay, be here at nine. But be careful. I have a feeling that whoever's behind this knows we're involved. And if they can't find you on their own, they may be watching us, hoping that we'll lead them to you. Judging from their bold actions thus far, I wouldn't put anything past them."

CHAPTER 34

A South African Airways 757 landed at cold, drizzly O'Hare International Airport with a bounce and a squeal. Two tall men in business suits, their faces as grim as the gray skies they descended from, were among the first to disembark. They each bore a striking resemblance to the other, appearing almost identical except that one had blue eyes, the other green. After clearing customs, they headed to the passenger pick-up zone where a black Suburban was waiting for them.

The driver did not say a word on the forty-minute drive to an abandoned warehouse on Chicago's South Side. Once they arrived, the driver handed the green-eyed man the keys. "Everything you requested is in the trunk." Neither of the two passengers responded. The driver exited the vehicle without saying another word, got in a waiting car, and drove off.

* * *

The research provided by Craven had been flawless, and the South Africans were able to round up three known associates of Ed Sulari in no time. Before the three men knew it, they were sitting on the cold floor of an abandoned warehouse with their hands cuffed and shackled to a water pipe.

The blue-eyed South African took one of the hapless trio, an obese Mafioso cliché named Fat Tony, into a room at the far end of the warehouse, while the other took the second captive, a wiry tough named Al, to a room on the opposite end. The third man, Stanley, of medium build and a notch or two less macho than the others, remained chained in the middle.

As screams of pain and horror began to resonate from both ends of the warehouse, the third hood, on the verge of tears, began to sweat and stammer. Five minutes later—which seemed like an eternity to Stanley—the screams were replaced by whimpers, and the blue-eyed South African who had taken Fat Tony emerged. Seconds later, the other one appeared. The whimpering turned to silence, and after a short, whispered conference about twenty feet from Stanley, the green-eyed South African grudgingly handed his partner, who had made his victim talk first, a crisp hundred-dollar bill.

With the prize stretched between his hands, the South African walked up to the remaining captive. The clicking of his hardsoled shoes on the concrete floor echoed through the warehouse.

"You're lucky—your *brus* gave it up quickly. Now all you have to do is confirm what they told us, and you'll be on your way."

Stanley wept. "Oh, god, I don't know why you brought me here. Ask me anything, I'll tell you whatever you want to know. I have a wife and a daughter. Please, I beg you."

"Where is Ed Sulari?"

Cuffed and restless, the man was barely able to catch his breath. The green-eyed captor flashed a wicked smile at his associate, pulled a pistol out of his jacket holster . . .

"No, no!" Stanley thrashed against his shackles.

. . . and fired a bullet through the kneecap of the screaming man.

After the cries of pain subsided, the questioning resumed. "I will ask you once more. Where is Ed Sulari?"

"He's . . . he's held up at my cabin. Near Lake Geneva," wailed the crippled man.

"Give us exact directions on how to get there."

"Yes, yes, just don't hurt me anymore."

* * *

Three murdered men with ties to the Chicago mafia lay dead in an abandoned warehouse on the South Side of Chicago as the two assassins headed north on Interstate 94. As they approached the Wisconsin border, the passenger turned to his partner. "I thought these mafia guys were supposed to be tough. Those three were a bunch of pussies."

"Yeah," the driver responded, "that fat *tsotsi* shat his bloomers before I even had a chance to cut his toes off."

"Craven says this Sulari is a pro, though. We shouldn't take any chances."

"He's not going to be expecting us," said the green-eyed South African, "although the cabin sounds as if it's got some security and a good field of fire."

"Surprise will win the day every time," the blue-eyed one said. "Every time."

* * *

Perched on a small hill, the A-frame was nestled into the verdant pine of the Wisconsin countryside. Heavily wooded, the area was blanketed by snow cover over a foot deep. The nearby lake lay frozen and foreboding, stretching out in the distance like a snow prairie.

Sulari had been living on frozen pizzas and coffee as he waited for Craven's wire transfer. He planned to head off to the Cayman Islands as soon as the money was sent to pick up his commission and forget his recent troubles. He kept the radio and TV off in case anybody tried sneaking up on him. The cabin was equipped with enough floodlights to light up Wrigley Field, but he felt it best to keep them off. The last thing he wanted to do was draw attention to himself while the heat was on. For now, he had one small lamp lit and the shades drawn.

Sulari was just starting to nod off at the table when his head jerked up, his skin crackling with the rush of adrenaline. *Footsteps! Motherfucking footsteps.* Drawing his weapon from his shoulder holster, he moved over to the window. With his gun trained outside, he flipped on the floodlights, lighting up the winterscape bright as day. At first he didn't see anything, but then a burst of steamy breath in the cold air gave away a big buck, standing rigidly at the edge of the woods. An instant later the beautiful animal made a quick, graceful turn away from the cabin and, in great leaps, crashed into the underbrush.

The thumping and slashing of brush was audible for several seconds as Sulari let out a sigh. "Jesus Christ," he said aloud. "I've had enough of this nature shit already."

He put his gun back in its holster, turned off the floodlights, and walked back toward the stove, shaking his arms and cracking his neck with a quick twist of his head. *No sleeping tonight— there'll be plenty of time to sleep when I'm on the plane.*

As he was fixing himself a fresh pot of coffee, he heard another noise out front. *That sounded awfully close to the front door,* he thought, adrenaline returning to his veins. *The deer wouldn't come that close.*

He drew his weapon and advanced to the front door in the moody glow of the lamp. This time he threw the door open and thrust his pistol into the darkness in the direction of the noise. Shots rang out, reverberating through the forest. The great buck, a quarter mile down the hill, came to a sudden halt and looked back toward the cabin.

Sulari dropped to his knees and fell face forward. Blood flowed from the two bullet holes in the back of his head, forming rivulets of red in the white snow. With his pistol still smoking, the blue-eyed assassin reached over and turned off the burner on the stove.

CHAPTER 35

Craven was not usually in a position to schedule meetings with Stedman, but things had changed. As in wartime, where the president caters to the five-star general in command, Stedman now needed Craven more than Craven needed Stedman. He even sensed in his boss's voice the unconscious shift in power.

When he entered the elaborate office, two executives rose from their seats and left without saying a word. At the moment, Craven was the most important person on the boss's agenda.

True to form, Stedman got straight to the point. "Catch me up," he said as he poured himself a stiff drink.

"The problem in Chicago is resolved. But—"

Stedman looked up from his drink. "There's something else?"

"On a hunch I decided to keep an eye on Maynard. I—"

Stedman cut him off. "We checked him out thoroughly years ago. He's as steadfast as they come, always has been."

Craven held up a hand. "Hold on. You know I don't do things flippantly."

But Stedman wasn't listening. "Just last week you had him intercept the package from Matthews. Doesn't that prove his loyalty and commitment to the cause?"

Craven's eyes narrowed. "Look, Mr. Stedman, you pay me not to trust anyone. You pay me to be suspicious when there's no clear reason to be suspicious. I have my reasons."

"Go on," Stedman said, nursing his drink.

"I had his phone tapped. Yesterday afternoon he took a call from Ryan Matthews and arranged a meeting with him for today."

"What did they talk about?"

"Matthews is ex-Bureau. They were both savvy enough not to say too much."

Stedman sat down. "I don't think there's anything to worry about. They have history. It makes sense that Matthews would go to him for answers. If Maynard refused to talk, it would make Matthews even more suspicious."

Craven didn't seem convinced. "Maybe, but they were speaking in code. They referred to a meeting place but didn't name it over the phone."

Either Stedman was trying to affect a sense of cool, or he was really convinced that Eric Maynard was not a threat. He locked eyes with his security chief. "Our men need to neutralize Matthews and Carver soon, along with any risk they may present. But we've worked on Maynard, and he knows what's at stake. He's not going to step out of bounds."

"I'm afraid there's more, sir. Last night, my security team did a complete audit on Maynard's computer and phone records from the past few months."

"What did you find?"

"We found out that he placed a call to Carver the night she first met Matthews. You remember, the same night that she was conveniently not aboard her uncle's yacht."

Stedman didn't show surprise often, but Craven's news put him at a momentary loss for words.

"And just last week, Matthews and Carver visited Maynard at his office. The next day they headed for Punta de Mita. You know I don't believe in coincidences, Mr. Stedman."

"So Maynard knew Carver?"

"From September through December of last year, Maynard placed eleven calls to Carver's old clinic in Chicago. However, we cannot find any record of calls before that time or since Carver resigned, and his division had no other business dealings with the clinic."

Stedman digested this news. "Is there anything else?"

"Maynard left work early yesterday. A search of his computer indicates that he accessed the files on Serapectin and the old files on Tricopatin. I think his old loyalties are resurfacing, and you know he could bring us down."

Stedman dropped his head into his hands. It was hard to tell if he was more upset by the betrayal or the loss of control. "Do whatever needs to be done."

Craven bolted up like a loaded spring. "That's all I needed to hear."

* * *

When Jordan and Ryan arrived at FBI headquarters, Crawford led them to a room set up with a TV and VCR. As they watched the video surveillance from Kalliburton, they were disappointed to see firsthand that the person who received the package was unidentifiable. The man seemed to know the range of the surveillance camera and was careful to avoid showing himself onscreen, with the exception of his left arm when he reached for the package.

Ryan's eyes were glued to the screen. "Jim, back up the tape to where the driver hands off the package." The footage was repeated twice. "Can you zoom in on the hand receiving the package?"

As Crawford manipulated the remote control, Ryan squinted at the enlarged image. "The ring," he said, his voice distant. "It's a Duke ring."

"So? I have to imagine that quite a few residents in this area wear Duke class rings."

"You're right, that really doesn't narrow the field down much. I just have a hunch." Ryan glanced at his watch. "I have a meeting but I'll be back in two hours." He turned to Jordan. "I'd feel better if you waited for me here."

Crawford stiffened with concern. "You need protection, too, Ryan."

"Not where I'm going," Ryan said, heading for the door.

* * *

By the time Ryan pulled into the parking lot of the Eno River State Park and hiked the quarter-mile trail to their scheduled rendezvous, he had already made up his mind.

He spotted Eric pacing along the riverbank. He was clearly agitated, and when he saw Ryan coming up the trail, he strode anxiously toward him.

"Look, Ryan, I found out some stuff. You and Jordan had better go underground. And I mean fast."

"Why?"

"You doubt me?"

"No, not really. I just want to hear you tell me why."

"Because you've pissed off some powerful people. And I think you know what they're capable of."

"You mean the same people who've been trying to kill Jordan and me ever since we met on Exuma?"

Eric frowned. "Come on, Ryan. Why play Mickey the Dunce?"

Ryan hesitated, his face contorted with emotion. "Because I want to hear it from you."

Eric did not offer a response.

"I'll never learn anything if I'm deep underground. Besides, our trip to Mexico provided a lot of answers. There's no way I can go underground now."

"If you don't, you won't stay alive. Please, Ryan, take Jordan and go." Eric's voice was pleading. "I'm telling you, amateur hour is over. They're bringing in the pros. These guys don't make mistakes."

"I know, Eric."

"There it is. I've told you what I know."

"You haven't told me shit. And I know more. In fact, I know it was you who accepted delivery on the package I sent to Dave."

Eric fell silent. Their conversation gave way to the churning river. Neither man knew what to say.

"I never meant for any of this to happen," Eric blurted out. "I'm so sorry about what happened to you and Cindy and—"

The first punch Ryan threw was badly aimed, but the next landed squarely as Ryan pummeled the smaller man. *Damn you, Eric, you were behind this all along!* Years of anger flooded Ryan's body, made worse by the betrayal of a dear friend. Tears filled his eyes as he swung at the man he once trusted.

Suddenly, Eric went limp and Ryan held his blows. Something was wrong. Eric's shirtfront was covered with blood, and his face had blanched as he slumped to the ground. Stunned, Ryan knelt down and gave the area a quick scan but saw no one.

Eric gasped for breath. "They told me nobody would get hurt," he whispered. Ryan heard, but could not concentrate on the words. "The key. Take the key. I . . . I started checking . . . I . . ." Eric's head turned slowly to the side, his eyes wide and glassy. Ryan knew he was dead.

Before Ryan could interpret Eric's message, he sensed what felt like a gun barrel pressing into his back.

"Okay, *bru*. Where's the goose?"

"Goose?"

"The girl. You know who I mean."

A tall, pale man with green eyes and dirty-blond hair carrying a sniper rifle with a silencer approached from the right. He tossed the rifle on the ground behind his blue-eyed partner and pulled a pistol, also with a silencer, from his coat. "We can't wait for your decision, *bru*. We're out of time."

Ryan heard the pistol cock. His back muscles clenched as he waited for the bullet.

"Last chance. Gonna talk?"

"Sure, mate," Ryan annunciated. "Right after you two queers are done fucking each other."

The assassins gave each other a surprised look before aiming their weapons at Ryan's chest. Before Ryan had a chance to speak again, the still air was filled with the sound of gunshots, and his body was covered with blood.

CHAPTER **36**

In shocked silence, Ryan stared at the blood on the front of his shirt. He clutched his chest with shaking hands and was astonished to discover that he was not hurt. He had not been hit! The blood splatter belonged to his assailants. A long breath hissed through his pursed lips as he pushed one of the dead assassins off his legs.

He heard a rush of footsteps and looked up to see Jordan running toward him, followed by Jim Crawford and his men. Without a word, Ryan turned his eyes up at Crawford. The FBI man, gun in hand, was smiling. "Good thing Jordan talked me into following you."

Ryan's eyes drifted over to Eric, his bloody body sprawled out on the ground next to the two killers. Except for his developing relationship with Jordan, the past three weeks had been a living nightmare. Now Eric, his longtime friend, college roommate, business partner, and the best man in his wedding, lay lifeless before him.

Crawford's voice was low, and all business. "I know you don't feel up to putting this all down in an official statement right now, but . . ." He spread his hands, palms upward, as if to say he had no choice in the matter.

Ryan knew the drill. "We might as well get it over with."

* * *

Back at FBI headquarters, a two-man team of hardtack senior agents conducted Ryan's interview. The relentless questioning was an eye-opener for Ryan as he experienced the role of the
victim for the first time. It was more frustrating than he had imagined, but he knew these guys were just doing their job. Still, by
the time Crawford showed up, Ryan was nearing the end of his
rope. "Jim, enough. Call your guys off."

Crawford motioned his men out of the room and sat next to
Ryan. "Sorry, Ryan, but you know the routine. It's a bitch if you're
on the wrong side of the desk."

Ryan finished off the lukewarm dregs of his coffee and started to get up. Crawford motioned for Ryan to stay put.

"As a rule, I don't provide victims with the specific details
of our investigation, but I'm going to make an exception. We've
been concentrating on learning who the hired guns were. I'm
hopeful that we'll be able to trace them back to their source. We
also followed up on the car they were driving. It belongs to a local
businessman. We contacted his wife, who told us that he's traveling on business and had parked his car at the airport. We checked
with airport security and located the surveillance video, which
caught these same two men in the act of stealing the car. A search
of their bodies revealed a small arsenal. In the car, we found their
personal belongings, along with another cache of weapons and
four passports with various aliases."

"I appreciate the update, Jim, but it sounds like a bunch of
dead ends."

"So far, it is. I've spent the past two hours trying to trace the
route of these men. We know that they boarded a South African
Airlines flight in Johannesburg Wednesday morning and arrived
at O'Hare the next day. This morning they used one of their bo-
gus passports as identification to board the plane from O'Hare
to RDU. I contacted some local sources in South Africa. They're

looking into their identities, but so far, we have nothing. These guys appear to be nameless ghosts."

Ryan pondered the possibilities. "Considering the arsenal and passports, those boys were professionals with some major cash behind them."

"I'll say. I've seen plenty of fake passports, and these were masterpieces. But what worries me most is the quality of their intel. Hell, *we* barely knew where you were, and these guys tracked you down within two hours of landing."

Ryan absorbed the implications of this before asking the unavoidable question: "Do you think there's a leak on your team?"

"I've worked with the same team for the past six years. My guess is they followed Maynard, and he led them straight to you." Crawford threw a glance at the two interviewers who were standing outside the door and motioned them in. "You guys about done?"

"We have a few more things to go over."

Ryan rolled his eyes. "By now they know more about the story than I do."

"Good, then they're doing their jobs." Turning to the agents, he added, "Give us another minute, and ask Dr. Carver to join us." The two agents left the room, and moments later, Jordan came in and took the seat next to Ryan. As the couple locked hands, Crawford grew serious. "Okay, here's the deal. Someone with an endless supply of money, high-tech intel, and ties to ruthless killers all over the world is out to eliminate the two of you."

"Sounds like the CIA to me," Jordan offered.

"Might as well be," Crawford said. "What makes matters worse is that we don't have a name or face to tie this to. Worse yet, there's not an admissible piece of evidence to even allow us a search warrant."

Ryan frowned. "Sounds promising, Jim. Any *more* good news?"

"The one piece of good news I do have is that we've kept the press at bay. They're still waiting for an official statement, but we need to talk about your futures first. As I see it, you have two choices. Go into protective custody, or get killed."

Ryan's frown was replaced by a sneer of disgust. *Running away is not in the playbook*, he told himself. Pausing to reassess, he thought, *Who are you fooling, Matthews? It's the end of the game. There are no other options.* "I'd just hate to see the bastards get away with it."

CHAPTER 37

Jacob Stedman was sitting at his desk, deep in thought, when Craven's phone call came in.

"Turn on CNN."

Stedman flipped on the TV. "Breaking News Story" flashed at the bottom of the screen. He sat up straight in his chair, his attention riveted. Sherry Roberts, the all-news network's latest blonde, was talking animatedly.

". . . but what we do know is that earlier today a triple homicide took place just a few hundred yards from where I'm standing." The camera panned the area blocked off by yellow tape. The caption read: *Eno River State Park, Durham, North Carolina.* "The victims have been identified as Eric Maynard of Chapel Hill; Ryan Matthews, formerly of Chapel Hill; and Dr. Jordan Carver of Chicago."

Stedman's eyes never left the screen as Sherry Roberts listened intently to her earpiece and then updated her viewers.

"Our sources tell us this is the same Ryan Matthews who, just two weeks ago, narrowly escaped a car bombing in Chicago. Following the massacre, a shoot-out ensued between federal agents and the two shooting suspects, resulting in the death of both assailants. The men have not yet been identified, but FBI officials believe them to be hired hit men. Hired by whom, the authorities won't say. Of course we will update you as more details become available. Back to you, Frank."

The screen switched to the network news desk. Frank Billings, a distinguished-looking anchorman with silvery white hair, said, "Five people dead. Two gunmen and their three victims. Have the police identified any links between the deceased?"

"Well, Frank, I have learned that the three victims were all highly placed executives in the pharmaceutical field. Eric Maynard was executive vice president at the pharmaceutical giant Fisher Singer Worldwide. Five years ago, Ryan Matthews was an executive vice president at the same company. Up until recently, Dr. Jordan Carver ran a medical clinic in Chicago. My sources tell me that many pharmaceutical companies frequently used her clinic as a testing site for experimental drug treatments under FDA review. Considering what has happened in the past, the tragedy today may be the result of some sort of power struggle."

"Excellent observations, Sherry," Billings said. "Let me add a new detail that just came in. According to reports, Dr. Carver was the niece of Wall Street magnate Henry Carver, who, along with his wife, Jennifer, was recently killed in an explosion aboard their yacht in the Bahamas. The explosion has been ruled a multiple homicide by local Bahamian authorities."

Stedman watched his TV screen without blinking.

"Frank, is there any indication that the explosion in the Bahamas could in some way be linked to these homicides in North Carolina?"

"Nothing concrete at this point, but it certainly seems possible. Evidently, Dr. Carver was *also* in the Bahamas the evening of the explosion. Police sources in the Bahamas tell us Dr. Carver might have been the intended target of that explosion. We'll have to wait for further verification as to whether any sort of commercial espionage is at play in this case." Billings stared into the camera with an appropriately grim expression. "We will keep you, the viewer, updated on this breaking story as more details become available. In other news . . ."

Stedman flicked off the TV and threw the remote onto his desk. "Assholes," he grumbled into the phone. "They talk about verification and then they go ahead and babble about commercial espionage. We're the next big boogeyman of American business."

Craven did not respond; always the good soldier, he waited patiently on the other end of the phone, several floors below his boss, for his orders.

"Get a hold of Gallagher and update him on what's happened," Stedman said. "Then I want the two of you to get up here right away. The vultures are en route, and I don't want any holes in our story."

Craven, along with Andy Gallagher, the company's chief of public relations, made it to Stedman's office within minutes. When both were seated, Stedman said, "No screw-ups on our response. 'We are deeply saddened by the loss of our friend and colleague . . .' " He stopped and focused his attention on Gallagher. "Remember, use the term 'friend and colleague' rather than 'our executive' or anything cold like that. It's 'friend and colleague.' Next, 'we here at Fisher Singer Worldwide are determined to get to the bottom of this tragedy and help bring the responsible parties to justice. In this regard, we will cooperate fully with local and federal authorities."

Gallagher struggled to jot down Stedman's dictation on a yellow notepad.

"Say no more than what I've given you. Make sure your field people get the word, and if in doubt, refer to Mr. Craven for further guidance. I don't want one shred of information going out of here unless it is approved."

Gallagher looked overwhelmed but managed to spit out a fairly convincing, "Understood, sir."

Stedman sat back in his chair. "Okay, Andy, that's all. Craven, you stay." When Gallagher had shuffled out, Stedman glared at his security chief. "You insisted that we bring in the South Africans." He hesitated, as if waiting for a response. None came. "You told me they were the best. And look what happened. A friggin' massacre! And now the Feds have their bodies to trace. Who knows how well we've covered our tracks. We—"

"Calm down, sir." Craven's voice was neutral, with no hint of fear or panic. He'd been in worse situations than this and had always managed to come out on top. "The important thing is that Matthews and Carver are out of the picture and the South Africans are dead, too. Dead men tell no tales."

Stedman sighed.

"The trail is as dead as they are," Craven reiterated.

"How can you be so sure?"

"Sir, when I insisted on the South Africans, it wasn't simply because I thought they were competent at their work. It was because, as true professionals, they were ghosts. They can't be traced to their mothers, let alone to us. That's why I picked them."

"What if the FBI figures out what Matthews and Carver were after?"

Craven knew how to pacify the increasingly jittery head of FSW. "Sir, my planning has gone even further than ensuring that there is no trail. You know that the attorneys have set this all up in such a way that it's impossible to trace any of this back to you or the company. Even if the Feds get suspicious—and they probably will—they won't find a shred of incriminating evidence. I can guarantee you that."

Stedman chewed on Craven's assurances. "But what about the people we used five years ago? They're still out there. If they're discovered or begin to develop a conscience after the pressure of these recent events—"

Craven interrupted. "Conscience? They have as much to lose as us. Why would anybody develop a conscience that drives them right into a life sentence or a date with the needle?"

"Since, as you said, I pay you to worry about things even when there is nothing to worry about, I say let's tie up all loose ends, no matter how remote the possibility that they will betray us." His eyes drilled into Craven. "And no more outside help. I want you to attend to it personally."

Craven leapt to his feet, his body language tantamount to clicking his heels. "Consider it done, sir."

CHAPTER 38

Sequestered at FBI headquarters, Ryan and Jordan spent their time watching CNN. The couple was amazed at the efficiency with which the FBI had erased them from the face of the earth. With Ryan and Jordan reported as dead, the Bureau would arrange for death certificates and make funeral arrangements. Since neither Jordan nor Ryan had any surviving family members, this part of the ploy would not be difficult. As far as housing was concerned, Crawford arranged for the couple to remain at the cabin on Lake Gastin for the next few weeks while things cooled down.

"What happens after that?" Jordan asked.

"At that point, we'll find you more permanent lodging along with new identities. You'll be deep underground. Think of it as an unofficial Witness Protection Program until we have a suspect in custody."

Ryan and Jordan exchanged a knowing glance. A life of isolation and hiding was nothing if not disturbing. They no longer held their own fate in their hands.

"I could use a drink about now," Ryan muttered.

"Coffee's down the hall."

"Not what I was thinking, Jim, but I guess it will do for now. Anyone else?"

"Please," Jordan responded.

Once Ryan left the room, Jordan turned to Crawford. "What

about my clinic? We're supposed to open next week. And what about my uncle's estate? Where will all that money go?"

"I'm not going to blow smoke at you. You will not be able to return to your clinic until the threat against you has been neutralized. Your uncle's estate will most likely end up in probate. I am sure we can pull some strings to keep the estate assets locked down until you are able to rise from the grave and make a legitimate claim. Our investigation is in the beginning stages, and building a case against this outfit will take months, if not longer. When it's safe and your identity is restored, you'll be able to resume life as normal. I know this is hard, but there's really no other choice."

Jordan thanked Jim for all he had done and then dropped her face into her hands just as Ryan returned. Crawford took Ryan's entry as an opportunity to make himself scarce. Ryan walked over to her and held out a cup of coffee.

"Don't be down, babe," Ryan said. "Think about the consequences. They were on to us. It wouldn't have been long before they got us."

Jordan sat on the edge of her chair. "The bastards weren't able to stop me with bombs and bullets and yet they've still succeeded. The clinic is my life's work. And what will I live on without access to Uncle Henry's estate?" She was holding back tears.

"I know how you feel," he said. "Honestly, I do. But we don't have any other options at this point. Frankly, we're lucky to be alive. And I have plenty of money for both of us."

"The money is not what I'm really worried about. It's the clinic."

Ryan clutched her hand. "I don't want to make Jim think we're ungrateful. We should really appreciate everything he's done."

Jordan's eyes sought his, an announcement at the tip of her tongue. "Ryan, I'm not ready to stop taking chances. And I don't want you trying to dissuade me, either. I'm *going* to be at the opening of my clinic." Her eyes flashed with determination.

Before Jordan could continue, the door opened and Crawford entered with a small box in his hands.

"There's a cell phone and charger in here. It's safe, untraceable—I think it even takes pictures. And," he said, reaching into his pocket and producing a set of keys, "you've got a new car. It's not the most stylish ride, but the point is to not draw any attention. I want you to hang out at the lake until you hear from me." He paused to let his orders sink in. "Okay, let's go check out the car."

On their way out, Crawford put his hand on Ryan's shoulder, slowing their pace to let Jordan get ahead. "I understand how she feels," he said under his breath, "but you've got to convince her she won't make it out there on her own."

When they reached the car, a bland off-white Chevy, the men shook hands as Crawford repeated his instructions. "Straight to the house, no pit stops and no movement until you hear from me."

Ryan gave Crawford a limp salute. "Yes, sir."

As they turned out of the parking lot, Jordan lashed out at Ryan. "This is just great. You've lived the last five years of your life like a hermit on another planet. This is right up your alley. This is probably how you wanted it to happen. Well, I'm not ready for that."

His voice quiet, Ryan said, "I wasn't ready either. It just happened."

"It wouldn't have happened if you hadn't given up."

"Don't judge me till you've walked a mile in my shoes, Jordan."

She turned away, staring vacantly out the side window. "I'm sorry, Ryan. That wasn't called for. But you know that if you weren't involved, I wouldn't give it another thought. I'd open my clinic and take my chances."

"I know," he said, his voice softening. "But I *am* involved."

"To what degree?" she asked, turning back to him.

He pulled the car to the curb. "To the point where there's no more me, no more you—it's just us."

She fell into his arms. "Oh, Ryan, I feel the same way. It's scary, but you're making me realize that I'm not living and making decisions just for myself anymore."

Ryan shook his head as he held her tight. "Even though you were right about me going into seclusion, I don't want you to do the same thing. To tell you the truth, I don't want to anymore, either."

"I had no right to say what I did."

"Yes, you did. We're in this thing together and there's no turning back."

"But I still feel guilty dragging you into this."

"You didn't. I'm in because I choose to be in."

"You're sure?"

"Yeah, I'm sure. I couldn't tell Jim that we were going to run off on our own. Who knows, the Feds may be able to force us into protective custody, considering they put their asses on the line faking our death. That's why I didn't tell him everything."

A sly smile formed on her lips. "Like *what* didn't you tell him?"

"Just before Eric died he told me to take a key. I didn't understand what he meant until Jim's men were pulling the dead assassins off of me. Then I found this as I was pulling myself up off the ground." Ryan pulled a key from his pocket and showed Jordan.

"Looks like the type of key you get at one of those pay-for-the-day lockers."

"Exactly. And the only place that has those lockers around here is the Greyhound station. And that's where we're heading now."

"I know you didn't tell Jim because you didn't want any more of his help, but—"

"There's also a practical reason," Ryan answered before she was able to finish. "The Feds would have to get a warrant to open the locker. That would involve more time and even more people. Too many people know too much as it is. Maybe I'm getting paranoid, but I don't trust anybody at the Bureau beyond Jim."

* * *

At the busy terminal, Ryan had tried the key in two-thirds of the lockers before he began to doubt whether the locker was even in this station. *Why am I so confident that this belongs to a locker here? There's no number on it, no indication, yet it matches the other keys in the unrented spaces.* He also started to worry that security might notice his suspicious activity. Jordan was on guard to cause a disturbance if a security guard came by, but they had no plan for the security camera, which looked down balefully upon his futile tinkering.

Inserting the key into locker 363, Ryan felt a pleasant rush as the lock yielded. *Pay dirt!*

Inside the locker they found a sealed manila envelope. Wary of the camera's Cyclops eye, Ryan calmly closed the locker and hastened Jordan out to the car to review the contents. In it, they found the business card of someone named Oscar Huggins, general manager of K-Dar Labs in Richmond, Virginia. The card was paper-clipped to photocopies of FSW ledger statements showing three separate payments to Oscar Huggins totaling one million dollars. The ledger statements were dated five years back. Behind the ledger statements, they found a printout containing a list of names and phone numbers. The list looked familiar.

CHAPTER 39

Ryan and Jordan spent the weekend holed up at the cabin on the lake. Other than their pit stop at the Greyhound Station, they followed Crawford's orders and did not leave the property. They forgot about reality for the next forty-eight hours. It was the respite they both needed.

* * *

It was 8:15 on Monday morning and Ryan was staring out the bedroom window with the phone to his ear. A Hawthorn tree swayed in the cool wind as cottony clouds chased each other across a low sky. Jordan padded up behind him, stretching her arms. "Any luck?"

He looked over his shoulder as she wrapped her arms around his chest from behind. "Maybe," he said as he covered the phone. "They're checking to see if Huggins is in. I—" He interrupted himself, holding up a finger as he returned his attention to the phone call. "Oh, I see. He'll be in later this afternoon? . . . Fine. . . . No, I'll just call him back then, thanks."

* * *

The interstate lay wide open before them after they escaped the morning rush hour. They picked up the blue-and-white highway signs and headed north to Richmond. As they crossed into Virginia, Ryan said, "I'm sure that the documents Eric stashed in the locker are in regards to the Tricopatin clinical trial."

Jordan looked skeptical. "And you think this Huggins is going to let us waltz in and scour his records?"

"No, but I know a way to at least get us into the lab. It's normal for FDA field inspectors to arrive unannounced, hoping to catch the labs unprepared. We can pretend to be FDA inspectors."

"I suppose they're going to let us march right in without any credentials?"

"I've heard some funny stories about how the inspectors show up at the back door and, just by mentioning they're from the FDA, scare the shit out of the shipping clerks. The FDA can shut down a lab for almost any reason. Do you think some shipping clerk or lab tech wants to risk pissing off an inspector by asking for ID?"

"You're right," Jordan conceded. "I remember once an FDA inspector showed up at our clinic. Before I even knew he was there, he had grilled several of my staff members. The little prick got enough penny-ante crap out of my nurses to just about trigger a full-blown audit."

"Intimidation is a powerful tool. The scared lab techs couldn't be more cooperative, running around and fetching the inspectors anything they ask for." For a brief moment, Ryan grinned. Their shared understanding of these things helped to make him feel even closer to her. The average person wouldn't have a clue about the intricacies of FDA rules and regulations. Even with this knowledge, Ryan knew his plan was risky, but at this point, it was their best option.

After a few more miles, Jordan looked up from the paperwork. "I've been scanning the list of names and phone numbers that Eric left for you. Although it's in a different format, the names are identical to the ones on the list we took from the NHCA clinic.

I think it'd be a good idea to call back the families of the patients we contacted from the Mexico list and give them our new cell phone number in case any of them have been trying to reach us."

"Yeah," Ryan said, "good idea. It can't be a coincidence."

As Ryan drove, Jordan, reenacting her role as an attorney representing the families of deceived patients who had trusted NHCA, began making phone calls. She encountered the same frustrating results as before. By the time they entered the Richmond city limits, they concluded that further calls were a waste of time. Everyone on that list was dead.

* * *

They arrived at K-Dar at 1:00 p.m. and went straight to the back door. They identified themselves as FDA compliance officers to the first lab tech they came across and asked to be taken to the file room.

As Ryan had predicted, the wide-eyed tech led them, without question, to a large, cluttered room before setting off to fetch his supervisor. The room was occupied by four lab technicians, several empty desks, and several rows of file cabinets. Jordan and Ryan situated themselves at separate workstations and waited. Within a few minutes, a middle-aged woman with the stiff and proper bearing of a drill sergeant arrived.

With a forced smile, she extended her hand. "Good afternoon. My name's Jane Zilles. I'm the assistant general manager. What can I help you with?"

Ryan spoke up first. "Just a routine follow-up visit. We're in the process of closing out a number of clinical trials, and we're here to do a final audit of your records for the Tricopatin trial that you did for FSW five years ago."

"Oh my," Zilles responded with surprise. "That was before my time here. Why is the FDA interested in trial data from so long ago?"

The question caught Ryan off guard and rendered him

speechless, but Jordan quickly intervened. "Another pharmaceutical company has submitted an NDA for a clinical trial for a new ovarian cancer drug. The Tricopatin trial resulted in some serious adverse effects, and we need to review the early data from it to establish a baseline for comparison."

"I see. Just a minute, while I try to figure out where to direct you." Zilles checked the computer to locate where the Tricopatin files were stored and then directed them to the appropriate section of the large file room. "Will there be anything else?"

Jordan said, "We'll also need access to your computer records."

Zilles logged her on at a nearby terminal and pulled up the Tricopatin database files. She then turned to the inspectors and asked, "Anything else? Coffee?"

Wanting this all to seem routine, Ryan smiled. "Coffee would be nice. Thank you."

Zilles took their order and left the room. Ryan turned to Jordan. "Let's start digging."

* * *

Back in her own office, Jane dispatched a clerk to get coffee and dialed the cell phone number of Oscar Huggins. "Oh dear," she muttered under her breath when he didn't answer. His outgoing message said that he would be in a meeting until three o'clock and would return his calls the next day. She left a message.

"Hello, Dr. Huggins, this is Jane. Sorry to bother you but there are a couple of FDA inspectors here auditing the Tricopatin trial that we did five years ago. That's before my time, and I'm not sure if I can answer their questions. Please call me as soon as you're free."

* * *

Craven jimmied the rear lower-level door of an opulent suburban home and slipped inside. Before creeping upstairs to wait for Oscar Huggins, he screwed a silencer onto the long barrel of his Colt .45. His senses went on full alert when he heard Huggins's car in the driveway. As he heard the garage door open, he slid into the study closet.

Huggins tossed his keys on the counter, grabbed a Diet Pepsi from the fridge, and then went to his home office. Sitting down at his desk and riffling through some papers, he dialed up his voice mail and put his cell on speakerphone while he went through his paperwork. Seconds before barging out of the closet and pulling the trigger, Craven heard the message from Jane Zilles playing in the background. Hearing the word "Tricopatin," Craven backed off the kill and began to plot his next move.

Huggins picked up the phone and dialed his underling. "Yes, Jane, I got your message. . . . Yeah, that's strange. Tell them I'll be there in about an hour, maybe longer if traffic's bad. If they ask you anything you don't know, tell them to wait for me. I'm on my way."

As Huggins prepared to leave, Craven snuck from the home the same way he had entered and sprinted back to his car parked two blocks away. *Not time to put this player to sleep yet. Got to follow him and see what these damn FDA inspectors are up to. Can't that Wiley control his own people? They're gonna fuck this up yet.*

* * *

Back at K-Dar Labs, Jordan and Ryan hadn't found anything to shed light on the mystery. They were both riffling through the Tricopatin files when the cell phone rang. Jordan answered on the second ring. To her surprise, it was Jessica Barringer, one of the NHCA patients. Since there were K-Dar employees in the room, she took the call in an outside corridor. She was, after all, answering as a tort attorney.

Mrs. Barringer had a mouthful for her. "You snakes are all alike. If it wasn't for that clinic, I would be dead today. My cancer has been in complete remission for the past two years. And it's not just me. Several of my very close friends who I met in the clinic have been cured as well. As far as I'm concerned, it's the best money I ever spent."

Shocked, Jordan tried to calm her but was cut off.

"Look," Barringer said, "I want you to stop calling me. If you sue the clinic, I'll be their star witness."

Jordan was about to speak when the phone went dead in her ear.

She put the phone away and returned to the file room. In utter disbelief, Jordan whispered, "You aren't going to believe this. That was Jessica Barringer, an NHCA patient so satisfied with her treatment that she's willing to lead a cheering section for the owners of the clinic. They did it. They're actually curing people."

Ryan was dumbfounded. "You've got to be *fucking* kidding me! That's not possible. Unless . . ."

"Unless what?"

"Unless Eric was telling the truth. I can't believe it. They successfully altered my formula."

* * *

Oscar Huggins arrived a few minutes past 5:00 p.m., just as most of the employees were leaving the building. He hurried to Jane Zilles's office. She looked up with relief.

"They've been here all afternoon, sir. They haven't asked me anything. That's a good sign, isn't it?"

"That's fine, Jane. I'll take care of things. Is there anyone else still working?"

"Everyone else has gone home for the evening. I'm the only one left."

"Okay. You can go home now. I appreciate you waiting around."

"Oh, no problem. Well, goodnight then Dr. Huggins."

Back in his office, Huggins hurried to his computer, brought up a file with a few keystrokes, and deleted it without hesitation. He smiled. *They haven't gotten to it yet.*

* * *

In the file room, Ryan looked over to see Jordan perusing a file, her face a mask of concentration. "What? Find something?"

"I couldn't find anything in the Tricopatin documents, so I decided to cross-reference your wife in the computer file. It led me to another file for Cindy, who was under the care of a Dr. Albert Seymour."

Ryan's interest grew. "Yeah?"

Jordan looked up at him. "The file includes the test results sent to the doctor."

"But I've already seen those."

"There are two sets of test results, Ryan. And the original one shows Cindy's cancer in complete remission." The air seemed to leave the room. Ryan felt faint.

"If you read them you'll find that the copy of the original has been altered. Look Ryan, as of her last test, Cindy's cancer was gone. There was no trace of it in the blood tests."

Ryan jumped out of his seat and grabbed the file. As he leafed through the pages, his anger boiled over. "Those sons of bitches! Why would they change her results?" His face began to redden.

Jordan stood and looped an arm over his shoulder. "Calm down. You look as if you could fall over." She took his arm and guided him back to his chair. He plopped down, his eyes scanning the file.

"Cindy would have lived. Jake and Karly would have lived," he mumbled. "They would have never gotten on that plane to Exuma. There would have been no reason to go to Exuma."

Ryan became lost in the past, going back to that awful day when he got the phone call: *There's been an accident. The plane you chartered has gone down in the ocean and everyone on board has been killed. We are deeply sorry for your loss.* He remembered the gut-wrenching feeling, the suffocating grief. How could he bear the unbearable? The only solution was the numbness he found in the bottle. His only solace was to avoid feeling anything at all. And he had remained numb, avoiding emotion for all these years. And he had never questioned anything.

"Ryan!" Jordan was looking into his eyes with concern, her hands on each side of his face.

"Somebody will pay for this," he muttered. "Somebody will *pay.*"

CHAPTER 40

Oscar Huggins walked into the file room with a confident smile on his face, prepared to dispense with the stuffed-shirt FDA inspectors. He introduced himself, holding out his hand.

Suddenly, he was set upon by an outraged agent, who grabbed him violently by his lapels and pushed him up against the wall.

"You son of a bitch!" Ryan spat. "You took a million-dollar payoff and altered my wife's test results!"

Sweat beading across his upper lip, Huggins blubbered, "Now hold on!" *Are these new FDA tactics?*

"No, you hold on! Here's the ledger from FSW showing the payout to you. Here are the altered test results you submitted to Dr. Seymour, and here are the real test results." With one hand still locked on Huggins's lapel, Ryan smacked the papers, file folder and all, against the man's face. Huggins fell against the wall as the folder hit him. "Sit down," Ryan roared. "Read it!"

While Ryan and Jordan waited, Huggins nervously picked up the papers. Consumed with fear—*these people are definitely not from the FDA*—Huggins was unable to focus on the paperwork. But he knew these documents well. When he thought he had reviewed the papers long enough to be convincing, he said, "I . . . I really don't know what to say. I . . ."

"How can you fuck with people's lives like that?"

Huggins ran his hand through his thinning hair. "I was just . . . I did what I was told. I'm not aware of anyone being hurt. The money. It was just—"

"Too good to pass up? And who 'told' you what to do? Have you done this more than once?"

Huggins dropped his face into his hands and looked as if he might faint. "Yes. I . . . I've done it several times for the big companies. But they told me it was just to get past the FDA bureaucracy."

Ryan was incredulous. "No, you just took the money," he shouted in disgust. "And now my wife is dead."

"I figured you'd crack, you weasel."

All eyes turned to the doorway. William Craven was holding a Colt .45 semiautomatic in his right hand, leveled at Ryan's chest.

"I have to hand it to both of you. You're not easy to kill. Bureau training is good." He sneered towards Ryan. "But it doesn't beat my training."

Ryan was curious. *Renegade Agent? Freelancer working for FSW? Who is this guy, and how does he know my background?* One thing Ryan knew for sure: the man was a stone-cold killer. He could see it in his eyes.

Recognition followed in an instant as his memory spun into action, and through his anger and confusion, he placed his opponent's face. "You were Stedman's chief of security, the thug who escorted me out of FSW."

The cold eyes brightened. "That's right. The last time I saw you I was hauling your ass out of Fisher." Craven was unable to resist talking about himself. "Of course, before this gig I worked Black Ops for Uncle Sam, cut my teeth on the Phoenix Program."

"Oh yeah, I see it in your eyes—Grade A nut job." Ryan was buying time to come up with a plan. He had to get the jump on Craven and hoped to provoke him into making a mistake. But Craven was too cautious, too cool, too deliberate. He kept them at a safe distance, even though he was armed and they were not.

One wrong move will earn me a quick bullet and a fast death. This sadist is enjoying hearing himself talk. Good, let him talk. I won't go down without a fight.

"And now you're a hired punk for some bigwigs, is that it?" Ryan challenged, his voice tinged with an equal dose of sarcasm and contempt.

"Oh, I'd say I'm more than that." Still smirking, he turned and addressed Huggins. "How convenient for me to find all of you here together. Give me that file, you little turd."

The terrified man was beginning to come unglued. "I'm on your side," he babbled. "Get rid of them and let me go. I won't tell anyone."

"You were supposed to destroy these test results five years ago," Craven said, staring a hole into Huggins. "I had a feeling a stupid little shit like you would hold on to the records. What were you planning on doing, blackmailing the company?"

"No, no, that's not it," Huggins wailed. Craven seemed amused by the terror that clouded the man's eyes. Like a whipped dog, Huggins handed the file to Craven, who promptly dumped it into a wastepaper basket. Pointing the gun at Ryan and Jordan, Craven motioned them away. He retrieved a cigarette lighter from his pants pocket, flicked it, and ignited the contents of the wastepaper basket. The papers caught fire and went up with a *whoosh*. A pall of brownish-white smoke emanated from the engulfed receptacle.

As everyone watched, seemingly mesmerized by the flame, Huggins made a dash for the door. It was a poor decision for an out-of-shape older man. Two quick shots from the Colt .45 dropped him in a crumpled heap in the doorway.

Taking advantage of the distraction, Ryan lunged at Craven, knocking the pistol from his hand. While Ryan was in shape, Craven was a raging bull. Soon, by way of brute strength alone, Craven had regained the advantage and was sitting astride Ryan. He grabbed his pistol from the floor and pointed it toward Ryan's head. Craven squinted with delight as he steadied the weapon.

Desperate, Ryan used both hands to grab his assailant's hand, as the barrel of the gun swung closer to his face. He considered cocking his fist and slugging the man, but he knew that he would have to release one hand, and before he could strike, it would be all over. Ryan knew the .45 was not a hair-trigger weapon, but it didn't take all that much pressure to fire it, either.

When he was nearly looking straight down the barrel, he saw Craven's finger begin to tighten. Beads of perspiration covered Ryan's forehead. His eternity was about to arrive on a high-caliber bullet to the brain when Craven suddenly collapsed. A trembling Jordan was standing over them, a dented fire extinguisher in her hand.

* * *

With his hands tied behind his back and his legs anchored to an office chair, Craven came to with a start, the muzzle of his own Colt .45 trained at his chest.

Ryan cocked the gun. Craven didn't flinch.

"Didn't think you were capable."

"Capable of what?"

"Killing a man in cold blood."

"There'd be nothing cold-blooded about killing the likes of you."

"A Bureau man all the way. A real hard-ass."

"You can buy yourself a few minutes by telling me something."

"And that would be?"

Ryan grabbed a lab chair, straddled it, and searched the man's eyes for a spark of compassion. "Why? Why would the company want to suppress a cure for ovarian cancer that promised to make them billions?"

Craven shook his head as if he were disappointed. "I guess your old buddy Maynard was right."

"About what?"

"About you. He said you didn't get it and that you never would. That you had a scientist's brain but no head for business. It's too bad. If you'd had a head for business and wasn't a former FBI agent, Stedman would have clued you in. In which case, your wife and kids would still be alive, and you'd be a millionaire many times over."

Ryan's gun hand shook from the tremors in his heart. He wanted to rid the world of this vermin. But first, he needed information. "My wife and kids died in a plane accident, you asshole."

"For the man who invented a cure for cancer, you're really kind of stupid."

Ryan pressed the barrel of the gun hard underneath Craven's chin.

"Your wonder drug worked, Doc. Your wife was cured. It was only a matter of time before you would have figured it out."

Ryan's mind whirled as his brain tried to absorb the information. "What are you saying?"

"If you just hadn't stolen the drug and given her the last injections, everything would have been fine. She would have died of cancer like all of the other patients who participated in the trial. But you did, and those final injections cured her. Before long, you would have figured it out and told your story to the world, and Tricopatin would have ended up back in clinical trials. And this time it might have actually been approved."

"So?"

"So the only way to stop you from figuring it out was to make sure she died. That's why I had her plane blown up over the Atlantic."

Ryan put the gun down, leaped at the bound man, and pummeled him with all the rage and fury that his tortured soul could muster. "Why did you have to kill my family? You bastard! You fucking scumbag!"

By the time Jordan managed to pull him off, Craven was bloody, his eye swollen and lip split. But being the hard man that he was, he remained conscious. His bloody lip was twisted into a wry grin, an outward sign of pride for being able to withstand the beating.

Ryan picked up the gun and pointed it at the man's head. "I still don't know why FSW didn't want to release a cure for cancer."

Craven spat his bloody drool to the floor. "Of course not. You're not a businessman. You'll never see what makes this country the richest in the world. You know nothing about the corporate culture that's made America great."

"And you believe what, that you're some sort of a patriot?"

Craven stared at Ryan through his good eye and, with all the coolness of a man in complete control, said, "I am."

"A corporate warrior, maybe, but nothing more than that. You're sure as hell no patriot."

Craven's grin was made even more sinister by the blood running out of his mouth. "I like the way that sounds. Yeah, that's what I am, a corporate warrior. I used to fight my country's battles on the battlefield. Nowadays, I'm fighting on the corporate battlefield."

Jordan stared at him in disbelief. "That's a sick philosophy."

Craven turned his beaten face toward her. "Not that I expect you to understand, missy, but there are as many enemies to our way of life that want to destroy our country from within as there are foreign. Without our wealth, would we be as great as we are?"

"Maybe, maybe not," Jordan responded. "But how are you defining greatness? And are you defining our wealth as a people strictly by how much money we have?"

Ryan interrupted. "Jordan, let's not dignify this piece of shit with the notion that his philosophy, whatever it is, has any relevance to human beings."

Ryan felt good drawing a distinction between people like himself, a dedicated scientist and researcher, and the corporate thugs he was battling. Of course, Craven only did the dirty work for the real corporate thugs. Guys of Craven's ilk were sadistic robots who got a perverse joy out of following cruel and merciless orders from men like Stedman, who were even more vile and despicable. They were evil men who would never give human lives more value than the almighty dollar. Profits had always trumped ethics in big business, and they probably always would. A large automaker would rather pay $100 million in legal claims for dead drivers than spend $300 million to recall a car with faulty brakes, just as a major pharmaceutical company would rather hide possible grievous side effects and risk hundreds of millions in lawsuits rather than pulling a multi-billion dollar per year blockbuster maintenance drug off the market. Ryan was glad he had never sold out his soul for a buck. The business end of things never had taken precedence over the scientific. Yes, he'd made money from his research—but at least he could live with himself.

Craven wasn't finished. In fact, he seemed eager to talk. "Listen, I'm no business genius, but the way I see it, it's simple. Sure, it sounds good on the surface to have a cancer cure to sell, and at first, the company might make a nice profit. But think about it, Matthews, Americans never have and never will pay for good medicine. They turn to the insurance companies to foot the bills, and do you think the insurance companies are going to pay what Tricopatin is really worth? Hell no. Tricopatin is worth millions of dollars per patient, but who's going to pay for it? Not the insurance companies, and certainly not your average Joe."

Ryan stared at him, dumbfounded.

"There would be a public outcry. The lobbyists for the major health insurance companies would pressure their bought-and-paid-for politicians, and before you know it, they'd be practically giving Tricopatin away. Poor Aunt Betty shows up with cancer and no insurance. What do you think would happen to the company if they didn't give her the miracle cure? No, my bosses are not about to let that happen. Not only would they take a bath on Tricopatin, they'd lose billions on the other cancer treatment drugs that they sell today. Why do you think they were willing to pay so much for your old company to begin with? They weren't going to allow you to cure ovarian cancer and rob them of the bil-

lions they make selling maintenance drugs to treat the same cancer. No, they bought Immugene with the sole intention of burying
Tricopatin. A couple hundred million is nothing compared to the
billions they would have lost if Tricopatin had hit the market."

"Incredible," Ryan said. "So that's it. Why cure people when
you can soak them with maintenance drugs for the rest of their
lives? I guess healthy people don't buy drugs, huh?"

"Hell's bells. You finally got it!"

"Yeah, I get *that*, asshole. But why peddle the drugs in Mexico?"

Using his shoulder, Craven managed to wipe some of the
blood dripping down his chin. "By killing the FDA approval and
selling it outside the U.S. for millions a pop, we get the best of
both worlds. Hell, Matthews, this is done all the time. Your cure
just happened to be a blockbuster cancer cure and not one for mi-
nor ailments. Do you really believe that the best the top research
scientists in the world can come up with is a pill you need to take
every single day just to get a hard-on?"

Ryan leveled the gun at Craven's head. "Are you done?"

Craven spat. "Yeah, I'm done."

"I'm more than happy to send you to hell with a bullet. Hell
is where you belong."

Though he was no sadist, Ryan nonetheless took delight in
watching Craven's face morph with its first outward sign of fear.
Or perhaps it was with his realization that he had been outsmart-
ed and overwhelmed by amateurs. Ryan knew that this bothered
Craven even more than the prospect of losing his life.

Craven watched Ryan's finger on the trigger, analyzing every nuance. As Ryan began to squeeze, the bound man shouted, "If you kill me, there will be hundreds more on your tail. I
burned the last shred of evidence and killed the last witness. The
company is untouchable, but you're not. If you kill me, you'll be
going to jail for the rest of your very short life. It'll be tough to
claim self-defense with me tied to a chair. Even if you untie me
afterwards, the forensic guys will determine I was tied up when

you shot me. Why don't you just let me go? There is no more evidence against Stedman, the company, or me. We have no reason to come after you. Hell, I won't even tell anyone you and the girl are still alive. You can just disappear." Craven was speaking with the desperation of a man who knew he was playing his last card.

Ryan became thoughtful, his rage subsiding. He looked at Craven and then, turning to Jordan, said, "Cut him loose."

"What? You can't mean that. Let this monster go?"

"Do it, Jordan. I know what I'm doing."

She grabbed a scalpel off of the countertop and slashed Craven's bonds, inching back beside Ryan.

Craven stood slowly. He stretched his arms over his head and, lightning fast, dove behind a shelf, making a half roll to the left and then to the right. With a lunge, he reached for his ankle holster and came up with a .38 aimed at Ryan. Craven squeezed the trigger, but nothing happened. Ryan opened his fist and flipped his hand over. As the bullets to the .38 clattered harmlessly onto the floor, he asked Craven one final question: "Looking for these?"

Craven's eyes went flat. His gun hand lowered and his mouth fell open as he waited for his own death.

Three shots rang out and Craven's body slumped to the floor, his cold blue eyes staring upward.

CHAPTER 41

"What a mess."

Jim Crawford was staring at Craven's bloodied body on the file-room floor. His gaze shifted a dozen feet to Dr. Huggins's dead body, still crumpled in a heap in the doorway. "Tell me something," he said. "How come the guy you shot looks like he was put through the ringer but you don't have so much as a scratch on you?"

Ryan grimaced. He did not feel an ounce of guilt for what he had done, but the evidence told a different story. "I got a little forceful with him while I was interrogating him," he said. "But what I learned more than made up for—"

"Evidence gained through physical interrogation doesn't stand up in court," Crawford said, cutting him off.

"I wasn't planning on taking him to court."

"We know who's been trying to kill me!" Jordan interjected, her voice laced with urgency.

"And that's only half of it," Ryan said. "We've got proof—or at least we *had* proof—that Fisher Singer Worldwide, along with orchestrating the attempted hits on Jordan, paid our dead friend there"—he nodded to Dr. Huggins—"to fudge results from the Tricopatin tests. My drug worked, and now they're selling it abroad under the name Serapectin."

"You *had* the evidence?"

"We had the test results, both the original ones that never saw the light of day and the altered ones that FSW fed me and everybody else."

"Where are they now?"

Ryan pointed with his eyes to the charred remains in the trash can. "Burnt to a crisp."

"Uh huh."

Ryan studied the look in Crawford's eyes. He couldn't tell if he was skeptical, frustrated, angry, or all three. What was obvious was that he'd had enough.

"You have to stop these people," Jordan said, clearly not ready to cede an inch.

Ryan knew they were out on a limb, but it was obvious she harbored no such doubts.

"Look, this is what I know so far," Crawford said. "I've got two dead bodies. I've got destroyed evidence. And I've got two witnesses—both of whom are officially dead, both of whom I've gone to a great deal of trouble to shield, and both of whom seem determined to make my job a living hell. In case you two haven't noticed, I actually have to report to someone, who, I might add, is *this* close to sending me packing. There's this little thing called the law, and every time you two get a wild hair and go off half-cocked, I'm the one who has to do damage control."

Ryan opened his mouth to plead his case, but Crawford cut him short.

"Don't say another word," he said, holding up his hand. "You two are coming with me."

"Where?"

"FBI headquarters in D.C. We're going to debrief you. We're going to get statements. We're going to make damned sure your story holds up. And we're going to—"

"Give it a rest, Jim." This time it was Ryan doing the interrupting. "We know the drill."

* * *

Ryan sat slumped in his chair in an interrogation room at FBI headquarters as Crawford paced on the other side of the table.

"So let's recap one last time," Crawford said, stifling a yawn. "You're browbeating Dr. Huggins at the lab when this Craven character shows up. Craven torches the evidence. Huggins tries to make a break for it. Craven puts a couple of bullets in his back. A struggle ensues, and Craven nearly takes you out, but Jordan saves your ass when she knocks the thug cold with a fire extinguisher. From there, you tie him up, hurt your hand on his face as soon as he wakes up, and pry an unrepentant confession out of him. Then, just when you're about to call me, he busts loose and goes for his hidden pistol, which you, despite your FBI training, somehow missed. You kill him before he kills you. Do I have it all?"

"More or less." Crawford had gone from supportive friend to bristly FBI agent. Ryan couldn't say he blamed him. He had pushed their friendship to the limit, and he wasn't done yet. "I want to go after him."

"Who?"

"Stedman. Somebody needs to take him down, and we're just the ones to do it."

"We. . . ?"

"We've come this far together. Why not finish the job?"

"Christ, you want all one hundred and fifty reasons?" Crawford shook his head, the corners of his mouth forming an exhausted frown. "I'll give you two for starters. One, I can't afford any more dead bodies on my watch. Two, neither of you are on the FBI payroll as far as I can tell."

"Let us help then," Ryan said.

Crawford ignored the request. "I'm still not clear on something."

"What?"

"I get why FSW is trying to off Jordan. They see her as a competitor, someone with scruples no less, who could seriously mess with their bottom line. But why bury the cure for ovarian cancer? Why not make a shitload of money from it? If I were Jacob Stedman, I'd make a mint from the cure, retire early, and head for the driving range."

"You don't think like these people," Ryan said. "That used to be my problem, too. I underestimated them—or overestimated them, depending on your perspective. They're not like us. It's not enough that they have wealth and power and everything money can buy. Stedman and his ilk want to rig the system so they'll always be needed, no matter what discoveries are made in the future. They're not trying to make people healthy. They're trying to keep them sick so they can treat their symptoms forever."

Crawford nodded thoughtfully. "A cure for cancer eliminates customers. But drugs that help people manage their illnesses, those you can sell for decades."

"Exactly."

"So in Stedman's ideal world, he strings patients along for years at a stretch, keeping them out of the grave and on the hook for more medicine, while selling a real cure off of U.S. soil, only to the mega-rich who can afford the multi-million-dollar price tag. It's a win-win situation."

"The man's a monster," Ryan said. "Which is why we need to nail him."

"I agree, but we're going to do this legally and by the book, which means you and Jordan are going to keep a low profile and give us room to do our job."

"But—"

Crawford held up both hands. "If you really want to nail Stedman, you won't risk jeopardizing the case further. Besides, I've got a hunch this goes deeper than one crooked CEO."

"Deeper?"

"Jacob Stedman is a powerful man with powerful friends. Who knows who he has working for him, or who he's working for? You took out his chief of security. My guess is that he already knows you and Jordan are back from the grave, which makes you a threat to his existence. He's going to do whatever he has to to eliminate that threat."

"How could he possibly know we're alive?"

"As I said, he is a very powerful man with powerful connections. Your escapades today have made it unlikely that your status remains covert. And the more people who know, the greater risk of a leak. Moving forward, I think it is best to operate under the assumption that he knows you and Jordan are alive."

"Then he also knows we are on to him and may have evidence to put his ass away. Which is why I need to finish it."

"Ryan, we've been over this already. You need to lay low. I'm going to put you up in a safe house here in town, and I'm going to put a couple of agents outside your door. But just in case . . ."

He nodded to somebody through the one-way glass, and an agent entered and handed him a bulky black plastic case. Crawford swung the case up onto the table and opened the latches, revealing a standard-issue revolver, plus ammunition. "It's not as powerful as the gun you took off Craven—and used on him—but it'll get the job done."

"A little unorthodox, no?"

"If you weren't a former Company man, you'd be on your own. But the boss seems to have taken pity on you. Not much. But a little."

"It's no fun being a marked man."

"Yeah," Crawford said. "But you're still breathing."

* * *

Senator McNally entered the private club in New York City alone. No assistant. No chaperone. He spied Stedman seated at a table in the corner and took his time closing the distance between them.

The senator had known Jacob Stedman for the better part of two decades—nearly the length of his political career. Though Stedman was his elder by a good fifteen years, the two had risen through the ranks simultaneously, him through the political establishment and Stedman through its corporate counterpart.

Throughout that time, McNally had considered Stedman a close associate. Not a friend, per se. But someone who could be trusted and someone whose opinion was worth seeking. Of course, since Fisher Singer Worldwide's rise to the top of the pharmaceutical world, Stedman had come to occupy a more prominent perch. A valuable contributor to the campaign coffers, he possessed the ability to raise significant funds on short notice and without scrutiny.

But he wasn't simply a cash cow. He was, for lack of a better word, an ally. At times, McNally wasn't sure who had the upper hand, and there had been moments, especially recently, when the senator had regretted their association, if for no other reason than the hefty price tag that came along with it. Stedman's support meant taking risks and embracing unsavory solutions, and the senator knew that by running with Stedman he was running with a dangerous crowd. But it was too late for regrets. Too late to back out. He needed to take control of the situation. And there was no time like the present.

"Two emergency meetings in one week," the senator said as he took a seat across the table from Stedman. "This is unprecedented."

"As are the circumstances," Stedman said.

"What's up, Jake?" The informality was a deliberate ploy and one intended to knock his ally down a few notches.

Stedman replied without hesitation, either overlooking or refusing to humor the use of his shortened first name. "It's Matthews again."

"Yes, I heard." The senator had enough friends at the FBI, not to mention in Stedman's own company, to know what was going on most of the time, although he wasn't always privy to the details. "I'm sorry to hear about William Craven. He was a great asset."

"I suppose he was," Stedman said coolly.

McNally was surprised at the detachment in Stedman's voice. He knew if he'd just lost his chief of security he'd be feeling awfully vulnerable, whatever his feelings for the man. "Do you have someone in place to take over for him?"

"Not at the moment," Stedman said. "That's why I called. I need your help."

"My help?"

"I want that SOB."

"I presume you're speaking of Matthews."

"Yes," Stedman replied, brandishing a menacing frown.

"My people aren't killers," the senator said. "You'll have to look elsewhere for that sort of help."

"I've been in touch with another team. But these guys will need time, up to forty-eight hours, to get here. And who knows how long it will take to track them down now that they're under federal protection."

"*Them*? I hope you're not including Dr. Carver."

"She knows as much as Matthews. Maybe more. She's a liability." Stedman leveled a cold gaze at the senator. "And not just for me."

McNally did his best to look unfazed. "This is the last time I'm going to tell you to steer clear of the Carver girl."

"Is that a threat, Senator?"

"Of course not," he answered quickly. "People in our position don't need to make threats. What I will tell you is that this quest of yours—to make Matthews and his cure for cancer disappear from the U.S. market—barely factors into a much bigger picture. You're trifling with more than you know."

Stedman opened his mouth to protest but the senator waved him off and kept talking.

"I can help you track Matthews's movements while you wait for your people to get into place. But you must promise to leave Carver to me." He paused before making his final point. "I share your concerns, friend, and I assure you she'll be dealt with before she can expose either of us. But you have to leave this one to me. Your future depends on it."

CHAPTER **42**

As the sun broke through the bedroom window, Ryan awoke at the safe house Crawford had sent them to the night before. The house was in Hillandale, Maryland, only ten miles from the FBI's D.C. headquarters, but it seemed like worlds away.

Lying in bed next to Ryan and staring at the ceiling, Jordan asked, "What do we do now?"

To Ryan's ears, Jordan's question sounded like a plea for help. It was clear she was running out of ideas. On her, hopelessness was a bad fit. She just wasn't the type to give up.

Maybe if she had more confidence in Crawford and the FBI to nail Stedman she'd be assuming a braver front. But she probably had, like him, the sneaking suspicion that they were largely on their own. Crawford and his men had saved Ryan's life back at Eno River State Park during his doomed meeting with Eric, but he couldn't help feeling like the suits were more often than not one step behind them. He glanced out the window. Knowing a pair of agents were posted somewhere outside didn't make him feel any safer—just trapped.

"Here's a question," Ryan said, answering Jordan's plea with a curveball. "Who's in Stedman's back pocket?"

Jordan gave him a quizzical look but said nothing.

Ryan continued with his train of thought. "Jim told me yesterday that he thinks this thing goes deeper than just Stedman, that he has in his corner some pretty powerful people. But who? If you're Big Pharma, who do you want working for you?"

Jordan chewed on the question for a moment, pursing her lips as she thought it over. "Somebody in government, obviously," she said.

"That's right. Somebody who can help you steer clear of all the red tape. Somebody who can streamline the process for you. If you're in the drug industry, who's your biggest nightmare?"

"The FDA," Jordan said. "Stedman has someone working for him at the FDA!"

Ryan smiled. "And not just a pencil pusher. Someone with clout. Who's the commissioner at the FDA now? Is it still Alex Mendel?"

"No, he retired a few years ago. He was replaced by Dr. Carl Wiley."

"That complicates things," Ryan said. "We'll start with Mendel. If he's a dead end, we'll go after Wiley."

Jordan sat up, turning towards Ryan. "You can't just *go after* the FDA commissioner. He's well insulated. So is his predecessor. It'll take time."

"We don't have time," Ryan said, jumping out of bed and heading down the hallway.

"Where are you going?"

"I saw a computer in the study."

* * *

As Jordan delivered coffee, Ryan was busy fleshing out a short but illuminating sketch of Alex Mendel. The former head of the FDA maintained an address in a Maryland suburb just outside of D.C.; since stepping down from his position, he had managed to keep an awfully low profile. Much of that had to do with extenuating circumstances. A mere four months had passed since his wife had died from—of all things—ovarian cancer. Mendel had retreated from the public spotlight to tend to her, only to witness her slow death. Throughout their ordeal, Mendel had given no interviews, and news reporters had crafted their stories on her condition from interviews with his friends and associates.

"I can't believe his wife died of ovarian cancer," Jordan said as she peered over his shoulder. "What are the odds?"

"Unfortunately, not as low as they should be," Ryan said. "Every year, thirteen or so women out of every one hundred thousand are diagnosed with ovarian cancer, and nearly nine of them die." Ryan suddenly felt sheepish. He didn't need to rattle off statistics to Jordan. She no doubt knew them well.

"Let's assume you get close enough to Mendel to ask a few questions," Jordan said. "What then?"

"I'll see how he reacts to my initial questions and play him on the fly."

"You won't torture him, will you?" Jordan asked with mock seriousness.

Ryan tried to laugh off the question. But it wasn't easy. He had behaved savagely toward Craven, whose thuggish demeanor had brought out the worst in him. Crawford had chided Ryan for his use of brute force, as well as for his newly acquired habit of working outside the law. And had he not reloaded Craven's backup weapon after he shot the man dead, Ryan would be facing criminal charges himself. Despite what Craven had done to his family, Ryan knew he was treading a fine line. But at the moment, he didn't give a damn.

"I have no plans of torturing an old man, but if he lies to me, I've got no problem letting him believe that the worst is yet to come. Mendel lives about ten miles away. Let's give him a visit."

"What about our friends?" Jordan asked, motioning toward the front door.

"Who says we're going out the front door?"

After getting ready, Ryan and Jordan exited through the rear door. The hopped the six-foot wood fence in the back yard, then jogged six blocks over to Powder Mill Road. Standing on the corner across from the Hillandale Shopping Center, Ryan spotted a cab driving on the opposite side of the road. He raised his arms and let out a loud whistle. The cabbie blew his horn once in acknowledgment and waited for an opportunity to make a U-turn.

Before the cab had circled around, a dark blue four-door sedan pulled up. The passenger-side front door opened and Jim Crawford jumped out. "What the hell are you up to now?"

"Listen Jim, I'm sorry, but we are not going to sit around for days on end at some safe house and hope that the FBI is going to solve our problems. I know you're trying to protect us, but we've both decided that we would prefer to take our chances."

Crawford looked at Jordan for confirmation.

"It was my idea as much as Ryan's, Jim," she said.

Crawford rubbed his temples and then ran his hand through his hair before opening the rear passenger door. "Get in, both of you."

They returned to FBI headquarters in D.C. where they spent the rest of the morning and early afternoon reviewing all of their previous official statements to the FBI. These statements were now typed up and ready for signatures.

Crawford entered the conference room where Ryan and Jordan had been stashed for the past four hours. "You guys won't accept my protection and I can't babysit you. Sign your statements along with our waiver form and you're free to go."

"What waiver?" Ryan asked.

Crawford tossed the document onto the table. "This waiver states that you have been made fully aware of the potential risks and dangers of declining federal protection, that you are of sound mind and body and yet are electing to decline such protection."

"Jim, you know how much I appreciate everything you have done for us."

"I know, Ryan. But I think you're a damn fool for risking your neck and I can't protect you if you decide to break any laws." Crawford tossed a pen on the table. "Still, if you get into any heat, you have my number."

With that, Ryan and Jordan signed their official statements

along with the waiver form and were out the door. They caught a cab and took it to the Hilton on Connecticut Avenue, where they rented a car from Hertz. After a late lunch courtesy of McDonald's, they jumped on the 495 and headed towards Chevy Chase.

* * *

Alex Mendel lived in a stately brick Tudor, which was nestled on a large well-manicured corner lot on a quiet tree-lined street in Chevy Chase, Maryland. Ryan and Jordan followed a winding path, paved with earth-toned flagstones, to the front door.

"Ready?" Ryan asked.

"Ready as I'll ever be."

Ryan knocked and waited for the sound of footfalls inside. Nothing.

"Try the doorbell," Jordan said.

He did as she suggested.

Still, nothing.

He was about to give up when he heard the mechanical sound of landscaping equipment fire up from the back yard. "Follow me," he said, leading Jordan around the side of the house, through a tall wrought-iron gate, and into a lush back yard that could have easily passed as a secret garden in the English countryside.

Mendel, a tall frail-looking gentleman with a bushy white mustache and eyebrows to match, was applying a hedge trimmer to a short hedge of boxwood that lined the path to the back door. He still had a full head of unruly white hair, although Ryan thought he looked noticeably older than the last time he'd seen him, several years ago, after Dr. Mendel had delivered a speech at a pharmaceutical conference.

Mendel caught sight of them in his peripheral vision and whirled around. "Can I help you?" he asked curtly as soon as he'd turned off the hedge trimmer.

"Dr. Mendel," Ryan said, moving to greet him. "My name is Ryan Matthews. This is Dr. Jordan Carver." He offered a friendly smile and extended his hand.

Mendel managed a tepid handshake in return. "Do I know you?"

"We've met before," Ryan said, "although I doubt you remember. I used to work for Fisher Singer Worldwide."

The old man eyed him suspiciously. "What do you want?"

Jordan cut in. "Dr. Mendel, we need to talk to you about a serious matter. We—"

"Whatever it is can wait," Mendel said, cutting her off. "Moreover, I don't appreciate the intrusion. If you had a legitimate reason to meet with me, you would have contacted me through the proper channels." He turned on his heels and started for the back door.

Ryan didn't bother to stop him but instead followed him inside, with Jordan close behind. Such aggressive behavior would only make the old man more wary of them, but it was better they move inside—beyond earshot of the neighbors—before beginning what was inevitably going to be an uncomfortable confrontation.

When Mendel reached for a phone hanging on the wall in the kitchen, Ryan moved to intercept.

"I'm calling the police," Mendel said, his feeble voice overflowing with indignation.

"I can't let you do that," Ryan said and removed the phone from his hand.

The old man did not resist, but turned and began moving towards the front door. Ryan, anticipating the move, took hold of his collar, gripping it as gently as he could, and guided him into the living room, which, with its plush carpet, tasteful decorations, and handsome furniture, looked like it still bore the stamp of a woman's touch.

Ryan steered Mendel toward one of the overstuffed chairs and kindly pushed him down. "Your wife did a wonderful job with this room," he said. "I was sorry to hear of her passing."

Mendel looked back at Ryan fearfully, his eyes bulging behind a pair of wire-rim glasses. "What do you want?"

Jordan intervened with her soothing voice. "We just want you to hear us out."

Mendel frowned, his bushy eyebrows nearly touching. "This is highly unusual."

"I know it is," Ryan said and let go of Mendel's collar. He grabbed a nearby footstool and plopped down in front of him.

Jordan followed his cue and took a seat on the edge of a black leather couch.

"Listen, you and I have a lot in common. I lost my wife to ovarian cancer, too. The odds were stacked against her, but I had a chance to save her." He forced back a tidal wave of emotion that suddenly threatened to engulf him. "And so did you."

It was the perfect opening gambit, and Ryan, having gained Mendel's undivided attention, used it to launch into a thorough explanation of his work with Tricopatin, FSW's successful move to bury it, and the ensuing roller coaster he'd been riding ever since the night, now almost four weeks ago, when he met Jordan. He told Mendel about Dr. Huggins and Craven. Once he had laid out all the facts, he decided to play a hunch.

"Dr. Mendel, I know about your involvement with the Tricopatin clinical trial."

"I had nothing to do with any clinical trial," Mendel shouted. "I was the commissioner of the FDA for god's sake. I didn't get involved with individual clinical trials. Those were handled by members of my staff."

"Now we both know that's not entirely true. You were given a directive and that directive was to halt the Tricopatin clinical trial and you complied."

"That's not true," Mendel retorted, his vigor diminishing.

"Think about it," Ryan said. "Your wife would still be alive today if you hadn't quashed Tricopatin. We could have saved her life."

The use of *we* was particularly effective; it put Ryan, Jordan, and Mendel squarely on the same team.

Mendel stifled a tear. "I had no idea."

"So you admit you helped kill my drug?"

"Yes and no," the old man said. "I saw the trial results—the real ones and the altered version—and I signed off on the ruse. But I don't remember a Dr. Huggins or a William Craven, and I only vaguely know of Jacob Stedman. I've never met him."

Ryan felt his short fuse burning again. He hadn't pushed Mendel into a confession only to get the runaround on who was pulling the strings. He was relieved when Jordan stepped in.

"I'm confused," she said. "If you weren't working with Stedman, then who was giving you your orders? Was it someone else at FSW?"

"No, no," Mendel said. "You've got it all wrong. I was never in the back pocket of industry. I worked for you, for the consumers."

"Then who told you to kill Tricopatin?" Ryan asked as gingerly as he could.

"The senator."

"Which senator?"

"Ed McNally."

Ryan felt his jaw drop. "Senator McNally?" he repeated. "I always thought he was one of the good guys."

Jordan crossed her arms. "You're lying."

Ryan was surprised. She'd gone from good cop to bad cop in the blink of an eye.

"I'm afraid not, young lady," Mendel said. "I got the order to sign off on the altered tests directly from Senator McNally. It was obviously a sensitive situation. When I questioned the order, the senator told me that it was a matter of national security and that I was to tell no one of my actions. The senator has a long history of working with pharmaceutical giants like FSW. He must have been repaying an old favor."

"That's quite an accusation," Jordan said angrily.

"And one that makes sense," Ryan said, glaring at Jordan. Ryan could tell when someone was giving it to him straight, and Mendel's confession was the real deal. How Jordan couldn't see that was beyond him, but now was not the time for a debate. He returned his attention to the old man. "Can you prove it?"

Mendel nodded solemnly. "I was not comfortable signing off on something so obviously underhanded, and found nothing credible behind the senator's national security reasoning. So I protected myself, just in case. I kept the original trial data and I taped my conversations with the senator."

"Where is this evidence?" Jordan demanded.

"Locked away in a safety-deposit box."

"The perfect bargaining chip if your role in this was ever exposed," Ryan said as he shot Jordan a knowing look. "That was a smart move. Now you get to cash that chip in and avoid being exposed."

Mendel glanced at his watch. "My bank closed an hour ago."

"That's all right," Ryan said. "We can go first thing in the morning."

"So you'll return tomorrow morning?"

"No," Ryan said. "I'm not taking my eyes off you until we've got that evidence firmly in hand. We're staying for dinner—and then spending the night."

CHAPTER 43

Senator Edward McNally stared at the drink in his hand and smiled. It wasn't quite the equivalent of a Rorschach test, but what the senator saw in the glass of single malt whiskey was certainly open to interpretation. Was he on the way up? Or on the way down? Was he working toward a better future for all Americans? Or just bargaining away his soul?

Tastes better than an inkblot, he thought as he downed the scotch.

With the television on and the late edition of the evening news soothing him to sleep, he realized it had been a long time since he'd simply crawled into bed with his wife, turned off the lamp on his nightstand in unison with her, and kissed the woman he loved goodnight. When he came home from work these days, *if* he came home at all, he needed distraction more than anything else. *Anesthesia.* Once he had sufficiently numbed himself, he required a quiet moment to reflect on the day's work. Had he succeeded in moving his agenda forward? The United States Senate had chewed up and spit out better men than him in the past—of that he was sure. But he liked to think he was special. Or at least luckier than most. He was going to make a difference regardless of the fallout. History would be the only judge that mattered.

"This country needs more team players," he said softly to himself. "People willing to—"

The ring tone on his private cell phone made him jump. He sat up straight in his easy chair and clumsily reached for his phone on the end table beside him.

"Sorry to disturb you at this late hour, Senator, but we have news."

McNally wondered if it was worth taking a stab at the nature of the news, but thought better of it. "Hit me."

"Matthews and your girl have had a busy day."

"Go on."

"They've found Mendel."

The senator inhaled deeply. "Christ."

"There's more."

"There always is," the senator said, reclining in his chair. "Go on."

"Mendel has evidence, including taped conversations between the two of you, locked away in a safety-deposit box. He's planning on turning it over to Matthews tomorrow."

In moments of crisis, especially when his luck had gone south, McNally prided himself on taking a counterintuitive approach. Rather than trying to stiffen his grip on the situation, he let go. Rather than go into hyperdrive, he slowed down. When in free fall, he reasoned, it was best to relax, like a drunk driver at the moment of impact, or like a cat gracefully turning in midair while falling from a second-story window. It was precisely his ability to embrace the darkest moments that separated him from his peers. When others panicked, he stayed cool.

"This is getting too dangerous." He paused to consider the implications before continuing. "Make it go away."

As he ended the call, he thought he heard someone in the hallway.

Sure enough, his wife appeared in the doorway, groggy and disheveled. "Did someone just call?"

He nodded nonchalantly.

"Was it important?"

He stood up and folded her into his arms. He could feel her

warm skin radiating through her nightshirt. Her breath smelled like sleep.

"No," he lied. "Not important at all."

CHAPTER **44**

The next morning, Ryan pulled into a passenger loading zone in front of Dr. Mendel's bank in the same affluent D.C. suburb of Chevy Chase. He gave Jordan's hand a reassuring squeeze as Mendel waited in the backseat. "We'll be back in five minutes. Keep the engine running."

Jordan unbuckled her seat belt, preparing to take his place behind the wheel. Ryan could only hazard a guess as to her mental state, but if hers resembled his at all, she was most likely trying—but failing—to keep a lid on her excitement. They were minutes away from possessing the smoking gun they needed to take Stedman down and break the Tricopatin case wide open. With a highly regarded senator involved, it was anyone's guess how things would shake out. The only certainty, Ryan told himself, was that heads would roll. No one would be safe, least of all the whistle-blowers.

Ryan followed Mendel inside, neither saying a word. The old man proceeded to the safety-deposit-box room while Ryan waited for him just outside in the secured corridor. They had rehearsed every detail the night before.

As he waited, Ryan pondered the fickle nature of fate. Mendel could have finished out the rest of his life in suburban comfort, more or less oblivious to his role in Stedman's cover-up. Or he could have refused to help, lawyering up and even pressing charges against Ryan and Jordan for trespassing and harassment. Instead, he'd opted to do the right thing. Having been given the chance to make amends, he was taking full advantage. It was possible that he was operating mostly from fear—fear of Ryan, fear of being exposed for his role in the cover-up, fear of spending what was left of his life in jail. But Ryan knew the guilt associated with the loss of a loved one. And being that Mendel's wife was dead because of his corruption, Ryan surmised that his change of heart was directly correlated with the gash in his soul.

Mendel returned moments later holding a dark brown file case. "Now," he said in a stern voice, "I want your word that I'll be kept out of this."

"You have my word."

His hands shaking, Mendel turned the file case over to Ryan.

Ryan opened the case and did a quick inventory of the contents. As expected, the file contained a copy of the test results— the same results that had been torched at K-Dar Labs—plus three mini-cassette discs.

"Are all three of these discs conversations between you and Senator McNally?"

"Yes. And what is revealed on these tapes will bury him."

That wasn't so hard, Ryan thought as he followed Mendel toward the exit. His next job would be to find Stedman—before he found them. But Ryan permitted himself a moment to savor their hard-earned success. Less than forty-eight hours had passed since Craven had destroyed what had appeared to be their only evidence linking Stedman and FSW to murder, fraud, and a host of other illegalities. But Craven's victory, seemingly irrevocable at the time, had proved ephemeral indeed.

Ryan patted Mendel on the back as they stepped outside into the bright sunlight. "You did good in there, Doc. I know you're uneasy about all of this, but you did the right thing."

The old man smiled for the first time, showing a toothy grin. "Thank you, Dr. Matthews," he said, pausing on the sidewalk. "This doesn't erase the mistake I made, but it's a small step in the right direction. You know, I've been thinking lately that retirement doesn't suit me. Maybe it's time I—"

A dark red, almost black, blot appeared in the center of Dr. Mendel's forehead, and a millisecond later Ryan heard the sickening thud of a bullet slamming into the old man's skull. The doctor crumpled to the sidewalk, dead before he hit the concrete.

Ryan instinctively bent over to check on him, but as he did, he felt, rather than heard, a second bullet whistle by, no more than an inch above his head, followed by a third, which whizzed past his right ear. He turned and scampered back inside, the glass doors shattering behind him. Customers and tellers gasped in horror, and Ryan, not wanting to see another person go down, hit the deck first, leading by example. With shards of glass still flying, soon even the security guard was face down on the gray tiled floor.

Jordan!

Ryan reached inside his jacket and fumbled for his cell phone. He hit Jordan's speed dial, but after four rings was directed to her voice mail.

"Damn it, Jordan," he hissed, "pick up!"

The firing finally came to a stop, bringing with it an eerie silence, and he gingerly lifted his head high enough to peer outside through the shattered front doors.

Jordan and the car were nowhere to be seen.

Ryan stood up, dusted himself off and pulled out his revolver. He was careful to position himself behind a pillar that stood between him and the glass, or what was left of it. If the shooter was still out there, he didn't fancy making himself an easy target.

Where was Jordan? His mind reeled against a backdrop of sirens. Maybe she'd been hit while trying to flee and was bleeding to death a few blocks away. Or maybe she'd been strong-armed by the shooter and taken hostage.

The police arrived, sirens blaring. Ryan tucked his weapon back in his pants just as a group of officers came barging inside. Seconds later, his cell phone rang.

"It's me," Jordan said on the other end of the line. "Are you okay?"

"I'm fine. Where are you?"

"Two blocks due east. When you ran inside, they started shooting at me. I gunned it and got out of there. I was gonna come back, but when I heard the police, I thought I should stay put. Can you make it out?"

Ryan eyed the growing assembly of policemen and medical personnel. "Wait for me." He hung up, put his head down, and tried to take advantage of the commotion to exit unnoticed.

"Hey!"

He turned to see a paunchy police officer, complete with extra chin, pointing at him.

"You! You're going the wrong way. Witnesses are giving their statements over there." The policeman motioned toward the far side of the lobby, where several shell-shocked bystanders had begun to gather.

"Thanks, Officer," Ryan said and started that way.

Street side, two medics raced toward Mendel's body, still sprawled across the sidewalk. As soon as the paunchy policeman turned to go outside and clear a path for them, Ryan backtracked and followed him through the exit, carefully sidestepping the shards of glass. With the policeman sufficiently distracted, Ryan hurried down the sidewalk and around the corner. He picked up the pace once he was out of sight and jogged the two blocks to Jordan, who in her haste had parked in a tow-away zone.

"We better beat it," Ryan said, flinging the file case onto the passenger's seat. "Or you might get a ticket from the meter maid."

Jordan's olive-toned face went ashen. "How can you joke at a time like this? We were nearly killed. And poor Dr. Mendel—"

"If it's any consolation, he died with a clean conscience," Ryan cut in. "And he didn't die in vain."

Jordan frowned. "I hope you're right," she said softly.

Ryan noticed a pair of bullet holes in the upholstery of the driver's side back door. "You want me to drive? We can pull over up ahead."

"No," Jordan said, "I'm fine. But where am I going?"

"Newark, New Jersey, home to the corporate headquarters of Fisher Singer Worldwide," Ryan answered as he opened the file case and pulled out one of the mini-cassette discs. "It's time we pay Jacob Stedman a visit."

CHAPTER 45

They headed north on I-95 and settled in for the four-hour drive that lay ahead of them. As they neared the outskirts of Baltimore, Ryan instructed Jordan to exit the freeway in a busy commercial district. Once off the freeway, they made three quick stops. The first was at Kinkos where Ryan made several copies of the documents contained in Mendel's file case. The second stop was at a mini-mart where they grabbed some prepackaged sandwiches and a couple of liters of water for the remaining three-and-a-half-hour trip. The third stop was at Best Buy, where Ryan purchased two mini-cassette players and a package of blank cassettes. He would use one of the tape players to preview Dr. Mendel's recordings as they drove towards Newark. He would then use the same recorder to play back any incriminating revelations to Stedman in an attempt to get him talking. The second device would be kept hidden—with the tape rolling. Whatever Stedman said would be recorded for posterity, as well as for the benefit of Crawford and the FBI.

They reached FSW headquarters at two o'clock in the afternoon and, after finding a parking space in the subterranean parking garage, rode the elevator up to the main floor.

Once in the lobby, Ryan marched straight to the information desk and addressed the receptionist. "We're here to see Jacob Stedman. We don't have an appointment."

The receptionist, a graying woman who looked old enough

to retire, gave him the once-over, staring at him over the tops of her bifocals. Her gaze shifted from him to Jordan and then back again. "I see. Your names please."

"Dr. Ryan Matthews and Dr. Jordan Carver."

The receptionist picked up her phone. "Yes, hello, Mary. I've got a Dr. Matthews and Dr. Carver here to see Mr. Stedman. They don't have an appointment." She paused for several moments before hanging up the phone. "Someone will be down shortly to escort you to Mr. Stedman's office."

Ryan opened his mouth to thank her, but the receptionist was already greeting the person behind them.

* * *

Ten minutes passed before a security guard finally arrived to take them upstairs. The guard looked only a few years removed from high school, but what he lacked in experience he made up for in size. He stood half a head taller than Ryan and sported huge hands and a linebacker's thick neck. He took them to the fifteenth floor. The elevators opened and they followed the guard down a long corridor. There were no other offices along the hallway, just two conference rooms. At the end of the walkway, they passed through a secretary's station and then arrived at a large corner office. The security guard knocked twice and waited.

"Enter," came Stedman's voice.

Ryan followed Jordan inside and threw a copy of the test results on Stedman's enormous black teak and mahogany desk.

The silver-haired Stedman took a cursory glance at the contents of the folder and excused his security guard, who turned on his heels and promptly closed the door behind him. Stedman picked up his phone. "Mary," he said as soon as his secretary answered, "I won't need you for the rest of the afternoon. You're welcome to go home early."

Stedman unfurled a predatory smile, his cold eyes revealing nothing, his square jaw showing ample resolve. "Please," he said, affecting a magnanimous tone, "sit."

"No thanks," Ryan said. He knew Stedman's type. A CEO like him never apologized, never asked permission. He was accustomed to running things his way, on his schedule. Even when put on the defensive, his first inclination would be to take control of the situation. Thus Ryan's only option was to go for the jugular first—and not let go.

"Craven told me everything before I killed the bastard," he blurted out. "I know that Tricopatin works. I know that my wife was on her way to a full recovery. I know that you feared that it would only be a matter of time before I figured everything out and told my story to the world. And then, Tricopatin would have been put back in clinical trials and approved. The only way to stop me from figuring it out was to make sure Cindy died, which was why you ordered Craven to take down her plane.

"Craven also filled me in on your motives. Americans never have and never will pay for good medicine, at least not according to your theory. They turn to the insurance companies to foot the bills, instead. And the insurance companies will not pay what Tricopatin is really worth. Before long the company would practically be giving Tricopatin away. And of course you were not about to let that happen. Not only would you lose out on Tricopatin profits, but you would lose billions on the cancer-coping drugs FSW sells. Why cure people when you can soak them for the cost of maintenance drugs, right?"

Stedman didn't bother to argue with the evidence. Instead, he stated the obvious. "In case you missed it, Dr. Matthews, I run a publicly traded Fortune 500 company. It's my responsibility to look out for the best interests of my shareholders. Yes, I made the business decision to kill the Tricopatin trials, but I never ordered anyone to be killed. Craven acted without my consent. He—"

"Craven wouldn't take a shit without your say-so. I know for a fact that Mendel was on the payroll. So is Senator McNally. And I'll bet Dr. Wiley is already reaping benefits as the new commissioner."

Stedman's right hand began to inch along the edge of his desk. When it was directly above his side drawer, Ryan pulled out the .38 revolver that Crawford had provided him the day before and aimed it directly at the CEO's chest. "Keep your hands where I can see them."

Ryan had to keep the pressure on, lest Stedman slither from his grasp. "I'm not here to convince you of anything or to force a confession," he said. "I already have all the evidence we need to send you to prison for a very long time. I could have handed it over to the Feds already if that was what I wanted."

"Then what do you want? Money?"

"No."

"What then?" For the first time, Stedman sounded annoyed.

"I'm here to watch you die for what you did to me and my family."

Stedman loosened his tie, swallowing hard. "You can't be serious."

Ryan raised the barrel of his gun from the CEO's chest to his face, massaging the trigger with his finger.

"Okay, okay!" Stedman said frantically, raising both hands in protest. "I admit what I did was wrong. I'm prepared to take responsibility for it, even if it means jail time. But please, hear me out. You must understand. I was only a pawn in all of this. If you want to nail the senator and Wiley—and a laundry list of other government officials—you'll need me to testify in court!"

Ryan could feel his hand shaking. Was he still acting? He could no longer tell. All he knew was that the trigger suddenly felt tantalizingly sensitive in his grip, practically ready to squeeze itself. Part of him wanted to pull the trigger, but another part wanted to see where this road led. He thought of Cindy and the children and felt his teeth grind. Stedman would never testify. He would find a way out. And he would never serve time. People like him never did. He would find a fall guy—and walk. Ryan thought of Dr. Mendel, who had been murdered before he could remake what was left of his life. Why should Stedman get a second chance?

A shot rang out, and Stedman, his eyes wide with horror, tried to speak, but his mouth moved silently. A bright red river ran south from a hole between his eyes, blood dripping from the end of his nose, and he slumped over in his chair, dead.

Ryan looked down at his gun in disbelief but saw that his finger, still on the trigger, hadn't moved. He turned to see Jordan, silent all this time, shaking violently, a gun in her hand.

"That's for killing my aunt and uncle, you son of a bitch."

CHAPTER 46

Jordan closed her eyes. She couldn't stomach the sight of Stedman, dead but still bleeding, his body awkwardly slumped in his chair. With his shoulders arched forward and his head drooping toward his desk, he looked smaller now. Almost human.

Jordan was an unapologetic animal lover, someone who went out of her way not to harm anything, be it a stray dog that had fleas or a fearsome spider that had made a home in one of her slippers. As for human life, she was devoting her career to helping the terminally ill recover from their illnesses, or at least die as gracefully and pain-free as possible.

But now?

There was no way to sugarcoat it. She was a murderer.

She opened her eyes to see Ryan methodically checking the safety on his gun before stowing it away in his jacket. He repeated the carefully orchestrated maneuver with her gun after gently prying it free from her grasp.

"I'm sorry," she said. "I . . ."

"You're shaking," Ryan said softly. "Are you okay?"

Jordan fumbled for an explanation. "I guess when I heard him pleading for his life, I got this sick feeling in my stomach that he was going to cut a deal, expose some political bigwig, and walk away with a slap on the wrist." She shook her head. "I just couldn't let that happen. He's the man responsible for my aunt and uncle's deaths, for the death of your family—given time, he would have killed us, too. We already have the evidence against the senator. If he's like most politicians, he'll simply expose someone else to save his own ass. That's what they do, isn't it?"

"Where'd you get the gun?"

"From Dr. Mendel's home. As you were securing him in his bedroom last night, I decided to search his study. While I didn't find anything incriminating, I did find his revolver and decided to take it, just in case."

"I was seconds away from pulling the trigger myself. But we have a dead body on our hands now, and several people know we were in this office. There will be no defense for what was done." He squeezed his temples and stood in silence before he spoke again. "Give me the gun. I'll take the rap. This was my fight first anyway, and I can't let you take the blame for what I should have done."

She took his hands in hers. "I can't let you do that." Then, suddenly, she had an idea. She motioned to Stedman. "What do you suppose he was reaching for in that drawer anyway?"

Ryan circled behind the desk and, mindful of the dead body next to him, carefully opened Stedman's desk drawer. With a bitter smile, he retrieved a shiny revolver. "It's loaded," he said after checking it.

Jordan moved quickly, pulling free a tissue from a Kleenex dispenser on the CEO's desk. After taking the gun from Ryan, she wiped Stedman's gun down and then pressed the weapon into Stedman's right hand, careful not to leave any fingerprints. She lined up behind Stedman, aimed the revolver at the door, and squeezed the dead man's finger until his weapon fired.

"Jesus," Ryan said, looking on in astonishment. "Where'd you learn that?"

Jordan shrugged. "I've seen it on TV a million times," she said. She stepped closer to Ryan, her lips almost touching his. "Neither of us deserves to be punished for eliminating this animal."

Ryan motioned to the door. "Let's get out of here while we still can."

CHAPTER 47

As they approached the parking garage exit at FSW headquarters, Ryan tried not to look guilty. He slowed to a stop at the gatehouse and handed his parking ticket to the middle-aged guard, who, unlike Stedman's security guard inside, looked like he'd let himself go years ago.

The guard took his time validating the ticket. "That'll be eight-fifty," he said.

Ryan resisted the urge to complain about the steep price for a two-hour visitor's pass and paid in cash. He eased his foot off the brake.

"Hold on a minute!" the guard ordered as the phone in the booth rang. He picked it up after the first ring, eyeing Ryan and Jordan as he listened to the caller.

Why would someone be calling the gatehouse? Had they already discovered Stedman's body? Ryan weighed his options, none of which were good. He did not want an overzealous security guard trying to detain them. And if he made a run for it, the local police would surely be called and the manhunt would be underway.

"Will do," the guard said and hung up. He returned his attention to Ryan but said nothing as he punched a few buttons on his cash register. Finally the machine spit out a receipt. "Here you go," he said, handing it to Ryan.

Once there were a few blocks between them and FSW, Ryan felt the tension in his muscles slowly recede. It was time to call Crawford.

"Where the hell are you?" Crawford barked as soon as the call went through.

"Newark. Had to pay a visit to Jacob Stedman."

"You don't know when to quit, do you? Ryan, I've bent over backwards to protect you so far, but if you—"

"He's dead."

"Don't tell me . . ."

"He pulled a gun on us after we showed him the evidence Mendel gave us."

"Mendel?"

"Dr. Alex Mendel, former commissioner of the FDA."

"The same Dr. Mendel who was murdered outside a bank in Chevy Chase Village this morning?"

"That's him. We met with him yesterday evening at his home. Turns out he signed off on the rigged Tricopatin results, although, in his defense, he wasn't fully aware of the implications. He got his orders from higher up. Once we filled him in on everything, he did the right thing and took us to the bank, where he had the test results plus a couple incriminating recordings stashed away in a safety-deposit box. We were leaving the bank when he was assassinated. The shooter tried to take me and Jordan out, too, but we got lucky. We then went straight to Stedman's office. I was trying to get him on tape confessing to everything and then planned on calling in you and your team to put this to rest. But he didn't take the bait and went for a gun in his desk drawer instead. I guess he didn't want to spend the rest of his life behind bars."

"Unbelievable. You guys are leaving a trail of dead bodies everywhere you go," Crawford said. "Listen, I want you and Jordan to find a safe place to hole up there in Newark before your luck runs out. We can be there in less than an hour by helicopter."

Ryan slowly exhaled. He wasn't quite ready to turn everything over to Crawford.

"Ryan," Crawford said, "you're through, okay? Time to let me do my job."

"I can't. Not yet. I've got one thing left to do before this is over."

"No! You're going to stay put and not do anything stupid, understand?"

"Don't worry, Jim," Ryan said, ignoring Crawford's pleas. "I'll call you as soon as it's finished and hand over the biggest fish in the bunch." He hung up before Crawford could get in another word.

Ryan looked over at Jordan, who was tapping her foot and biting her lip. "It's all right," he said. "We're on the home stretch."

Ryan's next call was to 411. After following the computer-prompted instructions, he was connected to the D.C. office of Senator Edward McNally. "I need to speak to the senator," he said as soon as a woman from McNally's staff answered.

"I'm sorry, sir," the woman said, "the senator's very busy. But if you have a comment or a question for the senator, you're welcome to use our online form—"

"Tell the senator that Dr. Ryan Matthews is calling and that I have in my possession several tapes given to me by the former commissioner of the FDA, Dr. Mendel. I'm sure he will be very interested in hearing these tapes."

The woman paused. "Just one moment, please."

After leaving Ryan on hold for several minutes, the woman returned to the line. "I will patch you through to the senator now, Dr. Matthews."

"Ryan Matthews," McNally said with a chuckle once the call had been transferred. "You've been on quite a little adventure, haven't you? The problem is, you don't know when to quit."

"My days of quitting are over, Senator," Ryan said. "I wanted to let you know that before you had Dr. Mendel killed, he handed over to me several pieces of incriminating evidence—evidence that will bury you for good."

"I suppose it's time we meet," the senator replied calmly.

"Where are you?"

"I'm just leaving Manhattan."

"Good. I'm close by. Meet me at the entrance to the South Mountain Reservation in one hour."

The senator paused. "I'm afraid I don't know where that is."

"It's not far. Tell your driver to put it into the GPS."

"All right," the senator said. "I'll see you in one hour."

"A couple more things."

"Yes?"

"I need your cell phone number. And if I get the slightest suspicion that you're planning another ambush, you'll never even see me and one copy of the tapes will go to the FBI and the other, straight to the *New York Times*."

* * *

The landscape slowly morphed from urban to wild as Ryan and Jordan neared the nature preserve in the Watchung Mountains.

"What's our plan?" Jordan asked.

"Well," Ryan ventured, "I'm not sure what we heard on the tapes goes far enough." He stopped himself. "If we were dealing with a normal citizen, it would be plenty. But the senator is a powerful man. We're going to need more to put him away. So my plan is to show him what we have and try to get him to make a specific admission regarding the Tricopatin trials."

"I just hope this doesn't escalate. Like you said, the senator's a powerful man."

"Don't worry. I've got it covered. His driver will certainly be packing, but we'll disarm him immediately and then strand him while we drive away with the senator in our car. There won't be enough time for the senator to bring in backup, and we'll be deep into the park by the time anyone else can arrive. Once we get a confession on tape, I'll call in the cavalry."

CHAPTER 48

The sun was sinking low in the sky when Ryan spotted the senator's black limousine approaching the entrance to the park. Ryan dialed the senator's cell phone number. "Have your driver pull over inside the main gate at the first parking lot. As soon as you stop, I want your driver to exit the car, remove his weapons, and lay them on the ground. And Senator, I know he will be carrying more than one gun, so I better see them all on the ground."

The black limo pulled into the largely deserted parking lot and came to a stop only twenty or so yards from where Ryan and Jordan sat inside their car.

Ryan waited with bated breath. Would the driver do as he had been told?

A stocky man wearing a black suit and sunglasses emerged from the driver's side front door. He reached inside his jacket and, using only his thumb and middle finger, pulled out what appeared to be a .45 and laid it on the pavement. He then reached down, lifted up his pant leg and, using the same two fingers, pulled a small revolver from his ankle holster and set it on the ground next to his other weapon.

Ryan stepped out of the car. "Toss your keys next to the guns!" he shouted.

The driver complied.

"Now get back in the car and keep both hands on the wheel at all times!"

As soon as the driver was inside, Ryan walked over to where the keys and guns lay and quickly scooped them up. He motioned for the senator to exit the limo.

The senator, whose tinted window was lowered halfway, calmly stepped out. He was a politician all right: cool, confident, and handsome. Ryan hated him already.

Ryan walked around to the back of the limo, tossed the keys to McNally and told him to open up the trunk. As the senator extended his hand to unlock the trunk, Ryan maneuvered around to the rear passenger side so he could keep one eye on the driver and another on the trunk. Ryan's gun was cocked. He was ready for any surprise the senator might have in store for him.

With the empty trunk opened up, Ryan called for the driver. As the driver circled around to the rear of the limo, Ryan used his gun to shoo the senator back several paces. Ryan frisked the man and then told him to get in the trunk. He complied without questions or hesitation. Ryan slammed the trunk lid closed and then led the senator to their car. He quickly frisked the senator before putting him in the front seat next to Jordan, who had taken over at the wheel. He then ducked into the backseat, directly behind the senator. "Go!" he said, and Jordan jumped on the gas.

No one said a word, and after they had covered several miles, with Jordan white-knuckling it the whole way, Ryan instructed her to pull off the main drag onto a narrow dirt road. They followed the dusty, deserted road a quarter of a mile or so before it ended at the mouth of a small grass meadow. Jordan stopped the car, and Ryan ordered the senator out first.

"How did you know about this place?" Jordan asked as they got out.

"When I worked for FSW, I often had time to kill after visiting the main office," he explained. "I'd come here while I was waiting for my flight." Ryan stepped toward the senator, who was waiting beside the car. "I used to work for Jacob Stedman," he said, addressing McNally, "but I suppose you already know all about me. I poured my life into a cure for ovarian cancer, and just as I thought I had a chance to save my wife, she and my children were taken from me. I blamed myself for years for their deaths, but over the past few days, I've found out the truth. And now I know that you, with the help of Stedman and the FDA, are responsible for killing Tricopatin."

Ryan carefully removed one of the mini-cassette players from his jacket, while the other one remained concealed, recording the conversation that was to follow. He began playing back McNally's incriminating conversations with Mendel. The tape played for ten minutes, with Ryan fast-forwarding through some insignificant dialogue, highlighting the exchanges between the senator and Dr. Mendel that involved incriminating evidence. By the time Ryan had stopped the recorder, it was clear that McNally was caught, on tape, instructing Commissioner Mendel to bury FDA submissions, delay various drugs, and generally do whatever he could to slow progress on the drug-research front.

"You're going to jail for a long, long time, Senator."

McNally didn't blink. "Do you know why FSW was willing to pay such a huge sum for Immugene when your fledgling company only had one promising drug in the pipeline, a drug that hadn't even made it into human trials yet?"

"Of course," Ryan said. "So FSW could gain control and make sure Tricopatin never received FDA approval."

The senator chuckled. "There are literally thousands of drugs that show success in animal studies but go on to fail miserably in human trials. If FSW and the other major pharmaceutical companies paid one hundred and fifty million dollars to acquire every little start-up biotech company that developed a potentially promising drug, they would be out of business in no time. You know better than I do that only one out of one thousand drugs that enter human trials earns FDA approval. Now I admit it could be a lot more, but twenty or thirty out of a thousand would be the best-case scenario, even if certain forces didn't exist to make sure they were rejected. No, FSW and the others only offer to buy the ones they know are going to actually pan out."

Ryan narrowed his eyes at the senator. "How in the hell would FSW—or anyone else for that matter—know if a drug works unless it has been tested on humans?"

"That's why companies like FSW have espionage departments that rival the CIA. Do you think the billions they spend on research and development each year are actually spent on scientists wearing white lab coats and running around with test tubes in laboratories? That may be a small piece of the puzzle, but the big bucks go into espionage and human testing, typically conducted in Third World countries."

Ryan thought he had heard it all from Craven, but McNally's revelation was one that he was not yet ready to fully comprehend. "What are you saying?"

The senator offered the same smile he used to woo voters and media. "Whenever one of these little start-up companies has a promising breakthrough, the boys in cloaks break in, steal the formula, and ship it off to some developing country. From there, another team finds a crop of volunteers who either have the disease or who are unknowingly *given* the disease. Then they test the drug on the infected, and if it works, they make the small start-up company an offer they can't refuse. If it doesn't—and most don't—they bury the dead and move on to the next drug and unsuspecting crop of guinea pigs."

Ryan was barely able to choke out a response. "Why in the world would you ever allow something like this to go on? Taking campaign contributions and doing illegal favors for big companies is one thing. But you're talking about endorsing mass murder. You're talking about turning a blind eye to the kind of ethics-free science practiced by the Nazis and the Communists. That's sick. That's . . ." He searched for a word that might have currency with the senator. ". . . un-American."

The senator shook his head. "Absolutely not," he said. "My responsibility as a U.S. senator is to protect the greater good of our country and her citizens. While I'm sorry for the people whose lives are sacrificed, I can't let their suffering distract me from the big picture."

Ryan was tempted to throttle McNally, but since the man was spilling his guts, he decided to continue to egg him on and see what else the now-doomed senator might reveal. "You talk of the greater good, Senator, but you go to unheard-of lengths to suppress drugs that would be of tremendous benefit to the American people. And all in the name of corporate greed." He shook his head, disgusted. "You're full of shit. You can't say this is done to find cures and then arrange to have those same cures suppressed just to protect the bottom line of your corporate masters, who would rather keep the people hooked on maintenance drugs than simply cure them."

"Yes, the pharmaceutical companies are oftentimes the beneficiaries of my efforts. But they don't set policy, and they have no idea of the greater goal. As far as they know, I'm nothing more than a dirty politician who's willing to get things done for a price."

"You're going to fry for what you've done, Senator."

Ryan expected a defiant response, but McNally remained calm.

"Do you know what the average life expectancy for an American citizen was just twenty years ago?" he asked.

"Seventy-two," Ryan answered. "What does that have to do with anything?"

"And do you know what it is today?"

Ryan sighed impatiently. "Seventy-eight, eighty, I'm not really sure. I get that people are living longer, no doubt thanks to better medicine. But they could live even longer and healthier lives if these cures weren't being suppressed."

"Indeed," the senator said. "You still don't get it, do you? Your wonder drug was not only a cure for ovarian cancer. Other researchers could have worked from your findings and developed cures for numerous other cancers. There was another drug we killed a few years back that promised to rejuvenate human organs. Hell, with just those two drugs on the market, it wouldn't be long before every disease known to man was cured and people were living one hundred and fifty years or longer."

Ryan was incredulous. The senator was beginning to wear him down. "And what would be so awful about that?"

"What do you think would happen to the American economy, and by extension the world economy, if people began living to one hundred and fifty? The Social Security system is already bankrupt. It wouldn't be long before the entire world was bankrupt, and we'd return to the Middle Ages. There wouldn't be enough food to feed the people or housing to house them or jobs to employ them or caregivers to care for them. The entire world would slip into anarchy, and the world as we know it would cease to exist."

"Everyone has the right to life and the best medical treatment available. I understand that increasing life expectancy rates could cause economic issues, but the picture you're painting is the worst-case scenario."

"If you have a solution to the problem that would not lead us down that path, I would love to hear it. Of course, you have been thinking about this for all of a few minutes now while I have spent the past decade studying the problem."

"Enlighten me, Senator."

"We could see this coming after the mapping of the human genome back in the nineties. This was a revolutionary medical breakthrough, and the entire scientific community was abuzz with the possibilities for new cures and new treatments. I was put in charge of a special committee by our last president to find a solution to the problems that could result from rapidly increasing life expectancy rates. We spent several years in think tanks with some of the brightest minds in the world. But the project was disbanded by the new administration after we failed to come up with even one viable solution after all our work. The only solution we offered was to limit the right of women to conceive. A national lottery system was suggested, but of course that meant the luck of the draw would determine the gene pool—and that was not going to happen, never mind the political consequences of trying to regulate the propagation of our species."

Ryan took a few steps back from the senator. "You're signing off on the wholesale slaughter of who-knows-how-many innocent people, you're suppressing cures to cancer, you're risking your career as a senator, not to mention your life as a free man—and based on what? A bunch of crackpot theories. Even if we find cures for every cancer known to man or learn how to grow a human liver, there's still Alzheimer's and AIDS and flesh-eating bacteria and a million other ailments that will keep us mortal, not to mention war, natural disasters, resource depletion, overpopulation—you name it. But my, how you talk! You'd think people were suddenly going to start living to one hundred and fifty tomorrow."

"Not tomorrow Matthews, but over the course of the next generation it would be possible if exponential revelations are made in medical science, which I am one hundred percent convinced could happen if left unchecked. Even if life expectancy increases to ninety over the next decade, Social Security is bankrupt under the current legislation. Unlike other politicians who only care about the next election, I am looking out for this country for the generations to come."

Ryan shook his head. "And how the hell are you going to control what goes on beyond our borders? China, Russia, Europe, India—they've got their own scientists and their own politicians. Please tell me you're on your own here."

The senator stuck his chin out. "You're the one who has his head in the sand. I'd rather be out front facing the world's problems than denying them. And I'm sure you'll be sorry to hear that I'm not on my own. I have a very powerful team behind me. You would be amazed to find out who all support the cause."

"Amaze me then. I'm all ears."

The senator laughed aloud. "Afraid I can't divulge that information. Of course, if you're ready to reenter society, we'd love to have you on our team."

Ryan had heard enough. "You're nuts. Get in the car, Senator. I'm taking you in."

McNally stood his ground. "I don't think so, Matthews. We were really hoping you would see the big picture and join our cause. But it's clear—"

"We? What do you mean *we*?" Ryan reached for his gun.

The impact came a fraction of a second before the blast, and before he knew what was happening, Ryan found himself on his back, the wind knocked out of him, his left ear ringing. He reached over with his right hand and gingerly touched his left shoulder. Warm blood oozed from a small but painful wound.

Confused and disoriented, he looked up just in time to see the smoking barrel of Jordan's gun staring down at him.

CHAPTER 49

Ryan lay on the ground, bleeding and bewildered. He searched for his gun and spotted it ten feet to his right. No chance at retrieving it from his position. He turned back and focused on the gun in Jordan's trembling right hand.

"I'm so sorry, Ryan," she said. "But we can't allow you to expose our mission. We're trying to save the world. I know it sounds crazy, but . . ." She wiped at her cheek with her free hand. "Please join us, Ryan."

The sight of Jordan towering over him with a gun in her hand felt surreal, and he briefly flirted with the notion that he was dreaming. For the second time today she'd surprised him, first by gunning down Stedman and now by turning her gun on him. The only thing keeping him tethered to reality was the pain in his right shoulder. He would need to stall for time, although he wasn't sure what he'd do with a few extra seconds.

"So you've been involved from the beginning?" he asked, unable to hide the disbelief in his voice.

"Yes," she said, "but—"

"But nothing. What about your aunt and uncle? They were killed by Stedman's people. And what about the other attempts on your life? If you were involved the whole time, why have they been trying to kill you?"

Jordan wiped another tear from her cheek, now stained with

streaks of mascara. "I know what it looks like, but Stedman and the senator were not on the same page. They were working at cross-purposes. Senator McNally tried to keep Stedman and his people away from me, but Stedman wouldn't listen. All he cared about was getting rid of me and my clinic. He couldn't afford the competition and was willing to kill me and my aunt and uncle— and you—to protect his bottom line. But even before we figured out that it was Stedman and his people who were trying to kill me, I couldn't tell you everything I knew because I would have exposed my role in the senator's secret project.

"The truth is that my clinic is being set up to ensure a long, healthy, and vibrant life for the high-powered supporters of our mission. We want those people who understand and support our work to be around a long, long time." The expression on her face morphed from regret to bitterness. "As far as Stedman is concerned, I took great pleasure in killing that greedy son of a bitch."

Ryan shook his head. It was tough to figure out a plan while digesting Jordan's story. It didn't help that his shoulder was bleeding profusely and radiating pain in all directions. "I don't get it. When I first met you, you surprised me—hell, you shocked me—when you said the FDA wouldn't recognize a real break- through drug if it drove up and parked in its ass. Did you really mean that? Or was that just a lie to get my attention?"

"It was not a lie," Jordan answered adamantly. "The FDA is one of the most manipulative governmental organizations out there—and that's saying something. I figured that out early on in my career. But it wasn't until I started having detailed discussions with the senator that I learned what I was up against. It's more than red tape. There are so many powerful forces—most of them regulatory but some of them within the industry—aligned against any real progress. I had no choice but to hear out the senator. And what he said made a lot of sense."

The sun had dropped below the tree line and darkness was looming. Ryan, still sprawled out in the dirt, brought himself upright into a sitting position, careful to prop himself up with his one good arm. With Jordan still waving her gun at him, he didn't dare rise to his feet. He looked down at his bleeding left shoulder and quickly assessed the wound. It didn't appear fatal, but it was likely serious, and he might go into shock if he kept bleeding at such an alarming rate. He glanced past Jordan at Senator McNally, who clearly had her back. McNally was unarmed but obviously had no intention of stopping her from pulling the trigger a second time. He looked bored by Jordan's tearful confession.

A wave of indignation washed over Ryan. *How had Jordan been taken in by this charlatan? Had the time they'd spent together over the past month meant nothing?* He wanted to argue with her, to set her straight, but he knew in his gut it was fruitless. The woman he had permitted himself to care so deeply for over the past month, if she had ever existed at all, was long gone. In her place stood a total stranger.

"How did McNally find you?"

"He didn't have to look far. He was a friend of the family for years. My uncle was a loyal supporter of the senator's father, and our families have been close ever since. We've talked on and off for years, and I often sought his advice, especially when dealing with the FDA. He encouraged me to move in a different direction—the clinic in Mexico. Our interests dovetailed: I wanted to save the terminally ill, and he wanted to secure a future for our country. You might disagree with his conclusions, but I'm convinced if you listened to him with an open mind you'd change your tune. Once I realized a true breakthrough is impossible the way things are now, I refocused my energy. I built the clinic, and I'll continue to develop and acquire new cures through any means necessary." Jordan was becoming more clear-eyed by the second, which meant Ryan was running out of time. "I know I can't save the world alone," she said, "but the senator has a master plan that I believe is our only long-term hope for the world."

"And what is the master plan?"

Senator McNally jumped back into the conversation, anxious to lay out his plan to Matthews. "I'll explain this to you in terminology you might actually understand, Matthews. Think of the four stages of ovarian cancer. Stage one was to get in bed with the international pharmaceutical companies in order to gain access to their discoveries. That was the easiest part of the plan. Stage two was setting up Jordan's clinic in Mexico with drugs we know are effective thanks to the pharmaceutical companies doing their drug trials in Third World countries. Stage three is to get my Social Security bill passed in both houses of Congress. And that is all but in the bag now."

"So what's stage four?" Ryan asked, his voice fading.

"What else?" McNally responded. "The death sentence. The United States will not survive with the elderly poor draining our money supply and exponentially growing our national debt with their monthly Social Security checks and Medicare expenses. Once one of our citizens is unable to support their own needs, they become expendable. Stage four is already well under way. We have already begun developing a virus that, once released, will spread around the world ending the misery of the habitually sick elderly population and stop them from sucking any more money out of their governments. Of course, before that virus can be released we need to have the antidote that will prevent harm to the world's productive citizens."

"And that is why we need you to join us," Jordan pleaded. "You're the greatest research mind of our generation, even if you insist on drinking yourself stupid. You invented Tricopatin, for god's sake. We need researchers like you to help with the completion of the virus and antidote along with the development of other cures that will ensure our continued survival."

"While hundreds of millions of people drop dead well before they need to?" Ryan questioned, still in shock.

"Yes," she said, "if that's what it takes to ensure the survival of humankind. These people would die anyway. We will be sparing them from the long-term misery that accompanies the end of life for so many while saving hundreds of billions of dollars that is spent each year keeping them alive."

"So you and the senator will be heading up the death panels?"

"Somebody has to step up and save us from ourselves."

"And Mendel? Did you kill him, too?"

Jordan shrugged. "He was a dirty ex-politician willing to expose the senator in order to save his own ass. He had to go. Please, Ryan, can't you understand? I care for you, and I want you to join us."

Her emotions seemed forced, as if she had already said goodbye. She had to know he would never sign off on the plan of a lunatic. There was no way to reason with her or the senator, who had begun pacing behind her. And he knew he couldn't fake loyalty to their madness. He was as good as dead.

"You're as crazy as the senator," he said, his jaw tightening. "I'll never join you people."

The senator rested a hand on Jordan's shoulder. "You tried," he said, affecting concern. "Now let's end it and get out of here before someone comes."

Jordan pointed the barrel of her pistol at Ryan's head. "Toss the tapes and both tape recorders over to the car," she said softly. "I don't want to rummage for them after . . ." She cocked her head to the side, training her ears toward a sound in the distance.

Ryan glanced past her and spotted two four-door sedans kicking up dust as they barreled toward them on the gravel road. Then three things happened simultaneously. Jordan turned toward the noise. As she did, the lead car flashed on its bright lights, temporarily blinding Jordan. Ryan rolled hard and fast towards his gun.

Seeing Ryan make a move for his weapon, Jordan unloaded her gun at him. The first two shots missed, but as Ryan came to a halt and Jordan regained her full vision, the third shot grazed his left shoulder, the same shoulder that had already taken a slug several minutes earlier.

Ryan shrieked as he lifted his revolver. He did another full roll, this time back to his left, just as another bullet whizzed by his head. He popped up into a sitting position, steadied his aim, and fired a single shot that struck Jordan in the center of her chest.

Jordan reeled from the impact, her shoulders slumping forward as she stared back at him, wide-eyed and in shock. She fell to her knees, and the gun slipped from her grasp. Before she could choke out a single word, she collapsed on her side with her back to him, her body a contorted heap on the edge of the grass.

Seconds later, the sedans skidded to a stop a few yards away, and Jim Crawford and his men jumped out, guns drawn.

CHAPTER 50

Ryan steadied himself and got to his feet. He tossed Crawford the tape recorder that had logged the entire encounter with Jordan and Senator McNally. "Take the senator into custody, Jim. What's on that tape will bury him. But trust me, you better be sitting down when you listen to it. The shit you're going to hear is unbelievable."

Stunned, Crawford stared at the tape recorder in his hands. He looked up at Ryan and then shifted his glance to Jordan's limp body on the ground. "But why did you shoot her?" he asked as one of his men knelt down beside her to check for a pulse.

Ryan knew the agent would find no signs of life. "It was her or me. Listen to the tape. It will explain everything."

Senator McNally, flatfooted moments ago and no doubt shocked by the sudden turn of events, suddenly came to life. "I don't know who you think you are," he growled, wagging a finger at Crawford, "but you're out of your depth." He motioned to Ryan. "I want this man arrested—now!"

Ryan suddenly felt the world closing in around him. If he didn't stop the bleeding in his shoulder, he would soon be headed toward an unconscious abyss, and there was no telling what the senator would do or say while he was out. He tore the sleeve from his shirt and tried to wrap it around his shoulder to staunch the bleeding.

"That looks bad," Crawford said to Ryan, ignoring the senator. "I'm going to call in an ambulance. In the meantime, I'll have one of my men dress it properly."

"Thanks." Ryan dropped back down on the ground. He was too weak to stand.

The senator, for his part, wouldn't give up. He lit into Crawford. "Do you know who I am? I'm Senator Edward McNally— *the* Senator McNally. If you want to keep your job, you'll handcuff this man immediately and then take my statement."

Crawford removed a pair of cuffs from his belt loop and unceremoniously clamped them around the indignant senator's wrists. "It's a pleasure meeting you, Senator. I'm Jim Crawford, FBI. While I appreciate the advice, I can handle it from here."

The senator protested as he was read his rights and then was ushered by one of Crawford's men to a sedan. Ryan looked up at Crawford, who was smiling down at him and shaking his head.

"You sure like to do things the hard way."

"I guess so," Ryan agreed. "How the hell did you find me out here?"

"We tracked you via your cell phone. Next time you want to lose us, turn it off."

Ryan managed a quiet laugh and gingerly lowered himself the rest of the way to the ground. He lay still, resting his head on the dirt, as one of Crawford's men dressed the wound. He was going to make it—he was certain of that. But he wasn't sure how he'd live with what he'd done. True, he'd had no choice, and that was what he would tell himself, over and over, in the coming days. But no matter how he spun Jordan's death, he would never forget the feeling of betrayal that had hit him as hard as the impact of the bullet from her gun.

He thought of Cindy and shuddered. His love for her had never waned. If anything, it had empowered him to find the courage to move forward with his life, to feel and to care and to be perfectly human once again.

EPILOGUE

Ryan stood outside Rosey's Place and admired the yachts floating in the marina. It felt good to be back in paradise, even if he was just stopping through. With his left arm in a sling and his right hand on the railing, he held his cell phone in the crook of his neck.

"Senator McNally was officially indicted today," Jim Crawford said on the other end of the line, "and will be going to jail for the rest of his life."

"That's good news, Jim."

"It gets better. McNally spilled his guts. The FDA commissioner, Carl Wiley, and several bigwig CEOs are about to be indicted. So, Ryan, if you're still looking for a job, I think several will be opening up real soon."

Ryan smiled. "Thanks, but I think I'll stick with research."

Before hanging up, Crawford added one more revelation. "Turns out Senator McNally's old man was fraternity brothers with Henry Carver in college. We even found a photograph in the senator's office of the two together on the Carvers' yacht," Crawford continued. "The Carvers and the McNallys go way back."

"Yeah, Jordan mentioned something about that just after she shot me," Ryan quipped. "That would have been useful information to have a few months ago."

"I'll remember to check that out next time buddy," Crawford shot back.

"Thanks, Jim. For everything."

Ryan sauntered into Rosey's and took a seat at the bar next to his friend, Franklin Rolle.

"Well, look who's back in town," Franklin said, shaking Ryan's good hand with both of his. "I heard the big news. Dat's great your drug is going back into clinical trials."

"Thanks. I'm looking forward to that day when late-stage ovarian cancer will no longer be a death sentence."

"So what's next? Are you going back to work in da States?"

"I think it's time, Franklin. I miss the research."

Franklin took a big swig from his drink. "We'll miss you in Exuma."

"No, you won't. I'm keeping my place and will be back to visit as often as possible. And hey, I'm not going anywhere for another three weeks. I need a vacation. So you'll just have to put up with me until then."

Rosey, who had just finished with another customer, greeted Ryan from behind the bar. "There he is, the man of the hour. What can I get you? The usual?"

Ryan considered ordering a double but caught himself. Instead, he steeled himself for the battle that lay ahead. "Iced tea," he said. "Don't bother with the lemon."

Rosey returned a moment later with the drink, the ice cubes clinking against each other in a frosty glass.

Just then a drop-dead gorgeous brunette wandered into the bar, weighed down with an armload of shopping bags. She had long legs, ample curves in just the right places, and lips as luscious as any Ryan had ever seen. As she struggled with her bags, Ryan took a sip of his iced tea, turned to Franklin, and put to rest the question on everyone's mind. "Not on your life."

AUTHOR'S NOTE

The fictional story you have just read was inspired by numerous true events, including the two news articles at the beginning of the book. There are other horrific tales that cannot be put into print due to a lack of verifiable evidence. However, like the news stories, the following is a verifiable true account of one of the top ten best-selling drugs of all time:

Tagamet, an anti-ulcer drug, was developed and marketed by the pharmaceutical giant SmithKline Beecham in the late seventies. Hailed as a medical breakthrough, this blockbuster drug gave relief to millions of people suffering from peptic ulcers. In 1977, the Food and Drug Administration approved Tagamet for sale in the United States.

Tagamet works by reducing the amount of acid released into the digestive tract, which reduces the pain associated with ulcers. Since the drug only masks the symptoms and does not cure ulcers, patients had no choice but to continue to take this maintenance drug on a regular basis for as long as the ulcer persisted (1, 2).

But patients who experienced significant pain relief from peptic ulcers didn't seem to mind, and insurance companies were more than happy to cover the drug cost, with higher premiums of course. Over the seventeen years following its introduction, sales of Tagamet exceeded $14 billion (3). In the early nineties, the anti-ulcer drug market was estimated to be over $8 billion dollars a year (1, 4). By any account, Tagamet was a true pharmaceutical success story—for both SmithKline Beecham and the millions suffering from peptic ulcers.

However, there is more to the story.

Soon after Tagamet (and other anti-ulcer drugs like Zantac) hit the market, two Australian physicians, Dr. Barry Marshall and Dr. Robbin Warren, were conducting research to determine the true cause of peptic ulcers, in hopes of finding a cure. In 1983, they announced that they had discovered the cause of almost all peptic ulcers, a tiny bacterium known as *Helicobacter pylori* (*H. pylori*). They determined that this bacterium is immune to the harsh acidic conditions of the stomach and is attracted to the stomach's lining. They found *H. pylori* in over 90 percent of the ulcer patients they examined.

Having discovered the cause of the ulcers, these physicians demonstrated that peptic ulcers could be cured by eradicating the bacteria with a combination of antibiotics over a two-week period. The scientific community reacted with extreme skepticism. But Dr. Marshall convinced them of the link between peptic ulcers and *H. pylori* with an unorthodox experiment. He intentionally ingested *H. pylori* cultured in his lab and developed peptic ulcers in his own body, which he was able to cure with antibiotics in a short period of time (1).

Although their research was published in 1983 in a prestigious medical journal, *The Lancet*, the pharmaceutical industry was in no rush to embrace the study's conclusions. If it became an acceptable practice to use low-cost antibiotics to cure peptic ulcers, the industry would lose billions of dollars a year in sales of anti-ulcer drugs. They were not about to let that happen without a fight. With pharmaceutical reps as the main information source for most physicians, word of this discovery did not spread throughout the medical community, and sales of Tagamet and other anti-ulcer drugs continued to climb for years after the *H. pylori* discovery.

Throughout the eighties and early nineties (a time when Tagamet had U.S. patent protection), antibiotic treatment of peptic ulcers was never accepted as standard medical practice. But that all changed in May 1994 when the patent protecting Tagamet in the United States expired. Without patent protection, Tagamet sales were doomed to collapse under competition from lower-priced generic drugs. With the impending decline of Tagamet sales, the use of antibiotic treatments on ulcers was no longer the great threat that it once had been. It was time for a new strategy, and the Big Pharma machine went to work.

Over ten years after the discovery of *H. pylori*, and three months before the Tagamet patent expiration, the linkage between the bacteria and peptic ulcers was finally acknowledged by the U.S. government. In February 1993, the U.S. National Institutes of Health issued a recommendation to all U.S. physicians to discontinue the use of anti-ulcer drugs to their patients, and instead endorsed a regimen of antibiotics to kill the *H. pylori* bacterium and thereby cure peptic ulcers (4). To maintain sales of Tagamet, however, SmithKline Beecham convinced the FDA to approve a watered-down version of Tagamet for a different application. One month after the patent expiration, Tagamet was approved as an over-the-counter treatment for routine heartburn.

The storm had been weathered. Big Pharma had kept a block-buster maintenance drug for the treatment of ulcers on the market throughout the seventeen-year life of its patent, while a known cure for ulcers was silenced for over ten years. And as for those two physicians who discovered *H. pylori* back in 1983 and were squelched for over a decade, they were awarded the Nobel Prize in Medicine and Physiology in 2005 for their discovery that peptic ulcers are caused by *H. pylori* and can be cured by antibiotics (5).

REFERENCES

1. Alper, Joseph. "Ulcers as an infectious disease." *Science*, Vol. 260, April 9, 1993, pp. 159-60.

2. Conwell, Carl F., et al. "Prevalence of *Helicobacter pylori* in family practice patients with refractory dyspepsia; a comparison of tests available in the office." *The Journal of Family Practice*, Vol. 41, No. 3, September 1995, pp. 245-49.

3. Freudenheim, Milt. "New Drug Era Begins as Tagamet Patent Ends." *New York Times*, May 17, 1994.

4. Vines, Gail. "The enemy within." *New Scientist*, October 15, 1994, pp. 12-14.

5. *Helicobacter pylori*, Office for Science and Society, Department of Chemistry, McGill University, 2003.

ACKNOWLEDGMENTS

My heartfelt thanks to my good friend and collaborator, Dr. Johnny Powers. It was his inspiration, insights, and technical advice, that helped bring my story together. Dr. Powers was the president of TriPath Imaging, a biotech company located in Burlington, North Carolina, before the company was sold to a major multinational competitor. In his career, Dr. Powers has dealt extensively with the Food & Drug Administration (FDA), has published numerous scientific research papers, and holds medical patents in both the U.S. and Canada.

Thanks also to my wife, Mary Ellen, for the countless hours she spent reading variations of the manuscript and offering invaluable insight, all the while remaining supportive of my efforts and devoted to the cause.

While I do not have the opportunity to name all of the others who participated in the editing process that was critical in producing the final manuscript, I want to offer a special thank you to Janelle Powers; my mom, Betty Shaw; my sister, Stefanie Longbrake; and my two brothers, Jim Shaw and Dr. Terry Shaw for their support and feedback throughout the process.

Finally, I wish to thank Dr. Nicholas Smedira and Dr. Harry Lever of the Cleveland Clinic for saving my life. I was diagnosed with hypertrophic obstructive cardiomyopathy (HOCM), a form of heart disease, prior to completing my manuscript. If not for the expertise in diagnosis of Dr. Lever and the surgical skills of Dr. Smedira, you would not be reading this now.